Boarding Pass

NAME OF PASSENGER **Moore , Montana**

FROM **Being Single**

TO **Getting Married**

CARRIER **Transcontinental Airlines**

CARRIER  FLIGHT CLASS  DATE  TIME

GATE  SEAT  SMO

**Void After 30 Days**

CKD  PCS  WT  UNCKD  BAGGAG

*Simon & Schuster*

# Baggage Claim

*a novel*

## David E. Talbert

NEW YORK   LONDON   TORONTO   SYDNEY   SINGAPORE

SIMON & SCHUSTER
Rockefeller Center
1230 Avenue of the Americas
New York, NY 10020

SIMON & SCHUSTER and colophon are registered
trademarks of Simon & Schuster, Inc.

Designed by Paul Dippolito

For information about special discounts for bulk purchases,
please contact Simon & Schuster Special Sales:
1-800-456-6798 or business@simonandschuster.com

Manufactured in the United States of America

10  9  8  7  6  5  4  3  2  1

Library of Congress Cataloging-in-Publication Data

Talbert, David E.
    Baggage claim: a novel / David E. Talbert
        p.   cm.
            1. Flight attendants—Fiction.   2. Women travelers—Fiction.
        3. Mate selection—Fiction.   I. Title.
    PS3620.A53B34 2003
    813'.6—dc21                                    2003054217

ISBN 0-7432-4718-3

*This book is dedicated to my wife, Lyn.*
*I will love you till there are no more words to say*
*no more notes to play*
*no more love to give*
*and no more life to live.*
—David

*One day all them bags gone get in your way.*

—ERYKAH BADU

Prologue

**B**eing a flight attendant for the last thirteen years, and looking for Mr. Right for almost as long, there are two things I know a lot about: men and baggage. Given the amount of time and travel spent with both, I've come to the conclusion that there are five kinds of men, like there are five kinds of baggage.

First, there's the overnight bag kind of man. Great for the pickup-and-go kind of girl. Spontaneous. Alive. Convenient. Never makes a plan because he never has a plan and expects you to drop whatever your plans are at a moment's notice. Most of the time you do, because you can always count on having a good time (or at the very least, some good sex). Problem is, Overnight Bag Man is not very practical. Eventually you're going to need more room for the stuff you've picked up along the way. You'll want him to handle more, but he can't—even if he wants to—because he simply doesn't have the capacity.

Then there's the garment bag kind of man. He's accustomed to the finer things in life. Handsome. Articulate. Well groomed. Went to the best schools, eats at the fanciest restaurants, and drives only European cars. Garment Bag Man often hangs framed pictures, articles, and certificates around his house that highlight his favorite person: himself. When it rains, he runs inside for cover. He sleeps with a scarf, and spends more time in the mirror primping than you do. Though Garment Bag Man is extremely fashionable, he isn't too sturdy. He can't cope with the hard knocks, the potholes, or the crash landings that life inevitably brings. At the first sign of wear, or the first rip or tear, Garment Bag Man falls completely apart.

Next is the executive bag kind of man. Briefcase Man. He's the hard-edged, box-shaped piece of luggage that you could drop from a ten-story building and it wouldn't break. Structured. Firm. The kind of man that is unwavering. Willing to fight for or even die for what he believes in. The only problem with Briefcase Man is that he can only fit what he can fit. You must conform to him. He cannot and will not conform to you. It's either his way or the highway, and if it's the highway you chose, he is more than gentlemanly enough to drop you off at the nearest on-ramp.

There's also the classic duffel bag kind of man. Loose fitting. Unstructured. Unfocused and usually arrives unannounced. Not part of the original set, but picked up along the way as needed. Willing to do whatever, whenever, and to whomever as long as it leads him to that which he seeks. Duffel Bag Man will always try to fit more into his schedule than is humanly possible. He thinks he has more game than Michael Jordan, Emmitt Smith, and Barry Bonds put together, and that his game can get him anything he wants and take him anywhere he desires. Because he wasn't part of the original set in the first place, he is easily replaced and quickly forgotten.

And last is the trunk kind of man. Rugged. Weather-proof. Well traveled. A self-made man. The kind of man that's been through a lot and has seen a lot. Carries a lot of stuff, a lot of history: an ex-wife, a dead wife, or a tribe of spoiled and dependent children. Usually older and worn but never tired or torn. An international kind of man. Listens to a lot of jazz. Watches very little television. Always smells good. A self-made man who marches to the beat of his own drum and has little interest in new band members wishing to play a tune of their own

Now, the perfect man is like the perfect set of luggage—strong, stylish, durable, and dependable. Adjustable, fit to travel, and fit to suit whatever the need at whatever the time. Full of compartments. So many that just when you think you've figured him out, and you've seen all there is to see, he surprises you with a hidden nook or a forbidden cranny.

Unfortunately, I haven't quite managed to find the perfect set of luggage or the perfect man. Only individual pieces. And not even matching ones. Just a bunch of random sizes, shapes, colors, and textures. Never the right pieces for the right purposes for the right predicaments. In fact, I've accumulated so much baggage from my past relationships, I'm starting to think that it's not a man that I need, it's a skycap.

*H*istory is repeating itself. Here I am once again sitting in the back room of a church, preparing for another wedding, not my own. Five times the bridesmaid, and never once the bride. It's not like I haven't been asked. It's just that the offers seem to come at the most insincere times. Like during sex: "Girl, you gon' make me marry you!" or, "Ooh girl, I got to have it like this till death do we part." You know the kind. The open-ended, always-pretended, but never-intended-to-be-a-proposal kind of proposal. Once I was even given a ring. Actually, it was a fax of the appraisal on a ring he was allegedly considering purchasing. I don't know which faded quicker: the ink from the fax or him.

But to date, no husband, no real proposal, and no actual ring. There was this one time in the third grade during lunch. My next-door neighbor, William, got down on his knees, his upper lip coated with milk, reached deep into his box of Cracker Jack, pulled out a caramel candy–covered plastic ring, and said those four magical words—"Will you marry me?" If I had known then that my proposal drought would last for another twenty years, I would've accepted his then.

I used to blame my drought on my astrological sign, which is Libra. They say that Libras can't get along with anyone but themselves. But then two of my Libra girlfriends—excuse me, ex-girlfriends— went and got married last month, ruining a perfectly good excuse for why I was still single. So, now I've got a new excuse: the unusual way I was born. My parents were on a plane flying home to Baltimore from Aunt Sybil's Seattle wedding when my seven months' pregnant soon-to-be mother started feeling contractions. Momma said it was the air turbulence that sent her into early labor. Daddy said it was the inordinate amount of mixed nuts that she mixed with club soda and ice cream. Whatever the reason, during the most inappropriate time at nearly 20,000 feet in the air, her belches of indigestion turned into moans of contractions and out came me.

There I was in 14C, lying on a plastic tray table. Naked to the world and the rest of the passengers on our flight. Floating high above the clouds, Utah to the right, Idaho to the left. Since neither was a fitting name for their newborn daughter, my parents settled on Montana. Montana Christina Moore. Which also explains why I became a flight attendant. I'm most comfortable in the clouds. Closer to God. Closer to Heaven. Maybe just closer to God so that He can help me *find* Heaven, which is, of course, in the arms of a loving husband. Okay, so that's my excuse and I'm sticking with it. And no matter how silly the excuse, if you're a female member of the Moore family, you'd better have at least one of the two: the excuse or the husband.

In my family having a husband is like Math, English, and Social Studies: a requirement. Being happy is the elective. A husband is a symbol of accomplishment. A treasured trophy of honor. At the very least, a human shield with the power to deflect the constant nagging of my four-times-married mother, family matriarch, and self-proclaimed relationship referee.

"You know, eggs don't last forever," she would say at holiday get-togethers as the family nervously laughed at what was obviously not meant to be funny. "Even the ones at the grocery store have an expiration date stamped on the side."

According to my mother's loose interpretation of the Bible, it was unholy, unhealthy, and downright blasphemous for a woman to be over the age of twenty-five and not married. She'd quote Galatians, Ephesians, Thessalonians, and any other book of the Bible ending in "ians" as she'd bellow, "You're not a lady until you're married and you're not a woman until you've had at least two children." By the time we were old enough to realize there was no such passage in Galatians, Ephesians, or Thessalonians, it was too late. The psychological damage had already been done. We had bought into it. And for that reason alone, no woman in my family dared go into her twenty-fifth birthday without a husband.

My sister Sharon, two years my junior, after three visits to the obgyn married her gynecologist, giving a whole new meaning to the phrase "sampling the goods." She seemed happy. Though I can't really tell. We weren't that close to begin with and then she and her husband moved to Ohio.

My sister Sarah, five years my junior, married the good Reverend Mark or Mike or Marty . . . I kind of forget. They met during a revival. He was old-fashioned, extra-Saved, thirty-nine years old going on sixty, and looking for a bride. Sarah, on the other hand, was naïve, inexperienced, twenty-three going on six, and looking for a free ride. Both saw in each other what they wanted, quickly married, and relocated to some small town down south. She never forgave my mother for remarrying after Daddy died so we don't see her very often.

My cousin Clarissa, on the night before she turned twenty-five, met a complete stranger in a nightclub and married him before the clock struck twelve. Of course, the next day they divorced, which was okay, since there was no shame in divorce. In divorce there was compassion. Sympathy. Being divorced was like joining a sorority where you could sit around during holidays eating potluck, sharing pain, and sipping on a never-ending supply of bitter aid.

But for some strange reason, which I have yet to discover, I dared to be single. I chose to be the sole Moore family rebel. To go against the grain. To challenge the family and their ridiculous rules. As a result, I have the unheralded dishonor of being the only woman in the family over twenty-five who has never taken the coveted stroll down the aisle. My maiden status is the favored conversation at reunions, birthdays, baptisms, and funerals. I've become my mother's sole whipping girl. And with a decade of putdowns, setbacks, and near-marriage misses, I have more stripes on my back than the entire cast of *Roots*.

The only unmarried sibling left is my baby sister Sheree. My favorite sister, Sheree. She's twenty-one and heavily into her studies at Temple. She wants to be a doctor, a lawyer, a dentist, or something professional that will require at least ten years of internships, research, and residencies. She doesn't even have a boyfriend. And if she did, she has absolutely no intention of getting married anytime soon. How could she and still become a doctor, lawyer, dentist, or something professional that will require at least ten years of internships, research, and residencies? Did I tell you how much I love Sheree?

So, whispered ever so gently, I'm thirty-five and single with no kids. And not because of any physical deformities. I'm attractive, shapely, with a jamoca honey nut almond color. Well, really, I'm medium brown, but jamoca honey nut almond just sounds more exotic. A size eight, though I always make the salesperson bring me a size six to try on first just so I can act shocked that it doesn't fit. I've got long, layered black hair and light brown eyes. My legs are sleeker than the lines on a 747, my skin smoother than a brother from the Nation. My teeth are floodlight bright, lashes naturally long, and there's just enough junk in my trunk to look like Janet, Miss Jackson if you're nasty. I'm smart, educated, pledged Delta at Morgan State University. Not because I wasn't fine enough to be an AKA, or smart enough to be a Zeta, but the Deltas on campus were cool and I was dating this *foine* brother who was the president of the Delta sweethearts and it just didn't seem like a good political move to cross party lines. Come to think of it, why *am* I still single?

A knock on the door pulled me out of my usual daze. It was Sharon's son, my five-year-old nephew Cedric, all dressed up.

"Auntie Montana," he said, beaming, "a man just brought you a letter." He handed me a FedEx envelope.

"Thank you, Cedric."

"You welcome."

"Cedric, can I have a kiss?"

"Uh Uh!!" He frowned and ran out of the room like I just asked him to eat a helping of okra and green peas.

I wasn't expecting any mail, especially not today. Who would be sending me a package . . . Graham? Oh my God, it's from Graham, the man that I have been dating now for five months, twenty-three days, ten hours, and nineteen seconds! Graham was my latest and my greatest. This year's most eligible candidate for the position of lifetime co-pilot. Graham was my deep-voiced, Billy Dee look-alike minus the mustache. My first class man, an executive bag/carry on. Kind and thoughtful. A gentleman. His signature was a long-stemmed red rose that greeted me on holidays, special days, and just-because-of days.

"You want my arm to fall off?"

Those were the first words that came out of his mouth as he stood gazing romantically into my eyes. On second thought, it was more like, "Excuse me, my arm is about to fall off!" As he stood there with a piercingly painful look as a tear fell from his eye. I had accidentally closed his arm in the door as he was exiting the plane. Oops. Disastrous for some but destiny for us. It was the spark that led to our further conversation.

Graham is a very successful commercial real estate broker who lives in a suburb outside Chicago. He's got a huge house, three fireplaces, and a German Shepherd named Duke . . . at least, that's how I imagine him to live. Since he's almost always on the road, I haven't had the pleasure of spending time with him at his home, which I guess would mean he has duffel bag tendencies. But at least he's a Prada duffel bag. Not that it's affected us much. Over time we've managed to develop a pretty healthy long-distance and occasional short-instance relationship. And nowadays, with cell phones, emails, and two-way pagers, we've been able to develop a promising relationship knowing that he's never more than an electronic device away.

I quickly tore open the envelope. Several rose petals and a handwritten note inscribed on the finest cut of linen parchment dropped from the package. Inhaling its fragrance, I began to read.

*Dearest Montana,*

*I hope all is well. Though you are absent in body, you are present in mind.*

Mmmph. Graham is not only fine, but he's poetic too. You go, Graham.

*I've had a change of business plans and I'll be spending Thanksgiving at home this year. I know it's short notice, but I would love for you to join me for an evening you won't soon forget.*

*Love,*
*Graham.*

Swiftly rummaging through the envelope, I noticed another surprise—a round-trip plane ticket to Chicago. Not that I needed it to travel, but the gentlemanly gesture speaks volumes to the kind of man Graham is.

Thanksgiving?! Chicago?! Graham?! Wow. God really does love me. Swooning with joy, I almost fell from my chair in disbelief. Graham has just invited me to Chicago for Thanksgiving weekend. Surely he realizes the implications. I mean, when a man just wants to kick it, he invites you to spend Labor Day, Groundhog Day, or maybe even Valentine's day. But Thanksgiving? No . . . he knows exactly what Thanksgiving means. Thanksgiving carries the aroma of love, the scent of commitment . . . the fragrance of family. A Thanksgiving with Graham means a weekend filled with fine dining, stimulating conversation, and a healthy serving of stank naked sex. Like Burger King, Graham could have me his way. Like a turkey, I want to be basted, buttered, slapped, and stuffed, legs spread till the juices ooze from within, filling the air with the aroma of hot roasted turkey, and what's left of my hot toasted coo—

"Auntie Montana, my momma said you should have your makeup on by now." It was my little nephew again, no doubt sent to make sure I was getting ready.

"Okay," I replied, looking guilty.

Watching him turn and leave, I kissed the letter, tucked it safely away, and attempted to focus on what I was here for. My mother. It was her wedding day and in one hour she'd be a November bride. Having already been an April bride, a May bride, a June bride, and a July bride, she'd run out of summer months and had now moved on to the holiday months. She loved being married, and hated being alone. By now she's had enough rice thrown at her to feed the entire continent of Asia. But I've gotta give it to her; she has no problem finding a husband and no problem skipping down the aisle as if it were her first time. Shameless is her middle name. Catherine Shameless Moore. She's always kept her first married name, though, not wanting her girls to grow up without an identity. But ever since my daddy died, it seems as if there's been a never-ending revolving door of replacement dads, shuffling around like little jokers in a game of spades, all vowing to fill the space. All trying to take our daddy's place.

First it was Deacon Orlando Scott, the senior deacon at our family church. Deacon Scott was nice. Not too tall, but not too short. Not too heavy, but not too skinny. Not too light, but not too dark. Now that I think of it, he was pretty generic. And he smelled. It wasn't a bad smell, just that old people smell. You know, the one when you walk into the church and it smells like mothballs mixed with Jean Naté. He had never been married, didn't have any children, and devoted his life to organizing the finances of the church. He and my mother were the same age and seemed to share the same passions . . . church, chicken, and gossip. He had known my father well and, after his death, Deacon Scott's frequent visits for consolation turned into even more frequent visits for her affection. They didn't seem like they were in love, rather in heavy like. Soon they were married.

It was weird having a man other than my father living in our house. I think at times he even wore some of Daddy's clothes. Not that they fit. No man ever could fit Daddy's clothes, but somehow, I think having another man in his clothes helped my mother feel as if he were in some way still alive. My mother said she didn't want her four daughters to grow up without a male figure in the house. So Deacon Scott served a purpose. Sleeping in separate full-size beds, I guess he served a purpose, however temporary.

Six months into the marriage, they divorced. We got a new church home and, six months later, a new replacement daddy.

Oliver Martin. Dark-skinned, big and burly, cuddly and warm, with a face more wrinkled than a pug. Oliver always sported a checkered hat and the aroma of cigar, which he tried to smoke in the house. I say "tried" because it didn't take him long to figure out that smoking in the house wasn't worth the week-long verbal lashing he would get from my mother. For the most part they got along well, and pretty soon a brand-new king-size bed replaced the two old full-size beds.

Oliver was a business owner. On Sundays, after we got home from church, he would preach about the benefits of being an entrepreneur and the trappings of owning your own business.

"Grapes always taste sweeter when you own the vine they came from," he would proudly say, "and having a vine begins first with planting a seed."

We would stay up for hours listening to him talk about the civil rights movement and how he used to march with Dr. King in all the big marches we read about during Black History Month. It really didn't matter whether or not he was telling the truth. What mattered most to us was that the stories always ended with a supernatural climax.

" . . . and in the middle of Dr. King's speech the lightning struck, the thunder started, and we knew that in any minute it was gonna start pouring rain. But not on Dr. King's head . . . uh uh. The rain started to fall and just as it almost touched the ground, Dr. King reached high up into heaven, pointed his finger, and the rain stopped mid-air." He finished with his own hand in the air for added dramatic effect.

Pretty soon, his story time with us gave way to more frequent arguing time with my mother over his extended hours at work and shortened hours at home. They divorced after three years. Surprisingly enough, they remarried a year later, lasting five more years until eventually she could take no more. She claimed that being married to a man who was never around was like holding on to a winning lottery ticket that had expired—not worth much more than the paper it was printed on. They called it quits for good.

Every now and then I stop by the liquor store for a soda and a civil rights story, both of which he is too eager to freely give.

Now on deck is my mother's fourth husband, Mitchell. Mitchell Carter. A gentle and soft-spoken father of two married sons that are both around my age. Being retired from the military, he speaks in 0800 and 0600 military talk. Besides that, he's okay, I guess. I haven't really been around him long enough to know or to care. That's her man. She's got Mitchell and I've got Thanksgiving. Thanksgiving Day Graham. There was another knock at the door. Uh oh. I haven't even started with my makeup. My mother's gonna kill me.

"Montana, it's me, William. Can I come in?"

Thank God, it's William. I yelled through the door, "Just a second, I have to slip something on!"

"I've seen them before, remember?"

"Not in almost twenty years you haven't."

"As of yesterday, they don't look like they've changed much to me."

"Ha ha. One second."

William has been my friend since forever. We started as boyfriend and girlfriend in elementary school and stayed that way through the eleventh grade when we both lost our virginity to each other. For as long as I can remember, William has always been there for me, never missing an event. Birthdays, holidays, or whatever days, he's been as sturdy and dependable as a Ford truck. An all around blue-collar man, a handy man, the black Brawny man. Outwardly tough as nails, inwardly gentle as a lamb.

To my mother, he was like the son she never had and the husband for me she always wanted. William and I would probably still be together if it hadn't been for my mother pushing it so hard. At sixteen, what girl wants to be with a guy that her family likes, especially her mother?

After we split, I began dating what seemed to be every deadbeat, no-count dog from Los Angeles to Louisiana. From Syracuse to Seattle. From Boston to Birmingham. Through each bad relationship William has been there. Through all the temporary good times in relationships, he's been there. Now that we're adults, it's probably best that we didn't hook up. I probably would've turned him from a good guy into a deadbeat too. Anyway, William's much more valuable to me as a friend than as just another ex-boyfriend, and I'm glad he's here. His presence makes these events more tolerable than they actually are. His friendship makes not having a husband easier to deal with. Though at times, it's still more than I can bear.

"Okay, I'm ready, come in."

He opened the door, peeking around first then finally entering.

"Wow, look at you. You look breathtaking."

"Maybe that's why I'm not married. I take men's breath away. By the time they catch it, they've moved on and married someone else. Note to self: Try not to make men lose their breath."

"You don't let up, do you? Still stewing over being single?"

"Stewing? No, I've now taken stewing to a much higher level. I'm now in a crock pot, pressure-cooking over being single. If you listen closely you can hear the steam coming from my ears," I said, laughing.

"It's your fault, you know," he replied. "You could have *been* married. I proposed to you twenty years ago, remember? But you said, let me see, what did you say . . . ?" He cocked his head in thought, then scrunched up his face. "'Nuh uh!!!' That's exactly what you said."

"William, you proposed to me in elementary school during recess. We were nine. You wanted my cookie, if I remember correctly, and the only way you thought you could get it was by giving me a ring from the bottom of your Cracker Jack box."

"Well, at least I was offering a ring for your cookie. That's more than I can say for the brothers you've dated ever since."

Sucking my teeth and rolling my eyes. "Yeah, okay, funny boy. Go ahead and make fun of me. It's your fault we're not married. If you hadn't been so nice, my mother wouldn't have liked you so much and our love would have been forbidden and dangerous, and you know you always want what you can't have."

"Oh . . . so is that why you didn't want me? 'Cause you thought you could have me?"

"I didn't think, I knew. And I *still* know," I said, looking way too confident. "But then again, that was in high school. I'm sure I don't still have it like that," I said as I continued applying my makeup.

"You know, if I looked real hard I could probably dig up that ring from the Cracker Jack box. It's not too late. I mean, you're already dressed. I could slip the preacher a twenty, steal a couple of your mother's flowers, put a couple cans on my truck, and together we could ride off into the sunset."

I looked at William standing there, looking as debonair as ever. Slightly over six feet, with cocoa-brown skin that matched his naturally hazel eyes. He was a looker. Unfortunately he was also incredibly boring. To William, a wild and adventurous evening meant ordering a pepperoni pizza and watching *Willy Wonka and the Chocolate Factory, Chitty Chitty Bang Bang,* or the original version of *Doctor Dolittle* with Rex Harrison. He was a kid at heart, but having inherited his father's construction business, William had become a living, breathing, talking routine. Like *The Truman Show,* his life was predictable, repetitious, and mundane. He stood poised for an answer and finally, I responded.

"As much as I would love to accept your offer, you'll be happy to know that someone is likely to have beaten you to the punch. I have a new man who happens to be a very strong candidate for marriage."

"Oh great, what's his name? Bob, Ted, Jim, Jack, John . . ."

"Ha, ha. His name is Graham and he's invited me to Chicago for Thanksgiving."

"Should I order my tux? You know, I've been meaning to pick one up for some time now. I just haven't gotten around to it yet."

"No, but you should probably order a stretcher for my mother. When she hears the news, she'll hyperventilate, fall to the ground, knock herself unconscious, and end up ruining the day she's been praying for since the day I was born a girl."

"Well, I better let you finish getting ready. Again, you look breathtaking. I mean, really beautiful."

Winking and smiling, he walked out the door.

With William gone my thoughts were now back to Graham. Thinking of Graham is the only thing that's going to get me through this wedding without losing my mind. Especially since I know that in any minute my mother is going to come barreling through the door.

No sooner had I thought it, than the door swung wide open and there she was. In a moment of dramatic pause she appeared in the doorway, adorned like the Queen of Sheba. A fabulous laced gown suited for royalty covered every inch of her body. She entered, twirling around like a schoolgirl, making me scatter through my purse searching for anything resembling tablets of Tums, Rolaids, or Pepto-Bismol.

"Isn't it fabulous?! Not bad for a fifty-eight-year-old woman," she said, grinning from ear to ear, as I thought to myself, you haven't seen fifty-eight in five years.

"So . . . what do you think?"

"About the dress? I like it. I mean . . . it's white. Bright white. Light bright halogen white. I mean as many times as you've been down the aisle, I would've expected battleship gray," I said with a smile and a grin, attempting to camouflage as a joke what was obviously truth. "Get it, Momma? Battleship gray?" I said, as my laughter grew increasingly faint. "Momma?"

My mother's face immediately froze. My joke sank faster than the *Titanic*. She stood, expressionless. Oh my God, what did I just say? It was a joke that just slipped out. It literally just slipped out from the green monster of subconscious envy and rage that had been steadily growing inside of me. I had just said one of the most cruel and insensitive things that a woman could ever say to another woman, and to my mother, no less. I mean, it's not her fault that she's accumulated more frequent flyer miles for her flights down the aisle than I've accumulated in ten years of cross-country travel. Oh my God, there I go again. Think Graham. Think happy. Think Thanksgiving. As she stood there with a blank look on her face, I could sense the overwhelming degree of pain that she was obviously in. Her pain became my pain as slowly, calmly, she responded.

"Whatever the color gown . . . at least I'm wearing one."

Ouch. Then she gave me that mother look. That look that needs no interpretation, explanation, or translation. She stared and I shrank. As I shrank even smaller she stared. And I shrank. And she stared. Until finally, when I was the size of a midget ant caught in a trash compactor, she broke the silence and in a soft whisper asked, "Could you zip me up in the back, please?"

I sighed. I was forgiven. "Sure, Momma! Of course!"

As she turned her back to me, lifting her veil, I discovered the few straining strands of fabric struggling to house a woman two sizes two big for a dress two sizes too small. Quickly, I began to shift and pull, tuck and grab, yank and grip the abundance of loose flesh. This was my only chance to redeem myself. It was either the zipper or me, and today it was going to have to be the zipper. So, I grabbed, and I pulled. As the veins popped from my arms and the sweat poured down my face I started calling on chants from the Buddha, physics from Sir Isaac Newton, and finally even the *Prayer of Jabez*, praying that the dress would enlarge its territory to fit my mother indeed. Pulling . . . tugging . . . squeezing . . . Got it! Whew!

"What was the problem?" she asked innocently.

"Oh, it must have been stuck on a piece of thread," I replied, almost fainting from the intense physical exertion. But it was more than worth it. My karmic debt was settled. My lie was a make-good that would surely render me guiltless of my earlier transgression.

As she stared in the mirror, I could only see myself. We looked so much alike it was frightening. Her bright eyes. Her warm smile. Though the years had been rough on her, she still maintained an elegant look of royalty. This was her day, and no matter how many times she was to travel down the aisle, she was my mother. Good, bad, or indifferent, she is my mother and I love her.

My Aunt Joann, our family's resident wedding planner, suddenly appeared in the doorway. "Ladies, it's two o'clock. Showtime."

Smiling, my mother looked to me. "Are you ready?"

"Am I ready?" I replied, somewhat thrown by her question. "You're the one getting married. The question is, are you ready?"

Pausing for a moment, she took both my hands, looked firmly into my eyes, and offered softly, "For a chance at love and security, no matter how fleeting, a woman is always ready."

For a moment, as she stared into my eyes, I began to swell with emotion. A tear almost rolled down my face. Luckily, I caught it just in time, since a tear would ruin my perfectly madeup face. Who knows what eligible man could be looming in the pews waiting for a chance to catch a glance at his future bride?

I fanned my eyes, gathered myself, and took my position at the front of the chapel doors. Slowly they swung open, revealing the opulent splendor. A church to rival the Sistine Chapel. Its high vaulted ceiling and bright colorful stained glass illuminated the entire room. The only thing missing was the Pope.

The organ sounded as I looked upon a church full of friends, family, and men. Hold up—not just men, but *foine* men. It was a church full of *foine* men and I was about to become their first vision of saint-like purity.

Wrapped in lavender, I was regal. I was Holy. Set aside. More important, in spite of my looming Thanksgiving nuptials, I was at present available . . . But I was wearing gloves. Gloves that would cover up my ring finger and conceal my availability. What better way to envision a bride than to see her walking down the aisle looking *brideish*? The gloves had just become public enemy number one; the only thing standing between matrimony and me. The gloves had become like the Grand Canyon, or the Great Wall of China . . . symbols of unreachable distance and impenetrable divide. But removing the gloves would ruin the look, the ambience, and the picture that my mother had so perfectly painted. Removing the gloves would be a direct sign to my mother and all in attendance that what was most important to me was my own selfish individual wants, needs, and desires. A sign of just how low I was willing to go to attract a husband. Removing the gloves meant shredding one of the few remaining strands of dignity I had left.

With my head held high, and my shoulders squarely facing the altar, I removed the gloves. And in a moment of shameless liberation, the angels sang, and a bright light covered my face as I heard the voice of God saying, "This is my beloved daughter, in whom I am well pleased."

Newly confident, with the grace of a she-tiger, I began my walk. As all eyes locked onto my glow, I walked. Like the Queen of England, I waved my ringless hand to my awed subjects and I walked. I waved and I, I—uh oh . . . I stopped. My dress was snagged.

Standing in the middle of the aisle, mid-promenade, I realized my dress was snagged. With hands waving, smile widened, face glowing, I was snagged. Snagged on a stray nail hanging from the side of a pew. Yes, the devil was busy. And as the music played and the single men gazed, I had to make a quick decision. Either reach back, bend over, and unsnag my dress, which would completely ruin the atmosphere I had so skillfully created, or continue walking and risk ripping the dress to shreds, which would again, completely ruin the atmosphere I had so skillfully created.

I paused. The music paused. Gaining a moment of clarity, I continued walking. And as I walked the dress snagged. It tugged and pulled and—*Screeeech!* It ripped. Still I continued walking and the dress continued ripping. And as the music played and the single men gazed, my long flowing dress had become a short flowing skirt. What had the potential of being my lifetime's most embarrassing moment turned into a loud outbreak of claps, whistles, and cheers as my gloveless, ringless hand and my seemingly velcroed gown-turned-miniskirt appeared to be a skillfully crafted stunt to add spice to an otherwise ordinary wedding.

I reached the altar and turned to my audience. For a moment, all eyes were on me, making me feel for the first time I wasn't just my mother's opening act. For this moment, I was the headliner, and it felt good. So good that I began to understand why my mother took every chance she could to capture the feeling. The emotion. No matter how fleeting, no matter how temporary, it was her moment. But today, for the first time, I felt like it was *our* moment.

And what a moment it was. A suspended space of captured time when it was impossible not to imagine Graham standing opposite me on my magical day. What style tuxedo would he be wearing? What color tie? Would he be clean-shaven or sporting a beard? How many babies would we have? Would they be boys, girls, one of each? Twins? What would we name them? Something Biblical like Ezekiel or Esther. Where would we live? What color house would we have? How many rooms? Surely if it's in Chicago we would have a wood-burning fireplace. Every Saturday morning, Graham would chop wood in the backyard in boots, shorts, and a red-and-black checkered wool coat. With every landing thud of the ax, I would quiver with the anticipation of his return. Thud, I'd quiver. Thud, I'd shiver.

Until I'd melt like a thousand-pound candle in the heart of a burning house.

Later he'd bring in the wood bare-handed, his chest and arms covered with stray chips and sap from the tree. The sap would stick to his fingers and I would pretend it was honey from a honeycomb, ever so sweet, ever so tasteful. And I would lick them.

Then in the spring we'd go hiking in the mountains overlooking the shimmering waters and nature's beauty. When I got tired he'd lift me in his arms, carry me step by step. As he would climb, he would grunt, and as he would grunt, he would climb. With each grunt, I'd quiver. Grunt, I'd shiver. And the more he grunted, I would become like a heated bowl of lava percolating hotter and hotter until finally, he would reach the top and lower me to the ground. He would grab my hand and lead me to the cabin. We would be warmed from the night's cool air by the fire. As the flames danced their intoxicating dance, we'd make love. And what a seasoned architect of love he would be! He would know all the right places. All the right things. With craftsman-like skill, he'd build a house of love, laying the foundation with tender wet kisses, then pouring the concrete with firm yet gentle strokes against my backside. Erecting the structure slowly and surely, slowly and smoothly, till finally our house of love was built.

As we both lay naked in our thoughts, our hearts open, he would look into my eyes, hold my face with his hand, and gently whisper in my ear—

"The flowers! Would you take these damn flowers?!"

Why would he say that?

"Montana, I swear, if you don't take these damn flowers!"

Uh oh. It appears I had drifted off so long I not only missed my mother's stroll down the aisle, but I had also missed her several attempts at trying to relieve herself of her bouquet of flowers so that she could begin taking her vows.

"What is wrong with you?" She said, obviously irritated. "And what happened to your dress? And put your gloves back on! You'll ruin my photo album."

Okay, back to reality. This day had absolutely nothing to do with me. This was all about her and well, it should be. It's her day.

"Do you, Catherine Oleta Moore, take yet another man to be your lawfully wedded husband? To have and to hold . . ."

As the words rang out and her response affirmed, she was married once again. Like a river, down the aisle she went, flowing out the doors and into her future. I couldn't help but cheer. She was the Babe Ruth of betrothal. And no matter how many times she struck out, my mother would fearlessly step to the plate again, expecting another home run.

For a moment that same tear that had earlier crept its way into my ducts reappeared, only this time, like Toni Braxton, I let it flow. Let it flow, let it flow, let it flow. The deed had been done. My mother was a bride for the fifth time.

"Montana . . ." It was Pastor Pendleton. "Are you all right?" Noticing the obvious flow of tears, he could see I was in an emotional state and, like a loving shepherd sensitive to the needs of his flock, he offered warm and loving words of comfort to a hurting sheep.

"Yes, I'm fine. Thank you, Pastor. But what about the flowers? I still have them. She'll need them for the ceremonial toss."

"Montana," he said with a look of conviction, "I want you to hold onto those flowers like you hold onto God's unchanging hand. There ain't a person on God's green earth that I can think of who can use the luck of the bride's bouquet more than you."

As the words eased from his mouth, I felt the last tear stop in midstream. No he did not just say what I thought he said. "Excuse me?"

"I said keep the flowers. Now, go in peace and sin no more." After making a sign of the cross, he strode ahead down the aisle.

My first thought was to hurl the flowers at that nappy patch of leftover hair in the middle of his balding ashy scalp. But instead I inhaled their fragrance and imagined myself for yet another moment as the headliner, the main attraction. Next time, thanks to God, and because of Graham, I would no longer be the bridesmaid, but finally the bride.

## Chapter 2

It was the busiest travel day of the year.

My announcements barreled through our 787 wide-body jet. "Welcome aboard Transcontinental Flight 592 with service to Chicago's O'Hare International Airport. All luggage must be properly stowed in the overhead bins or underneath the seat in front of you. Our flight time is two and a half hours."

Needless to say, the attitudes on the plane were as high as the altitudes. Most passengers were angry for having been bumped twice due to oversold flights. Others were disgruntled because their fit-for-a-king first-class comfort cove had been downgraded to a fit-for-a-peasant second-class coach coffin. But me, I was happy. Nauseatingly happy. I was "Oh Happy Day when Jesus washed my sins away" happy. So happy I had begun to irritate already irritated passengers attempting to board.

"Good evening, welcome aboard!" I said with a "Hey, Kool-Aid!" smile.

"Why in the hell are you so happy?" growled a passenger covered in sweat hoisting two oversized pieces of luggage over his shoulders.

"I'm happy because for the first time in my life I can hear the birds singing. Three birds named love, happiness, and commitment. Like the Love Unlimited Orchestra, all joining together in one fabulously orchestrated symphony. Melodic, harmonious, and glorious."

"Bitch, please. Don't nobody want to hear about no got-damn birds."

"Alrighty, then. You have a wonderful flight." Yes, I was happy. So happy that the mean-spirited verbal assaults of angry passengers rolled off my sleeve like summer rain on a vaulted windowsill.

For on the other side of Flight 592 was Graham. Graham my husband-to-be Jackson. Graham, my chocolate knight in shining armor, who would surely meet me at passenger pickup and whisk me away through the snow atop a towering Clydesdale.

"Yah! Yah! Yah!" he'd shout like a bronze-toned Ben Hur in the Roman coliseum. "Yah! Yah!" Galloping down the Dan Ryan Expressway. "Yah! Yah!" Trudging through the snow. "Yah!" Trouncing cars and SUVs on our way to his palatial estate. "Yah!"

And when we reached Casa de Jackson, he'd dismount the mighty Clydesdale like a prize jockey in the Kentucky Derby. A path of rose petals leading to his front door would be laid out before me, with every step unleashing the aroma of Mediterranean roses flown in from the Congo that morning. When we reached the grand entrance he would sweep me into his arms like a lover stealing away with one of Pharaoh's most prized concubines. There we'd enter into the holiest of holies, his love's lair, where he would baptize me in a pool of blazing hot passion.

"Good evening, welcome aboard. Welcome aboard. Good evening."

"Girl, where the hell is Sam? He's fifteen minutes late. I swear, this time, I'm gonna report his ass."

It was Gail Best, my best girlfriend and fellow flight attendant, who came storming from the rear of the plane. She had little tolerance for whatever or whoever got in the way of her pre-flight flirt time. Time that she could use to scope out potential millionaires, hundred thousand-aires, or anyone in the air willing to finance a good time for the duration of her layover.

Perennially thirty-nine, Gail was blessed with a body like Jessica Rabbit, but cursed with a face like old Br'er Rabbit. Luckily, gravity had served her well. Like a naval cadet, her breasts saluted all who dared to look, and anyone who dared gaze on them long enough became frozen, like Lot's wife, then powerless to her will. By the time the flight began its final descent Gail had options. Many options. So many that she hardly ever ended up at the airport hotel with the other flight attendants. She was my friend. A friend in need and an ear indeed. A loyal confidante who knew almost as much about my business as I did. Too much, if I really stop to think about it. Momentarily shifting focus from Sam's lateness, she moved on to her true passion—men.

"Girl, look at 27B." She never used names, only seat numbers. That kept it impersonal. "Girl, 27B is fine, ain't he? And he's paid! See, they think sitting in coach is gonna throw me off the scent, but I can sniff a man with money a mile away. And besides, the P.I.L. never lies. Girl, he might be tonight's layover."

The P.I.L. was the passenger information list that was supposed to be confidential and for ticketing agents' use only. But, in exchange for an occasional buddy pass (or an occasional piece of Gail's buddy ass), she got access to every passenger's name, address, and more important, their frequent flyer information. Once she loaded those details into her homemade formula, she could pinpoint who was paid and most likely to get laid.

"Um hmmm." Her eyes lit up. "Give me a bag of peanuts, girl. Stand back, and watch a pro. And uh, check your watch, girl, I'm going for the record."

Like Christopher Columbus, Gail was an explorer, but unlike the New World, her male passengers had no problem being explored. Swiftly she began her patented move. She sashayed down the aisle toward her unassuming prey. She leaned in to offer 27B a bag of dry roasted peanuts and accidentally dropped them between his legs. Then just as quickly, Gail started to apologize and began her efforts to retrieve the mishandled bag of peanuts. Slowly she began sliding and gliding the loose bag of nuts side to side, caressing and pressing her elongated fingernails against his inner thighs, massaging his manhood, left to right, right to left, like pocket pool, bumping, grazing, bumping, grazing, tossing the bag of nuts to and fro as she charted her course through his mountainous terrain. I could almost see the blood rushing through every crevice of his body faster than Carl Lewis in the 40-meter dash.

After several moments she gazed into his eyes and mouthed, "Now, sit back, relax, and enjoy your flight." Judging from the smile on the face of 27B, he had more than forgiven her blunder.

Switching back down the aisle, she returned to where I stood, looking as if she needed a cigarette. "Check the watch, girl." Up until now, her record had been two minutes and twenty-five seconds.

I looked at my watch. "Two minutes and fifteen seconds."

"Damn, I'm good," she said.

"Hey, girls!" It was Sam, dressed in a hot pink satin top pulling a custom made overnight bag covered in pink chiffon. Sam Benson was my other best girlfriend. Well, sort of. When I first met Sam, I made the mistake of addressing him as Sam Benson, the flight attendant. I was quickly corrected and informed of his preferred moniker—Sky Goddess. His true calling is his special engagement performances where he transforms himself in full drag into the black Barbra Streisand.

One time, Sam showed up late, still in full Barbra drag, and received several thunderous encores for his a cappella performance medley of Barbra's hit songs "People," "The Way We Were," and Sam's favorite from the movie *Funny Girl*, "Don't Rain on My Parade." The airline executives weren't so pleased when they received a letter from a passenger complaining that on her flight, Barbra refused to sing her favorite, "Papa, Can You Hear Me." Sam was fined and placed on probation. The fine was later reversed when they received letters from the NAACP, Operation Push, and Turner Classic Movies citing allegations of race discrimination, sexual orientation discrimination, and discrimination against the in-flight viewing of classic films—all of which, surprisingly enough, either starred or had their theme songs sung by, you guessed it, Barbra. Ever since, he's used every opportunity to defy rules and regulations, daring the higher-ups to mutter a word. In his latest act of insubordination, Sam replaced the Transcontinental standard-issue black Hush Puppies with backless clogs, and instead of a low-groomed haircut, Sam sported a blond teacup bob.

Sam dared to be whom and what he aspired to become, a diva. In many ways it made us kindred spirits. Both dreamers. Both seekers. Both having no problem hurling ourselves, caution abandoned, impending crash course ignored, into any situation that we deemed worthy. We were both daredevils. Me for love, and Sam for . . . Barbra.

"Hey, girls, did you miss me?" he said, eyes gleaming.

"Hey, girls my ass, you're twenty minutes late!" Gail replied with both hands hugging her hips.

"Is someone speaking to me?" Sam looked around to the left, to the right, and behind him, acting as if Gail was nowhere around. "Hi, Montana, happy holidays! You look fabulous as ever."

"Sam, you hear me." Gail grabbed his arm, spinning him around to face her. "I said, you're twenty minutes late. Don't make me report you."

"Gail, beauty takes time. Fashion is a voyage, style is a journey. Some of us prefer to be oven prepared, baked to perfection. Then there are those"—eyeing Gail from head to toe—"who prefer the microwaveable TV dinner look. Present company included."

Ding Ding! The gloves were on. Round one had begun with haymakers and shots below the belt.

Fuming, Gail responded, "Why, you little flying flame!" Gail didn't waste any time. But Sam wasn't easily flustered.

"Oh, Gail, Gail, Gail. Wait. What is that awful smell? Has the first class menu changed? Are we serving fish today? Oops, I'm sorry, Gail, that must be your new perfume, Jean Paul Halibut." Grinning and giggling, Sam knocked Gail to the canvas with his first punch.

"Guys, guys, please, it's almost Thanksgiving," I interrupted, needing to break this up before the cuts went too deep.

"You calling me a fish?" Gail replied.

"If the worm fits, honey, then hop on the hook and slide!!!"

"Sam, you ashy-ankled, clog-heel-wearing, Barbra Streisand wannabe. You just mad 'cause you weren't born a woman."

"Well, that makes two of us. 'Cause a real woman wouldn't be caught dead with curly red highlights and doo doo brown roots, you section-eight little orphan Annie. Can somebody say *touch up!* Woo hoo!!! Touch up!!!"

As the argument headed into overdrive, the fasten seatbelts sign illuminated.

"Flight attendants, prepare doors for departure." It was the voice of the captain as our flight was about to begin. Sam grabbed the microphone and began speaking.

"Ladies and gentlemen, the captain has now turned on the fasten seatbelt sign. All passengers must be seated with their seatbelts fully fastened."

"Give me that microphone, Pinky. I'm working first class tonight."

Gail yanked the microphone from Sam's hands and took over the announcements. "At this time all overhead bins must be closed and tray tables locked and in their upright positions."

"First you got to *have* class first before you can work in first class. Give me this microphone you nappy-headed cow." As they scuffled for the microphone, I stepped in and relieved them both of their announcement duties.

"I'll make the announcements. Sam, you work business class, and Gail, you take coach."

They both mouthed ill-fated death wishes to each other while taking their posts.

"Our captain today is Pilot Tim Watts," I continued. "We'll be flying at an altitude of 35,000 feet. Our flying time is approximately two hours and thirty-five minutes. We now ask that you direct your attention to the monitors located in the front of each cabin for important safety instructions."

Finally we were in flight, on our way to the bright lights of Chicago's windy city. Home of Jordan and the Bulls. Payton and the Bears. Sosa and the Cubs. But none could compare to Graham. Graham was my all-star. The NBA championship ring, the Super Bowl ring, and the World Series ring all paled in comparison to the sparkle of the ring that awaited me.

"Cream and sugar? Just a moment, coming right up."

I poured the coffee and served the tea. All was well on Flight 592.

"Girl, I can't wait to get to Chicago. I'm gonna get my party on!" Sam exclaimed, beaming with cheer.

"You too?"

"Yes, girl. Ain't no party like a Chi-town party! But why are you so happy to get to Chicago?"

"Oh, no special reason," I said, letting out a brief giggle while I continued pouring coffee.

"Was that a giggle?"

"No."

"Then what was it?"

"It was a . . ." Again I giggled. "It was nothing."

"Wait a second, girl. Did I just see some magical pixie dust fall from your eyes?" Grabbing my hand, placing the coffee mug back on my tray, Sam led me to the galley area. "Excuse us," he said to the passengers nearby.

"Okay, Montana, dish it, tramp. What's the T? You are giggling way too much for my taste."

Suddenly I found myself giggling uncontrollably, my brown skin turning a vibrant shade of red. It was hard to keep a secret from Sam, he knew me all too well. And really, I had been waiting for the perfect opportunity to tell him what was anyway.

"Sam!"

"Girl, what is it?"

"Sam!"

"What, girl?!"

"Sam!!!"

"Bitch, spit it out! What is it? As happy as you are, you'd think you were wearing a gown, a satin garter, and a veil, headed down the aisle."

I held my breath, frozen by his words.

"Girl, no!" Noticing the look in my eyes and the weight of the pregnant pause. "No, Montana! You're getting married?! You better not be getting married and I ain't in the wedding party!"

"Sam, I'm not getting married."

"You better not be, 'cause I was about to go postal. Gay postal, at that. Dish it, girl!"

"Well . . ." Just as I was about to spill the beans, Gail came stomping into the galley.

"What are you two talking about? Got me working back in the plantation wing."

"Gail, will you shut the hell up, Montana is about to tell me about her fiancé!"

"Sam, don't you—fiancé?! What fiancé?!" Gail's nosiness had just saved Sam from his verbal lashing.

"I don't know," Sam retorted. "'Cause as usual, you interrupted us. Don't you have some crotches to massage or something?"

"No, we ran out of nuts," she returned.

"That's a first for you, I'm sure." Rolling his eyes, he turned his attention back to me. "Montana, now tell me about your fiancé."

"I know you weren't about to tell Sam and not me. When did you get a fiancé and why didn't I know about it?"

"I don't have a fiancé . . . yet. That's why I'm going to Chicago."

Like major league catchers with bases loaded in the bottom of the ninth, both assumed the position: perched and eager, waiting intently on my next pitch.

"I'm going to Chicago to visit Graham."

"Graham? Real estate Graham? Upper-six-figure-a-year Graham?" Barely able to pull herself together, Gail suddenly became more excited than I was. Though sex obsessed, loud, and overly aggressive, underneath it all she was just like me. A simple girl searching for a simple life with a man she could simply love. Though she'd never admit it, she lived vicariously through my near brushes with happiness. Deep down, I believed that she found hope for herself in me. The closer I came to finding someone, the closer she came.

"Big baller, shot caller Graham?" Almost hyperventilating, she nearly dropped her pot of piping hot coffee to the ground.

"Gail, please! Would you calm down and let her finish the story?! Go on, Montana."

"Well, he invited me to spend some time with him at his home for Thanksgiving in Chicago. And . . . well . . ."

"And well, hell!" Gail shouted. "It's gonna be more than the turkey getting stuffed tonight!"

"Must you reduce everything to sex?" Sam shrugged with disgust.

"Yes!" she joyously responded.

"It was a rhetorical question, Gail. Montana, this is just like *Funny Girl.* You're Fanny Brice, Barbra Streisand's character, the little songstress slash actress that could, and Graham is Nick Arnstein, Omar Sharif's character, the mysteriously handsome slash charming slash successful businessman. I'm about to cry!"

"I'm about to cry if you keep comparing Montana to them lily-white movies that ain't nobody ever heard of, let alone watched."

"Spoken from a woman who threatened to picket the Oscars because *Booty Call* wasn't nominated by the Academy." Turning back to me, "Montana, I'm *so* happy for you. I hope everything works out." Reaching under his shirt, he revealed a thin silver chain. From it dangled a sparkling sapphire broach.

"This was one of the original pieces of jewelry worn by Barbra in the movie *Funny Girl.* I bought it on eBay. I take it with me everywhere I go as a good luck charm. I want you to have it. From this day forward I crown you diva for life . . . diva for love." Tearing up as he placed the pendant around my neck, Sam paused, then looked at Gail. "Project Annie, it's your turn. Don't you have something lucky? A Boones Farm bottle top? An empty slug from your baby daddy's gun? Anything?"

Shrugging Sam off, Gail turned in earnest. "Montana, go get your man, girl. I'm jealous. I wish it were me. Give me a hug, girl."

"Group hug! Group hug!" we all shouted.

As we all stood hugging and sniffling the intercom rumbled and the ever-present, seemingly majestic voice of the captain announced, "Flight attendants, prepare your doors for our final descent as we approach Chicago's O'Hare International Airport."

As the voice of the captain faded, what echoed through my mind were my mother's words just moments before her fifth stroll down the aisle: "For a chance at love and security, no matter how fleeting, a woman is always ready."

## Chapter 3

Happy Thanksgiving. Good-night. Good-night. Happy Thanksgiving."

The last two passengers exited and I was left there standing alone. Finally it was time. Time for me to exit the plane and enter my future. Graham's world.

Danger! Danger! Overload! Overload! It was too much. Too much too soon. Too much right now. I needed a few minutes to let what I had *willed* catch up with what I had *wanted* to catch up with the thing I had *waited* for all of my life.

I grabbed a stack of plastic garbage bags and began straightening up the first class cabin, checking overhead bins, under seat stowaways, seatback pockets, and whatever else I could find to stall time. After having completed only two rows, I felt a hand touching me on the shoulder. It was Pilot Watts.

"Montana, tomorrow's Thanksgiving. Go."

"But—"

"Go. They'll get to it tomorrow. It's the last flight for this plane tonight anyway. Go enjoy your Thanksgiving." I made a few more insistent responses but he stared me down and ushered me off of the plane.

Grabbing my overstuffed rolling bag, I exited the gate and made a beeline to the ladies room for a moment of prayer. Even though I

31

was anticipating an evening of hot buttered sex on a platter, I still wanted to pray. Finally finding an empty stall, I paused for a moment of reverence. "Lord . . . right now I'm just asking for two things: one, that you bless the end. Two, that you forgive me for the means I intend on using to get there. Amen, Amen. Amen, Amen."

Leaving the stall, I stopped for a quick mirror check and took a deep breath. I popped in a mint and took another deep breath. Squirt, one, two, three of the perfume and one more deep breath. Out of breath and excuses, I was off.

Like a princess headed for her coronation, I was off. My head held high and eyes opened wide, my heart beating, pulsating, beating, until like the green-furred, love-emblazoned heart of the Grinch, it too had grown ten times its original size. But no. This is all too good to be true. Surely I would faint at the first sight of Graham, bounce my head on the ground, and spend the weekend unconscious in the emergency room. Or he would be at the wrong baggage terminal, wrong gate, wrong airport, or wrong state. Something *has* to go wrong. Nothing could go right. Nothing right. Something wrong.

I played these words through my mind over and over, until I succeeded in numbing my expectations. Like the Jedi mind game, I had reversed my thoughts from love and commitment to pain and remorse. Nothing right. Something wrong. Once again I was at peace. The peace of not expecting things to be right, thereby avoiding being crushed when they ultimately went wrong. Nothing right. Something wrong. Like a Buddhist chant, those words rang over and over in my mind.

Finally reaching the baggage claim terminal, I exited the revolving security doors and . . . and . . . and . . . there he was—Graham. He was dressed in a thick camel-colored cashmere overcoat that stylishly complemented what lay beneath: a chocolate-brown suit with light caramel pinstripes. Oh yeah, it was Graham. Hat cocked to the side covering his rich dark hair, skin glistening, and teeth neon white. Fo sho nuff, it was Graham. Holding his signature single long-stemmed red rose, thank God from whom all blessings flow, it was Graham.

As he stood there with one arm extended, posing like he had just been crowned *Ebony* Man of the Millennium, he slowly opened his lips and mouthed, "Do you want my arm to fall off?"

With the majesty of Mufasa, Graham made his approach. When he reached me, he gently stroked the side of my face. With a baritone voice that vibrated throughout the terminal, while simultaneously sporting a smile that could melt the entire continent of Antarctica, Graham spoke.

"Montana." Always taking time for a dramatic pause, again he called my name. "Montana . . . you look unbelievable. More beautiful than I remember."

Coy and playful, I responded, "You must not have a good memory," as we both stood gazing into each other's eyes.

Locked into the moment, he grabbed both my arms firmly and in a warm yet intense tone whispered, "My hope is that soon our opportunity to spend time together will be dramatically more frequent, and I won't have to rely on my memory."

I felt the earth move. Graham led me through the airport's sliding doors into the crisp Chicago evening as the words "nothing right, something wrong" vanished and were instantly replaced with the words "frequent" and "opportunity." At last, I could exchange my frequent flyer miles for a frequent flying man. Frequent. Opportunity. Maybe Sam *was* right. Maybe I *was* Fanny Brice and holding my hand *was* Mr. Arnstein. Frequent. Opportunity.

Quickly we arrived at the parking lot where, just as I had imagined, Graham drove a Benz. Not just any Benz. The big one. The big black one. God, if this is a dream, may I never ever wake up. Graham popped his trunk with the remote, took my bag, and placed it in the trunk. He then walked over to the passenger side and opened my door. Graham opened my door first. For that alone, I'm gonna give you some. Graham was good. He was a gentleman. Easing his big black cashmere-covered body into his big black-leather seat, Graham was good. All good.

"Is the temperature okay?" he asked as he wrapped his big black hands around his big black steering wheel.

"I'm fine, thank you," I responded, wrapped in my coat like Nanook of the north.

Driving down the Dan Ryan, Graham *handled* that big black car. Swerving and dipping, he was in a hurry. Passionate, focused, and intent on reaching his destination. "Run, Forrest, run!" He wasn't about to let car, truck, bus, or anything else get in his way. "Drive, Forrest, drive!"

Soon I began to feel like a Planters peanut as I began slowly roasting. "Turn down the heat!" I thought to myself, but then, why would he keep a lady cold? Not Graham. Graham is much too good for that. Graham has class. Why not make a lady warm? The warmer I was, the more willing I would be to undress. Ooh, Graham, you naughty boy you.

As if the fire needed any more fueling, Graham further intensified our clandestine expedition with the sounds of Wynton Marsalis funneling through his state-of-the-art speakers. The jumping red lights from his Nakamichi sound system were hypnotic as the intermittent levels began to take the rhythm of passionate lovemaking. Wynton was dancing the forbidden dance. Improvising the one-two, three-four patterns of bass, drum, piano, and horn.

As the bass went lower and the highs went higher and the seat got hotter, like a teakettle, I simmered, almost drowning in my own pool of lustful anticipation. Damn, Graham is good. "Drive, Forrest, drive! Drive this big black car till you can't drive no more!" Owwww! I howled to myself, biting my fist, muting my moans. Owww!

Our silence screamed as I gained a greater appreciation for the unspoken. It was obvious that our union was more than contrived small talk. It was spiritual. It was soulful. Like the upper room, we were with one mind and on one accord. I shrank in the seat, willing to go with his flow.

Half an hour into the ride we pulled up to a dock. "I hope you like seafood," he said. Being from Baltimore, and having spent most of my teenage life between the Inner Harbor and Lexington Market, it was impossible for me not to like seafood. "Of course," I responded.

"Good, then you'll love what's being prepared for dinner." I watched the cashmere from his coat stroke his seat as he exited the car. Trying to have some class, I stayed in my seat, not wanting to deny him an opportunity for another bout of chivalry. Like clockwork, he opened my door, and then reached for my hand. Raising from my seat, I exited his big black chariot and we began walking toward the dock.

"You have a boat?" I asked. Which was probably a stupid question given that we were standing on a deck looking at a sea full of boats.

"Yeah, just a little something. I hope you like it."

We walked fifty feet farther and what stood before us was not "a little something." It was a big boat, like the Love Boat, with black stripes and gold sails that reached heaven. Fitting colors, seeing that Graham was an Alpha man.

"You like it?" he asked as he stood petting its nose like the proud father of his firstborn child.

"Yes, I love it."

Before I could even take it all in, someone, noticing our arrival, came from the inside to greet us.

"Good evening, Mr. Jackson. Dinner is almost ready." It was an older Asian man dressed in all black with a white hat.

A chef? Graham had a chef, a boat, and a big black Benz. Frequent. Opportunity. Frequent. Opportunity.

"Dinner will be ready in a few minutes. Let's go up on deck. It's a little chilly, but if you don't mind standing close to me, I'm sure our bodies will keep us warm."

We gazed across the shimmering, mirror-like waters of Lake Michigan. Reaching for my hand, Graham opened my palm and placed in it a small stone that he pulled from his pocket.

"Montana, I want you to throw this out as far as you can," he whispered softly.

I flashed back to the many days spent by the pond at my grandmother's house where skipping rocks was our pastime pleasure. I walked over to the edge of the deck, wound up like Satchel Paige in the Negro League World Series, and with all the strength and might I could muster, hurled the rock deep into the distant darkness.

Barely seconds after it left my hand, Graham grabbed my waist and said softly in my ear, "Now what do you see?"

"I see ripples caused by the rock. Ripples that seem to go forever."

"That rock is you, Montana. And the ripples are what happened six months ago when you walked into my life. That's what this visit is all about. I wanted to make sure the ripples are still as intense."

I returned his pointed stare and threw caution to the wind asking the obvious question.

"So, are they? Are the ripples still as intense?" I held my breath. It was clear to me that our future together and the success of my entire visit to Chicago hinged on his response.

While the brisk Lake Michigan breeze whistled through the air, causing a gentle mist to appear from his mouth, he spoke, "As if someone dropped a rock the size of the state of Illinois in a pond the size of my palm." Unsure of what, if any, my response should be, I stood silent, in awe.

"Montana, what I'm saying is, just like the ripples that continue in the distance, I want our lives to be a series of ripples that last a lifetime."

Suddenly, the words "frequent" and "opportunity" no longer ruled. There was a new sheriff in town, and his name was "lifetime." Like Clint Eastwood in *Unforgiven*, "lifetime" stood tall. Brave. Mighty. Fearless. Standing frozen in the moment, the word "lifetime" kept echoing through my mind, washing over the negative haze of improbabilities infiltrating my bones, giving clarity to the entire evening. I exhaled. Finally, my maiden voyage had reached its Plymouth Rock.

The chef returned with a plate of warm and succulent appetizers. It was calamari sautéed in a lemony sauce. After one bite, my senses were again aroused. He fed me, I fed him, and we fed each other. After several moments I couldn't tell whose hand was whose. Drunk with desire, I was intoxicated by the moment.

Toasts were made and dinner was served under an amazingly clear sky full of bright glistening stars. Underneath the platinum-covered serving trays were heaping portions of white fish covered with a lobster glaze. Strips of tender bacon covered what had to be the *Guinness Book of World Records*' biggest lobster. There were crab cakes stuffed with shrimp, and a dark sauce with just enough bite to let you know it was there. More drinks were poured and more dinner was served.

"Have a good evening, Mr. Jackson." The chef's words faded more quickly than he himself had as again the word "lifetime" repeated over and over in my mind like a broken record.

Graham and I were suddenly and completely alone. The captain and his east coast stowaway. No cleverly crafted, adjective-filled, lust-induced daydream would compare to the taming my body surely awaited. Placing my hand in his, Graham slowly lured me into the den of his passion's iniquity.

Sharp winding stairs descended lower and lower until we reached his underground cavern: a dimly lit room no less than twelve feet underwater, walls moist from engine heat. In the center of the room, obviously bolted to the floor, was a brushed steel bed covered in pillows, fit for a king. To my right, I noticed a portal in the wall that revealed a glimpse of the mystical underwater world that lay just beyond. Damn, Graham was good.

He placed his big black hand on the small of my back and slipped his index finger inside my skirt's waistband. He fiddled with the button and my skirt fell lifelessly to the ground. His big black hands slid over every crevice of my jamoca honey nut almond colored body. Slowly, very slowly his fingers continued, gliding inch by inch around my navel as my panties descended lower and lower, past my knees, over my calves, until they were no more. Then shortly thereafter, Victoria's Secret was told as my bra fell silently to the floor. Slowly he laid me on the bed. By now, like silk panties in a delicate cycle, I was spinning ever so slightly, ever so gently. While he was standing over me, I watched as his buckle came undone. He was hypnotic. Soon his pants and shirt joined my panties and bra, and he climbed in the bed beside me. Damn, Graham is good.

His lips gently moistened my body with warm wet kisses from

my neck to my nose, from my chest to my toes until, like the walls, I was dripping in the steamy sea of ecstasy. Then slowly, Graham began his descent. Kissing my quivering lips, once, twice, three times, he went down. Licking my neck with his tongue, licking from side to side, left to right, east to west, he went down. Grazing the tip of my breast with his hand, circling my navel, he went down. Like Jacques Cousteau he not only went down but he stayed down as the mysteries of my deep underwater world he explored. With no oxygen tank he explored. For over half an hour he explored. Wrapping his big black hands around my inner thighs until, like a molten mound of lava, I erupted. My non-stop flight had made its first connection, and with a little more luck, and a little more fuel, we would take flight again. Hot damn, Graham is good.

I lay there in a pool of my own femininity, singing his praises, high-fiving his oral prowess. My body quivered with sensation as a warm wet slice of peach brushed gently over my nipples, causing them to throb with excitement. Soon after, I felt heat as hot fudge covered my belly. And then, strawberries and cream, sliced bananas, and sprinkled nuts. As I lay there, half conscious, he leaned down and whispered, "Dinner isn't really complete until you've had dessert." No, this brother hadn't just made himself a human sundae. What can I say? Graham is good.

But Graham wasn't the only one with a sweet tooth. Being taught that it was far more blessed to give than to receive, and believing with every ounce of my being that he was destined to be my husband, I decided to return the favor. Leaning him back, I began gently moving my fingers up and down his spread thighs, kissing his stomach, licking his pelvis. Then I slowly removed his thigh-hugging Calvin Klein boxers. My, my, my. Graham's Benz wasn't the only thing big and black. Like a bowl of Rice Crispies, the snap, crackle and popping sound of his toes gave me every indication that Graham was more than pleased with my affinity for most things chocolate, and all things mouth watering. I may have been done, but he was just getting started.

Slowly he climbed on top. I groaned slightly as he entered my underwater tomb. To conquer was no easy task. I, too, was a warrior and understood that no real warrior enjoys the chase without the challenge. I wrestled and tossed, running my jamoca nut hands through his silky black hair, then across his big black chiseled body, making him fully aware that I was no easy win.

We tussled and tossed. Tossed and tussled. Moaning, panting, hugging, rubbing. As the boat rocked, our ships docked and we both screamed with fulfillment. My non-stop flight had suddenly made multiple connections. I was sure that I had finally found my forever. Then, for what seemed like an eternity, we lay in each other's arms, lifeless.

Suddenly Graham looked at his watch. "It's getting pretty late. We'd better be going." We showered, dressed, and were once again riding down the Dan Ryan. Only this time, Wynton had turned into Luther.

I fidgeted in my seat like a child on Christmas Eve, content in the fact that we were headed to his house where he would propose, making formal his intentions. But then the car slowed and made a turn. I hadn't anticipated the possibility of any delay. What's this? A detour?

Graham seemed to be making a momentary pit stop at the downtown Ritz Carlton. Being a successful businessman, his real estate prospects usually stayed at the finest hotels. In Graham's business, perception was everything and since class was his standard, he chose only the best for his clients.

Leaning over close to my face, Graham whispered softly, "Montana . . . Montana . . . I had a wonderful evening. I'm booked on a flight that leaves at six a.m. and I've still got tons of paperwork to review, so I figured staying here would be best."

Uh oh, seems there's been a slight shift in cabin pressure. Though momentarily thrown, and looking forward to the tour of his home, I was fine with our stay at a hotel instead. So, naturally I asked the obvious. "Oh, so we're staying here tonight?"

"No, *you're* staying here tonight. I've reserved one of the best suites in the hotel for you. I'll call you when I get home." My head spun 360 degrees as the needles jumped and the cabin pressure plummeted out of control.

Easing his big black body from his big black seat, he popped open the trunk of his big black Benz. He came around and opened my door, then grabbed my overstuffed rolling bag from the open trunk.

"I had a really wonderful time," he said, as I stood there feeling like I was the lead actress in a poorly written romantic comedy turned dramatic horrordy.

Quickly he jumped his big black body back into his big black Benz. The engine roared, the exhaust pipe fumed, and the words of Luther singing "Love Won't Let Me Wait" grew more distant until I heard only the final chord of "wait . . . wait . . ."

"Wait!" I yelled. "Wait! You forgot something! Me!" I yelled and chased after his big black Benz, "Wait! Please, wait!" It was to no avail. In the distance he reentered the Dan Ryan and his car faded into the hazy abyss.

Something had obviously gone god-awful wrong. Suddenly there I was, my forehead still warm from Graham's kiss in the middle of the street, trying to chase down a big black Benz with an overstuffed rolling bag behind me. I had become love's crack ho and Graham was my pimp, slanging hope and dealing promises of a future. I had prostituted myself for love. I was Trick Baby, and Graham was Iceberg Slim. But wait, how does this work? He's the one that took me out to dinner on his yacht. He wined and dined *me*. So he's the ho, and I'm the pimp. But then again, obviously sex was what he wanted, so I'm the ho. Now, I'm confused. Who's the ho?

"Can I help you with your bags?"

Startled, I turned. It was a bowtie-wearing bellman. "Good evening, sistah, can I help you with your bags?" he offered again.

"Yeah, but . . . do you mind if I ask you a question first?" He nodded. "Who's the ho? The one who gave it up and liked it, or the one who wanted it and took it?"

Expressionless, the bellman paused for a moment of contemplation. Then with the poise of a Muslim minister from the Nation and the precision of a Harvard professor, the bellman began his dissertation on Ho-ism 101.

"Ho-dom, my sistah, is not in the journey, but in the destination.

In each of our very own lifetimes, we have all in some way prostituted ourselves in pursuit of an earthly pleasure. According to the Honorable Elijah Muhammad, it is time for the ho to become the pimp, and the pimp to become the ho. Bean pie, my sistah?" I shook my head no, and he continued. "You see, the white man . . ."

Deciding to depart mid-tangent, I pulled my own bag into the lobby of what had to be the most fabulous hotel on the planet. Vaulted cathedral ceilings, bright glistening chandeliers, Niagara Falls–size water fountains, and warm courteous smiles, willing to provide me with whatever I needed. Suddenly I wasn't feeling so bad after all.

Quickly, my thoughts of ho-dom were replaced with a new philosophy: dropping me off at a hotel was a sign of respect. Of chivalry. Clearly a signal from Graham that I was more than just the hot buttered piece of Thanksgiving meat. Yes, Graham was a gentleman, and I was a lady. His lady. Like a Hindu cow, I was sacred. He was preserving me for the greater good. A deeper love. A lifetime love. Graham was saving me from myself, for unlike my old self I was now a lady. His lady. To be praised, to be honored, to be worshiped.

Reaching the front desk, I was handed my room key and pointed in the direction of the elevator.

"What floor would you like?"

They even have an elevator attendant. A cute one too. "Eleven."

"Oh, the penthouse suite. Yes, ma'am," he replied with a slight twinkle in his eyes.

My only desire was to get in the room, relax, take a hot bath, and reflect on Graham's earlier talk of lifetime. The room was spacious. It had a foyer and a hallway that led to either the bedroom on the left, or a full living room to the right, a wet bar, and what looked like a one-thousand-inch television screen. Tired and worn, I chose the bedroom to the left. There was a custom-made king-size bed with thick and fluffy pillows. Ruffled burgundy drapes opened to a view of Michigan Avenue's Magnificent Mile. Even the bathroom was grand, with two sinks, a sunken tub, and a separate steam shower. The perfect atmosphere for reflecting.

Reflecting... reflecting... "RRRRRRRRing!!!" Oh my God. It's Graham calling. It has to be Graham. He's had a change of heart. He changed his mind and was waiting for me downstairs, calling to tell me that he wanted to take me to his house. "RRRRRRRRing!" Where *is* that damn cell phone? I rummaged through my purse as if the phone were a check from the Publishers Clearing House Sweepstakes and Ed McMahon himself was standing there to cash it. Yes, I rummaged. With peach-scented sweat dripping from my now not-too-freshly-*did* do, I rummaged. "RRRRRRRing!!"

Please don't stop ringing. He'll think I've fallen asleep and then not call back. He'll shut off his phone and the night will be ruined. Where is that damn phone?! Phone, please, phone please. There it is! Quickly I snatched the flip open, nearly breaking it, rushing it to my ear.

"Hello!!! Hello!! Hello!"

"Girl, are y'all doing it yet?" It was Gail. "Girl, I know y'all doing it. Is it good? Does he hook it to the left or to the right?"

"No, we're not doing it," I replied, deflated with disappointment.

"You're not?!"

"No! And if we were, I sure wouldn't be answering the phone."

"I would."

"I'm sure."

"Why y'all not doin' it yet?" Since it was Gail on the phone, I had to respond with something good or she would never let it go.

"Gail, we're not doing it right now because we've already done it. We had a wonderful evening of fine wining and dining on his boat and because he's got to get up early in the morning for a flight, he put me up in a fabulous five-star hotel, which to me is very honorable."

Silence filled the airwaves as I stood, fingers, legs, and toes crossed, hoping that Gail would buy the explanation I was selling.

"Umh hmh," she moaned.

Just the response I had feared. No good was to be gained from an umh hmh. Umh hmh was part of the universal language of women. No matter what the situation, its meaning was clear. In this case, Gail obviously wasn't buying it.

"Don't umh hmh me. Gail, nothing is wrong!" I pleaded, hoping not to sound flustered.

"Oh, it's something wrong, girl," she replied. "That man did not ask you to fly all the way to Chicago on Thanksgiving to put you in a hotel room to spend the night alone by yourself. And who in the hell flies anywhere on Thanksgiving morning? Isn't he from Chicago? Ain't his people in Chicago? I smell a rat, girl. A big ole stuffed Thanksgiving Day rat."

Two things Gail was not: trusting and mature. Not to mention her every motivation in life had something to do with the pursuit of sex. I had to be the bigger person. I had to be the adult. I had to face the accusation she was aiming at Graham head on with the proper dignity and class he commanded.

"Good night, Gail."

"Good night? Girl, don't you hang up on—"

*Click.* Okay, so maybe hanging up wasn't all that mature, but it was a quick fix and the only way I could prevent her from planting any more negative seeds in my head that would grow faster than the ones I had already planted and watered myself.

"RRRRRRRing!!!"

"What, Gail?" I answered, knowing it was her.

"Gurrl, he probably got a page from another woman and dropped you off so he could dip his turkey neck in another woman's Thanksgiving gravy. Montana, don't let that man play you like that. Go over to his house and clown his ass!"

"Gail, I'm going to sleep. I'll see you tomorrow."

"Girl, wait a second, Montana, don't you—"

*Click.* I hung up again. I don't care what she says. Graham is honorable and I am fortunate to have a man like him in my life. Honorable. Fortunate. Honorable. Fortunate. Honorable. Fortunate.

I kept repeating those words over and over as I grabbed my coat and headed back down the elevator toward the front desk. Honorable. Fortunate.

"Excuse me," I said to the front desk attendant. "I'm trying to reconcile my credit card accounts and I'm not sure which credit card my travel agent used to book this room. Do you mind if I see the printout?" Honorable. Fortunate.

Looking at me like I was crazy, the front desk attendant punched in the room number and handed me the printout.

"Thank you so much. Happy Thanksgiving."

I had obviously hit an all-time low. There I was, huddled up in a corner of the hotel lobby, scanning the hotel printout for Graham's credit card information, hoping to find his home address. What little class and dignity I had left was slowly vanishing into the night.

This is ridiculous, Montana. Put down the hotel printout and pull yourself together. Put down the printout and reclaim your pride. I said all of this to myself while still scanning. Put down the printout and reunite yourself with the respect you once had *for* yourself. Bingo! Reunion cancelled. His address: 3546 Mike Circle, Olympia Fields, IL, 60461.

Quickly, I hopped in a cab and was off. At 2:45, we reached a residential neighborhood. I had done the unthinkable. I was in front of Graham's house.

"Girl, I'm here," I whispered into the cell phone to the only person who could relate firsthand to the hellish depths I had descended.

"Here where?" Gail responded, sounding too happy to have received a returned phone call.

"At his house."

"Whose house?"

"Graham's house."

"Graham's house?"

"Yes, Graham's house."

"Oh . . . he came back and picked you up?"

"Well . . . yeah . . . kinda sorta."

"Guuurrrlll, please tell me you did not go over to that man's house without being invited!" I pulled the phone from my ear as Gail shouted loudly, even startling the cab driver who by now was staring at me through the rearview mirror wondering if he may possibly be part of some FBI sting gone bad. I handed him an extra twenty-dollar tip.

"You said something was fishy."

"Yeah I did, but I didn't tell you to buy a pole and go fishing! Girl, I hope for your sake he lives alone."

Knowing Gail, her concern was merely a smoke screen, an obligatory lead-in to getting the information she was really seeking. After several moments of silence she could stand it no longer.

"Girl, how many square feet is it?" I was right.

"About four thousand," offered the cab driver. "I visit a lot of these homes, so I know."

"Thank you," I replied.

"You're welcome."

"About four thousand," I repeated to Gail.

"Four thousand?! *Guuurrrlll . . .*"

Handing the cab driver another twenty to hide around the corner and wait, I eased out of the car and cautiously approached Graham's driveway, trying to avoid being spotted by nosy neighbors.

"What're you doing now?" Gail asked.

"I'm standing in his driveway, looking up at his house."

Truly, Graham was a man of means. He lived in a brick covered palace. Custom lighting set the mood, bouncing off his landscaping. His front lawn was manicured to perfection. If the neighborhood's property value were to decrease, it wouldn't be because of the color of his skin or the condition of his lawn.

"What're you doing now?" Gail asked again.

"I'm walking around to the back. I see some lights, so I'm just going to take a look," I shamelessly replied.

"Montana, that's breaking and entering. That's a crime."

"It's only a crime if you get caught. You know what, you're right. I'm being silly. I'm going to just knock on his door and find out for myself."

"*Guuurrrlll,* don't you do that!!"

"Why not?"

"'Cause you'll look like a stalker. Right now you just look desperate," she answered. "Trust me, I know, I've been both. Now, go around the back and find a window where you can see inside. That way he'll never know you were there."

Her advice sounding good to me, I eased the side gate open and walked slowly, gingerly, around the back.

"What's his backyard look like?"

"It looks like a backyard."

"Girl, don't get smart. What does he have back there?"

"He has lawn furniture, lots of trees, and grass. And a dog, a big dog," I answered, nearly having a heart attack as I imagined myself being mangled to shreds by the dog and later being identified in the police report as an ex-lover turned crazed stalker turned chocolate puppy chow.

As the sound of the barking grew louder and the dog came closer, there I stood, still, with both eyes closed. Maybe if I couldn't see him, he couldn't see me. Then the barking stopped just as suddenly as it had started. Opening my eyes, I realized it was the dog next door, staring, peering, and growling.

"Girl, are you dead?"

"No, I'm not dead."

"Oh good. 'Cause so close to the holidays, that would have been a mess. That his dog?"

"No, the dog next door, thank God. But he's looking at me like he's about to come through this fence."

"Give him a snack. That's the only way you'll get the dog to leave you alone. If you don't, Graham will know somebody is outside and come looking."

Reaching in my pocket, I found an old peppermint. Slipping closer to the fence, I offered it, and to my surprise he accepted. Whew. Silence. For a moment the coast was clear. Then the back door opened and the porch light came on. I could see through the trees it was Graham. Standing ever so kingly in a gold emblem–emblazoned, burgundy cotton robe, even in moral question Graham had style.

"What are you doing now?" Gail asked.

"Needing somewhere to hide. Graham is walking toward the fence but there's nowhere to hide," I replied as I frantically searched for cover.

"Is there a trash can nearby?"

"Yeah."

"Well, get in it!"

"Gail, have you lost your mind?! I am not getting in the trash can!" There had to be a point where I drew the line and this was it. There was no way in hell I was climbing inside of a garbage can.

"Girl, get in the trash can! If I'm wrong about Graham, which I seriously doubt, and he is on the up and up, he'll never forgive you. And if he catches you, you can forget about getting married! Get in the trash can!"

Sinking to an all time low, I slowly, quietly, eased the lid from the trash can, climbed inside, and lowered it closed.

"What are you doing now?" Gail asked.

"Shhh. I'm in the trash can."

"You in the trash can?! Have you lost your mind?!"

"Well, you told me to get in the trash can!"

"Yeah, but I didn't think you was stupid enough to listen!"

"Shhhh! And it's not a trash can anyway, it's a recycle bin. Okay, he's gone." Quietly, I climbed out of the trash can and spotted a window above me.

"Now what are you doing?" Gail asked.

"Trying to pull myself on top of this garbage can so I can see inside."

"Be careful, girl. They got alarms on windows. I know, that's how I got caught."

Slowly I peered over the windowsill, hoping to go unnoticed. Finally, I was able to see inside.

"Gail, it's beautiful. Even more beautiful than the outside."

"Any panties on the floor?" Gail asked.

"No. It's spotless. Like you could eat off the floors. His fireplace is lit but nobody's in the room. Wait. It's him." My voice fell to a whisper. "There he is, walking in the room. He's got a portfolio in one hand, and a coffee mug in the other. He's sitting down."

"By himself?" Gail asked.

"Yes, by himself. Gail, he's alone. You were wrong, girl. Graham is alone, preparing for his business meeting. Just like he said he would be."

Gail was wrong. I was now staring at my future through a double-paned window. Through all the years of searching for that special someone, my forever someone, there he was, alone. He was honorable and yes, I was fortunate. And he was honorable. Fortunate. Honorable. The words continued ringing and ringing and ringing until they began to sound like an actual bell ringing and ringing and ringing and . . .

"Girl, what's that ringing noise?" Gail asked.

"Those are words Gail, ringing in my mind," I replied, feeling emancipated from my racing imagination.

"In your mind?! Well, if they're ringing in your mind, then how come I can hear them?" she replied. "Them ain't words, that's a doorbell."

She was right. Snapping myself from my daze, I realized the ringing and ringing and ringing was a doorbell ringing and ringing and ringing. Glancing quickly, focusing my eyes, I watched as Graham stood, put down his portfolio, took one final sip from his coffee, and headed for the door. I ducked. After a moment, his front door swung open and in barrelled one over-zealous dog, two over-thrilled children, and one . . . one . . . one very overly lucky woman with her arms loaded with luggage.

"Who is it, girl? Who's at the door? Montana? I know you hear me, girl." Gail continued to call my name over and over as I waited what seemed to be an eternity for the room to clear. I had crash landed. The man that I had glorified as being first class had turned out to be a two-carry-on limit, in other words, *scum*.

Carefully I eased off of the trash can and headed out of the side gate, thinking all the while of my most recent mantra. In a way, a somewhat crazy kind of way, I still felt fortunate and honorable. Fortunate that I found out the truth. And honorable . . . honorable . . . well, that one's gonna take a minute.

## Chapter 4

Sorry, the flights are full."

"We're overbooked. Sorry."

"I'm sorry, we just sold the last seat five minutes ago."

Crazed and overworked, every ticketing agent delivered the same unsettling news as I desperately searched for the first flight out. Any flight out. If not a plane, maybe a train or an automobile. Right now I was willing to skateboard home if I had to. Finally, I heard my name over the intercom.

"Montana Moore, please report to the ticket counter. Montana Moore." Rushing to the counter, I flashed my tags and headed for my gate.

"Welcome to Transcontinental Flight 404 with non-stop service to Baltimore's BWI airport." Emotionally drained, exhausted, and confused, I boarded the plane. I hoisted my overstuffed rolling bag into an overhead bin and sank into my seat, contemplating this evening's events and the range of emotions I had experienced. From extreme joy to intense pain, love's pendulum had swung, destroying all in its path. I was numb from disbelief, hardly able to speak.

"Montana, would you like a snack?" asked the very accommodating flight attendant who noticed my credentials hanging from my bag. "We're all out of dinners, but I have some fresh fruit. We've got peaches and srawberries and. . ."

Quickly cutting her off, I replied "No. No, thank you. No fresh fruit." I attempted (unsuccessfully, I'm sure) to return her comforting smile.

What went wrong? What could I have done differently? How could I have prevented what happened from happening? How could I have been so oblivious to the signs? How could I have allowed my heart to be served on a platter, only to have it splattered to the ground? How could I be so damn stupid?

What about his wife? Does she even realize her husband is leading a second life? A secret life? For six months he was mine. For six months we laughed, we shared, we exchanged emotions and desires and plans. For six months we were, in my mind, singular. I wonder does his wife feel like me: cheated on? Robbed of her future? I wonder if I were in her place, would I know? Does a woman ever know? Are there women who do know, but don't care?

The craziest thing in the world is that I feel more sorry for her than I do for myself. I know that sounds stupid, but I do. At least I *know* he's a dog. She could be sitting there thinking that he's the ideal husband, and that his business trips are actually spent doing business, not pleasure. I feel sorry for her. But then . . . the other craziest thing is that honestly, if I was her and didn't know, would it be all that bad? Would it be all that bad coming home with a dog and two kids to a four-thousand-square-foot house, welcomed by a hug, greeted with a kiss, soothed by the crackling sounds of a warm fireplace? Would it be all that bad if, even though I wasn't the only one, he made me feel like I was? And if he was going to end up being the low-down, two-timing snake that he was, why did he have to be so damn good in bed?

By now I was really tired. I was mentally drained, and even more confused as these thoughts and a hundred thousand more went swiftly spiraling through my head, faster than the speed of sound. Even more alarming was the fact that I had been bragging to almost the entire east coast about my trip to see Graham. I had made him my Superman, immortal and invincible. Now, I had to make him mortal. Fallible. And even worse—unavailable.

Woe is me. That was my plan. Woe is me, poor me, who believed that he could, and trusted that he would. Woe is me. I had to make myself the victim. I had to make myself the universally sympathetic, embittered woman, jaded, angry, and broken. For in my family, there was honor in heartache at the hands of a man. There was camaraderie in emotional ruin.

Thankfully for my sake, this flight was a connection from Dallas that got me into BWI a little after 7 a.m., which meant I would get to my apartment shortly after 8 a.m. and have a good five hours alone before I had to face the world. Five hours that I desperately needed to work through my lie.

When the plane landed, I hopped into a cab and headed down Interstate 95. Past Camden Yards, making a right on Pratt Street, then a left up St. Paul Street, until I finally reached my apartment building. A tall white brick building. It wasn't the Ritz Carlton, but it was comfortable. And it was mine.

The sign on the elevator read "Out of Service," so I grabbed my bag and headed up two flights of stairs to my apartment, my cozy hideaway overlooking St. Paul Street.

I slid my key into the lock, turning it ever so gently. I was truly exhausted and couldn't wait to run the bathwater and begin scrubbing away the scent of pain, peaches, and strawberries.

"Meoowww! Meoowww!"

Greeting me at the door was my best friend in the whole wide world, Muggly, a black shorthaired alley cat with yellow eyes. A gift from William on my twenty-fifth birthday, Muggly was found in the pipes at one of his construction sites. And ever since she's been a trusted friend, confidante, and companion. And even more important, a snuggle buddy.

"Hi, Muggly. "

"Meoowww."

By the look in Muggly's eyes, she knew that my trip was a bust. I couldn't lie to her. She knew me oh too well. I immediately flopped on the couch and started crying. And when I cry, Muggly cries. After almost an hour of our whines and tears it was time to focus on the here and now. It was up to me to concentrate, look at my life for what it was, and focus on what mattered most: a good excuse for why I'm home on Thanksgiving.

"Okay, Muggly, we have to come up with something good. Any ideas?"

Muggly always had the right answers. I was convinced that the day I learned to speak cat, my romantic woes would come to an end. But until then, I suppose I had to figure things out for myself.

Okay, Montana, what are your options? I got it. I got it. I'll just hide out here and act like I'm in Chicago. She'll never know the difference. That's it!

"Meoowww."

You're right, Muggly, that's not it. Knowing my mother, she'll call to wish me a Happy Thanksgiving and before I can respond, she'll immediately want to know how things are going with Graham. I moved on to option number two. Thinking. Thinking. Thinking. Got it!

I'll call her from my cell, tell her that I'm in Chicago, but things sorta kinda didn't work out. And I decided that it would be best for us both to stay friends and not pursue anything further. That's it!

"Meoowww."

That's not it, huh? After six months of hyping him up, there's no way things didn't work out unless he didn't want them to work out. I'm left with only one option: tell the truth.

"Ye shall know the truth, Muggly, and the truth shall what? Set you free!" I'm a grown woman, and I'm gonna tell her the truth.

"Meoowww!"

At that very moment, I heard a key being inserted into my front door, the doorknob turning, and then slowly opening.

"Ahhhhhh!!"

"Meoowww!!"

It was my mother and baby sister, Sheree.

Catching her breath, holding her heart, "My God, Montana, you nearly gave me a heart attack. And you nearly scared Muggly to death too. Unlike me, if she died, she has eight more to go."

I made the mistake of making my mother Muggly's caretaker

while I was on the road. Ever since, she's given herself license to show up unannounced, acting like she's there to feed Muggly, when really her true purpose is to pry into my love life, and rummage around my house looking for romantic leads.

"Momma!" I said, feigning my own surprise, "what are you doing here? Hey, Sheree."

"Hey, Montana," Sheree replied, looking a bit awkward.

"What do you mean what am I doing here? I'm here to feed Muggly. I bought her some gizzards so she could have a Thanksgiving of her own. But a better question would be what are you doing here? I thought you were in Chicago having ham with Graham."

"Meoowww."

That was my cue from Muggly to tell the truth.

"What am I doing here?"

"Yes, what are you doing here?" she asked again, eyebrows raised, eyes bugged.

"I'm here because . . . because . . . oh Momma, it was . . . tragic."

"Meoowww."

"What was tragic?"

"The accident."

"Meoowww."

"What accident?"

"I got on the plane to go to Chicago, 'cause that's where he lives, and you know he has a roof, over his house, and the strangest thing happened."

"What?"

"The snow fell from the sky and fell on his roof and his roof collapsed on his legs, and his legs had to be amputated. That's why I didn't stay. He told the doctors that he didn't want me to see him like that. He said I deserved to be with a whole man, not just half of one."

"So, you got dumped? Again?" she said, looking expressionless.

"Yeah, pretty much."

Surely a lecture was forthcoming. Either that or some cleverly twisted scripture that would make me feel worse than I was already feeling.

"Well, Montana, God works in mysterious ways. His ways are not our ways. God closes one door so that He can open another. And when God opens up a door, no man will ever be able to close it."

At that moment my heart instantly started to mend. She was comforting. Uncharacteristically kind. It was a breakthrough. A sign that good things were soon to come.

"Wow, Momma," I responded, starting to get choked up with emotion, "Thank you. That was one of the nicest things you've ever said to me. You're right. That door did close, and I believe God has another one waiting to open for me. For us all."

"Us all who? I got a husband. And Sheree has a surprise."

"What's the surprise?" I said, picking up the pieces from my cracked face.

"Sheree, show Montana your hand!" my mother said, egging her on.

Her hand? Why would my mother be asking my little sister to show me her hand? The only reason she would show me her hand was if . . . was if she was . . . in slow motion Sheree's arm swung wide, her hand outstretched, wobbling from the weight of her hand. A sudden burst of light beamed from her finger, illuminating the entire room.

"It's two and a half carats," my mother blissfully pronounced. "Not bad for a twenty-one year old, huh? I didn't get my first carat until my third marriage."

I couldn't believe my eyes. It was as if I had walked into an episode of *The Twilight Zone* and I was this week's special guest star. My twenty-one-year-old baby sister was wearing a ring on her ring finger. A two-and-a-half carat ring. My sister was engaged. The one I had nearly raised since birth, whose diapers I'd changed. The one who had two years left before she recieved her degree, and four more years left before she'd be eligible for the Moore family curse of the unwed daughter. God, this can't be happening.

"Aren't you going to congratulate her?" my mother asked as my sister stood silent, almost as uncomfortable as I was, knowing she had gone against her promise to give me at least one month's prior notice before getting engaged. She knew that I was caught off guard with no time to come up with a suitable and mature response. A response like, "Hey, Momma, I'm moving to Morocco," or "Momma, did you know I was joining a convent?"

My mother's eyes pierced through me like an infrared light. I was going to have to dig deep down for my obligatory overwhelmingly joyful response. So I dug. With all my might, I dug. Like an Egyptian excavation team searching for King Tut's tomb. Like an Arab drilling for oil. Like a South African mining for diamonds, I dug. I dug and I dug. And as the seconds ticked by slower than a snail crossing the desert, neither striking diamonds, nor oil, nor jewels, I dug.

Still digging.

Still digging.

Still digging.

"Say something, Montana!" My mother snapped.

Managing to manufacture a smile, I faced my little sister, who stood with what appeared to be her own pre-packaged look of excitement.

"Congratulations, Sheree."

"Well it's about damn time. Damn is in the Bible. God knows I would have thought you would be next, Montana. I've been praying and praying but He answers prayer in His own time. Praise God. Well, it's time to get Thanksgiving dinner started. Come on, Sheree. Some of Mitchell's family is coming over and I want everything to be just right." My mother quickly skipped toward the front door, whistling, giggling, and enjoying the moment. Almost immediately my sister attempted to follow.

"I'm right behind you, Momma," she nervously shrilled.

"No, Sheree, why don't you stay *here* so we can talk," I said with teeth clenched. "Momma, we'll be right behind you."

"Are you sure, Sheree?"

With me pinching her arm, she responded in a high-pitched voice, "I'm sure."

"Okay, but hurry up. And Montana . . ." she pulled me over for a private sidebar and whispered into my ear. "I know that misery loves company, but since it's a holiday, leave misery at home. Are we clear?"

"Crystal."

Releasing my arm, her mood instantly changed. "Well, I'll be running along. See you both shortly." She left the apartment.

"What the hell is going on, Sheree?" I said angrily, trembling in rage, as Sheree stood, barely able to look me in my eyes.

"Sheree, look at me." I forced her to look me in the eye. Almost immediately she started to cry. "Don't cry. Answer the question. What's going on?"

"I had to do it, Montana. I can't deal with the pressure, I'm not as strong as you," she exclaimed as the tears ran swiftly down her face.

"Sheree, you are only twenty-one. What do you know about being married? And who in the hell are you marrying?"

"I don't know anything about being married. But every time I listen to Momma talk about you, I know about how it feels *not* being married!"

Staring into Sheree's eyes, I realized that she was more willing to save face than to find love. Instantly, we both burst out in tears, hugging and crying. Even Muggly began crying. Finally, after there were no more tears to cry, we sat on the couch in silence.

"Do you want to know his name?" Sheree asked.

I playfully responded, "No, I just want to show up at the wedding and refer to him as 'what's his name' or 'who's the guy.' Of course I want to know his name."

"His name is Jalen. Jalen Howard. He's very good-looking. Smart. He's a pre-med major at Temple. He wants to be an ophthalmologist and start his own private practice. He has his own townhouse that his grandfather left him, so it's not like we have to even start out living in an apartment. He has his own car. Not a new car, but it runs. He has—"

"Sheree," I cut her off. "Enough about what he does and what he drives. Do you love him?" I asked, afraid of her response.

"What kind of question is that?"

"One that I want you to answer. Sheree, do you love the man you're about to marry?"

"No, Montana. Okay? No. Not yet. But that doesn't mean that

over time I won't grow to love him. I like him. I like him a lot. That's a start, right? I mean, after hearing Momma and the rest of the women in the family talking about how overrated love is, I figured it wasn't that important."

The only word that seemed to fit the moment was "Wow." Staring at me, she awaited my response. Even if in my mind what she was doing was ruining her life, I at least owed her my support. "Well, little sister, I can't say I agree with this, but I'm your big sister and I love you. And no matter what, I'm always going to be here for you."

"Thank you, Montana. You don't know how much that means hearing you say that."

"Well, I'm glad."

"There is one thing that would make me happier than anything in the entire world," she said, her eyes twinkling.

"Sure, what do you need? I could probably get you a free honeymoon trip to Hawaii or someplace. Do you need some help with money? Whatever it is, I'll do what I can."

"Mo, I want you to be my maid of honor." I gasped, holding my chest, feeling like I had been struck with a five-ton brick flung from a hundred-story building.

"You want *me* to be your maid of honor?"

"Yes!" she hurriedly replied. "Momma already scheduled our engagement party for Christmas Eve, and the wedding is in May. May seventh, the anniversary of when she and Daddy were married. So, would you? Please?"

How could I say no, she was my baby sister. "Of course I will. It would be my honor."

"Now, I'm thinking the color of the gowns should be fuchia," she said, eyes bright. "Momma wants peach, but I don't care what she wants, it's my wedding. I want the bridesmaids' gowns to stop right above the knee. And laced chokers around the neck. For my gown I'm thinking backless, long and flowing. I want my hair to be pinned up with a laced sash, and I want my shoes to be . . ."

As she went on and on into that zone so typical of brides-to-be, I slipped into an out-of-body experience. It was like I was standing across the room watching myself sitting there talking to her. I imagined my future. Year after year, bride after bride, I would be the one sitting there listening to another Moore woman plan for their special day, when they would be the headliner, the star of their own show. And there I'd be, just like Aunt Joann, the wedding planner, getting older, growing colder. There I'd be . . . the last living Moore family child born female who had never been married.

## Chapter 5

It was a beautiful late autumn morning. Vibrant shades of golden orange leaves covered the trees outside my window. The sun's piercing rays shone through the glass, bounced off my hardwood floors, ricocheted off my hanging mirror, and finally found its way to my face. My eyes squinted as the pouring light illuminated the room.

A week had passed since my disastrous ordeal with Graham and the double blow of finding out about Sheree's engagement and ensuing party. I had fully digested my Thanksgiving meal but I had not yet fully digested Graham. Thoughts of him still lingered, haunting my body like bad beef. Tired of feeling bad, I was determined that this day would be the first day of the rest of my life.

This would be a day free of yesterday's grief, devoid of yesterday's Graham. Today I would focus on my healing. The key to healing was admitting your pain and taking responsibility for your own actions. Focusing on your own personal role in creating your pain, not on the perpetrator of your pain. Now, it's not like I'm some expert on putting the emotional pieces of one's life back together, but I heard about the process on *Oprah*. And since her show is the infallible, undeniable, unadulterated gospel of pain and suffering, I figured it's at least worth trying.

Slowly, I lifted my cozy cotton sheets and fluffy down comforter, hopped out of bed, stood in front of the mirror atop my grandmother's refurbished wood dresser and with the courage of an alcoholic at an AA meeting, I admitted my pain.

"I, Montana Moore, am in pain."

So far so good.

"I'm in pain from being too trustworthy, too giving."

I'm pretty good at this.

"I'm in pain for believing that Graham was God's ebony angel and not the low-down, good-for-nothing, snake in the grass, cousin of Satan that he turned out to be!!"

"Meeooowwww!"

I had obviously strayed from my path. That was anger, not healing.

"I'm supposed to be focusing on the part I played. Dealing with my issues. Right, Muggly?"

"Meeooowwww!"

Okay, here goes again. I took a minute to roll my neck from side to side and shrug my shoulders. Then I planted my feet firmly on the ground, gritted my teeth, and once again admitted my pain.

"I, Montana Moore, am in pain. Pain from allowing myself to believe that being married was the single most important event in a woman's life. I am in pain from believing that being single, successful, and a good person wasn't enough. As a result, I allowed myself—" Taking a deep breath, I continued.

"I allowed myself to—" Taking another deep breath, noticing Muggly in the corner with her paw over her eyes.

"I allowed myself to be blinded by the conniving, deceitful, treacherous ways of a low-down, black bastard, good-for-nothing, slimy slithering face full of dirt, low to the ground, reptile snake in the grass!!!! I hate him! I hate him! I hate him! I *HATE HIM!!!!*"

Feathers from my down pillow filled the air. Screeching meows like sirens echoed through the room, as I continued beating the bed with the pillows until I was covered from head to toe like Frosty the

Snowman. But I felt good. I felt really good. Oprah was right. But then again, Oprah is *always* right. I was laughing, crying, and looking ridiculous all at once, but feeling a lot better. Even Muggly looked refreshed.

I was tired of thinking of Graham, so my thoughts moved to Sheree. It was less than a month before her engagement party. Less than a month before I had to face my disgrace and lose the last tattered strand of my already low self-esteem. Okay, Montana, focus on something else. Focus on something good. Something positive.

My brain scrambled and scrambled like a hard drive seeking a file. Finally . . . it stopped. Work! Focus on work. Work is always a good distraction. A quick and good fix. And with a ten-day schedule of all-day cross-country flights ahead of me, I would have more than enough time to shift my focus. So I began packing, stuffing my bag with enough clothes to keep a person warm in a Russian winter. I showered, watered my plants, hugged Muggly, jumped in a cab, and raced to the airport.

Work. Work. Work. Work was my focus. My cure. No mention of Graham, no thoughts of Sheree. That was my new mantra. Over and over I repeated it as I rushed through the airport waving at agents, winking at vendors. No mention of Graham. No thoughts of Sheree. Finally reaching the plane, I exhaled. My will was strong. My resolve impenetrable.

"Sheree is getting what?!! To who?!" Gail exclaimed, almost in shock as she nearly burnt her arm on a pot of coffee.

Okay, so maybe I wasn't as strong as I thought.

"I don't know, I haven't met him yet and I can't remember his name. It was late when she told me."

"When did all this happen?"

"Last weekend, I guess."

"And you ain't never even met the guy?!"

"No."

"Flight attendants, prepare your doors for departure" rang through the air, as we were about to begin our ascent. We were on a short hop to Detroit, which was more than enough time for Gail to cheer me up, make me laugh, or at the very least, convince me that her life was in much worse condition than mine. I began my announcements knowing full well she wasn't near ready to let it go.

"Welcome aboard Transcontinental Airlines Flight 606 with non-stop service to Detroit's Metro Airport."

"You can't remember your sister's fiancé's name? How can you not know his name? You're about to be related!" Gail attempted to whisper while covering the intercom.

"Sheree barely knows his name. All she knows is that he drives a car, owns a house, and wants to be an optometrist. And more important, that he's willing to be married. To her."

I removed her hand from the intercom. "All luggage must be properly stowed in the overhead bins or underneath the seat in front of you."

"Montana, I don't mean no disrespect, but your family got issues." She yanked the mic from my hand. "No, ya'll got more than issues," she said with greater attitude than before. "Ya'll got the full years' subscription. Your family shops for husbands like a sale at the mall. A closeout sale. Buy one husband and get one free, taking the extra husband home as a gift for your cousin, auntie, grand-mamma . . . whoever!"

"It's the curse."

"What's the curse?"

"The Moore family curse," I replied as I snatched back the mic. "Our flight time is one hour and fifteen minutes. Thank you for flying Transcontinental Airlines, where we promise to get you there safely or the next flight's on us."

"What the hell is a Moore family curse?" Gail asked as we began serving coffee in the first class cabin.

"Here you go, Mr. Ashley, would you like sugar and cream?" I didn't want my emotional state to interfere with my job.

"What curse?"

"The curse of the Moore family rules."

"What rules?"

"According to my mother, you're not a lady unless you're married on or before your twenty-fifth birthday. And you're not a woman unless you've had at least two kids. And if you're not a lady, and you're not a woman, then you're like Gail, a whore. Mrs. McPherson, would you like cream or sugar with that?"

"Your momma called me a ho? Hold up, hold up, *hold up!* Montana, I know your momma did not call me a ho?"

"No, Gail, she did not call you a ho. She called you a whore."

"What's the difference?"

"The word 'whore' is in the Bible, the word 'ho' is not."

"Thanks," Gail sarcastically replied. "Now I feel a whole lot better." She stood there, face twisted and arms crossed.

"Gail, this is not about you. This is about my stupid family and their stupid rules. Hello, Dr. Julion. Cream or sugar today?"

"I can't believe your *mother* called me a ho."

"Whore."

"It's the same thing!" she shouted, startling the first class passengers.

"Gail, let it go," I whispered, attempting to calm her down. "You know how crazy my mother is. And besides, she's called you a lot worse."

"Than a whore?!"

"Gail, it doesn't matter. What matters is that in less than a month my sister is having an engagement party where the whole family shows up and showers the bride-to-be with gifts and well wishes. It's a pre-reception party so just in case you don't make it to the final wedding date, you know, like if the groom-to-be pulls out, then you will have at least gained points toward being exempt from the curse. There's an addendum to the rules. Three engagement parties equal one wedding."

"I have never ever been called a whore. I've been called a slut, tramp, even a trollop. But a whore? A whore?"

"Gail, what am I gonna do?" I said, ignoring her rant. "If I show up at that party without a man I'll be the laughingstock of the entire family. Professor Previtt, would you like one sugar or two with your coffee today?"

"Two, please."

"Just get you a fiancé to bring to the party."

"What?"

"That's the only thing I can see that will solve your problems. But then again, given your luck with men it'll probably be easier to hit the—"

"Wait!"

"What?"

"That's it!"

"What's it?"

"That's it!"

"What's it?!"

Nodding my head, affirming my thoughts. "I'm getting engaged in less than thirty days. Yep, that's it! I've made up my mind. Three weeks from now, I, Montana Christina Moore, will announce my engagement to my family and the entire unwed world."

"Engagement, to who? Graham?" Sam asked gleefully, catching the tail end of the conversation. "So the weekend went well, yes?"

"No," I responded, sadly shaking my head. "Graham had a prior commitment."

"To who?"

"His wife."

"Okay," he replied, looking perplexed. "Then who, pray tell, are you getting engaged to in three weeks?" he continued, flashing his award-winning smile, as he was now even more intent to know.

"She don't even know herself," Gail said, slightly irritated.

"I'm sorry," Sam replied, turning to Gail. "When did the horse learn how to talk?"

"Sam, I swear, don't start with me today. I'm not in the mood," she answered, cutting her eyes.

"Hello!" Sam said with his hand on his hip. "Montana, how are you getting engaged in three weeks if you don't know who the hell you're getting engaged to? And more importantly, why the rush?"

"'Cause of some stupid rules," Gail retorted. "Rules that her momma's momma's momma came up with that's jacked up *all* the women in her family, as you can see." Cutting her eyes at me. "In her family, you're not a lady until you're married on or before your twenty-fifth birthday. And you're not a woman unless you've had at least two kids, and according to her mother, if you're not a lady, and you're not a woman, you're—"

"A whore," Sam added.

"Right," Gail countered.

"Like you," Sam said. Gail's eyes, ears, and nose matched the color of her fire-red hair as she stood there boiling, rocking, gripping her hands, and seething with rage.

"I am not a whore."

"That's right, Gail, keep on saying it to yourself over and over until you start believing it. And don't forget this one: 'I like myself. I'm a good person. I matter.'"

"Look here, you flying flaming air fairy, I am not a whore!"

"Gail, please, your legs are like the neighborhood liquor store: conveniently located and open all night." He then turned to me all emotional, hugging me tight. "Montana, I feel so bad for you. This is just like the movie *Funny Girl*. You're Fanny Brice." I was thrown, thinking the movie had a happy ending. "Mr. Arnstein based their whole relationship on the outcome of a poker game and when he lost the game, they lost each other. See, Montana, love is your poker game, and heartache your dealer. Up until now, heartache has dealt you a handful of jokers, poking fun at your expense. But the dealer will soon change, heartache will be replaced with happiness, and your hand will be full of kings with aces riding on horses, strutting for life, galloping for love. Montana Moore, *your* king will soon come along, and your fate won't be in the hands of the dealer, for in your heart you will possess the entire deck, a royal flush of truth, love, happiness, and commitment." He pulled me close, squeezing me tight. In his words I found comfort.

"What about me?" Gail uttered softly, as she herself was getting emotional. "I want to play poker too. When's happiness gonna deal my hand?"

"Oh, please, Gail," Sam lashed back, "we're having a moment. Don't you have some peanuts to go plant on somebody?"

"Nobody ever thinks of me," she remarked, swelling up with

emotion. "Has anyone ever stopped to think that maybe I want to be happy too? First I'm a whore, then I'm a liquor store. I just want to be happy too!"

Seeing Gail at the point of a nervous breakdown, Sam showed compassion for her. "Aw, come on, Gail," he said, reaching out and grabbing her by the arm. "Group hug. Group hug," he exclaimed as we hugged, laughed, cried a little, hugged, laughed, and cried a bit more. Then suddenly, Gail broke from our embrace.

"All right now, that's enough," Gail shouted as she pulled out her mirror and began fixing herself up. "You about to mess up my makeup."

"So, Montana," Sam asked, "what do we do about this engagement party in three weeks?"

"I don't know," I replied, "but I've got to show up with a ring on my finger and a man on my arm. If not, I'll never be able to show up to any more holiday gatherings, baptisms, weddings, or funerals."

"I have an idea! Why don't I go as your date to the engagement party?" Sam gleefully asked.

"She said she needed a man, not Peter Pan," Gail shot back.

"In that case, Gail, why don't *you* take Montana? If you go without plucking your facial hairs for a week, nobody will ever know the difference," Sam sneered with a villainous grin.

"I'm about sick of you, Sam."

"Touché!"

Before the catfight became fully blown, I quickly shifted the focus back to my dilemma. "Guys! Guys! Yoo, hoo! Engagement party? Three weeks? Remember?!"

"Montana, you're right. And I apologize. Gail, apologize."

"For what?"

"For being mannish!"

"You apologize."

"I just did!"

"Guys, guys!"

"I'm sorry, Montana. Gail, I call a truce. Montana needs us right now."

"Truce accepted," Gail replied.

"Montana, if you just have to have a man to show up to your sister's engagement party, then that's simple. I'm sure any man would love to be your escort," Sam said.

"Yeah, especially if you promise to give him some later that night," Gail offered.

"Wrong answer!!!" Sam exclaimed with an irritating high-pitched shrill. "Unlike you, Heidi Fleiss, Montana is no longer prostituting herself for love. Wait, I have an idea. Montana, get your phone book."

"Why?"

"Girl, just do it." Not knowing his plan but trusting his motives, I reached in my purse and pulled it out, only to have it instantly snatched from my hands. "We'll flip through the book and narrow your choices down to one."

"One?!" Gail shouted. "She can't pick just one. She'll need at least ten. A woman's always got to have backup."

"Ten isn't backup, ten is a posse. All right, so we'll pick two, then."

"No, we'll pick eight."

"No, we'll pick four."

"Six!"

"We'll pick five!" I said, figuring it was the happy and most reasonable compromise. Five single, eligible, and available men that are willing to become engaged in three weeks. We started with A.

"Aaron. What about Aaron?" Sam asked.

"Aaron . . . Aaron is incredible. Well spoken, smart, handsome, but . . . married with five kids."

"Married?" Gail replied, "Well, why is he still in your phone book? That's a waste of space. He's got a wife and an NBA team." Quickly ripping him out, balling him up, and throwing the page in the trash, we moved on.

"Allan! What's the deal on him?" Sam asked.

"He's very considerate. Always very well put-together. Sends a card on my birthday every year since we met . . . But, he's gay."

"Oooh, girl," Gail said, ripping out the page. "He gets slam-dunked in the garbage can."

"Give me that page, Gail. Just because he's gay does not mean he's garbage, you Raggedy Ann–headed goat. Allan has potential," Sam added, snatching the page from Gail and smoothing out its wrinkled creases.

"Not for Montana," Gail shot back.

"I know, heifer. For me!" Sam responded, stuffing the number in his pocket.

This went on for what seemed an eternity as Sam and Gail cussed, fussed, and pages went ripping and flying in the air. Through the K's they fussed. Through the M's they cussed. Now, through the P's Sam fussed, pulling out a plastic knife and threatening to saw Gail's weave. Through the T's, Gail cussed back, holding two cans of mace pointed at Sam.

Finally we hit Z. Phone book paper was piled to the airplane's ceiling. Exhausted and worn, we poured some wine and toasted to our success. We had chosen five men. From Atlanta to Los Angeles. From Oakland to Philly. From New York to D.C. Five men, all eligible, all single, and most important, men I had previously dated who had hinted at the possibility of a future together.

"Great."

"Great!"

"Wait," Sam said, stopping Gail and me in mid-celebration.

"What's wrong?"

"Yeah, what's wrong, Sam?"

"Three things. Time, opportunity, and access. Everybody we chose is very busy and their social calendars are full, not to mention, they're spread across the entire country."

"That ain't no problem," Gail offered. "If the mountain won't come to Mohammad, then Mohammad must go to the mountain."

"I can't go chasing after these men. They'll think I'm desperate."

"Montana, you need a husband in three weeks! Hello! If that's not desperate, then what is? A man has too many options to be fooling around chasing a woman. The ratio is already thirteen to one. And that's thirteen to one nine-to-five working, paycheck to paycheck living, public transportation riding kind of man. Don't get one that's got a little something going for him. That's got a house, got some money, or even worse yet, that's got a dream. Don't let him have a little status, a little notoriety. Then you're really in trouble. 'Cause then, it's like a thousand to one. See, you've got to make yourself stand out so that in that thousand, he only sees one."

I was in shock. For once, Gail was saying something that made sense. Standing before me was a new Gail. A sage. A master. Love's Dalai Lama. A spiritual guide to help me navigate through love's uncharted waters. She was my teacher and I was her pupil. Gail had the answers, the solutions, and the cures to my woes.

Like a humble apprentice, I asked the next obvious question. "So, teacher, how do you make yourself the one?" I pensively asked, anxious to soak up her wisdom and insight.

"Hell if I know. Do you see a damn ring on my finger?" Okay, now this was the Gail that I knew.

"You know, Montana, I really hate to say this. I really, really, really hate to say this. But Gail's got a point. Most men want to be hunted, but also need to feel as if they're doing the hunting. Most men want to fight the wars, slay the beasts, and come home blood-drenched, tattered, and torn, falling helpless, unconscious, into the arms of a loving, nurturing woman. You have to make a man feel like he can fly, believe that he is stronger, faster, and wiser than he really is. The woman that learns to appease her man conquers her man." Sam was dissecting the male psyche with Freud-like skill. You go, Sam.

"Look at Samson and Delilah," he continued. "Now, I don't agree with Delilah, but you have to admit she was on to something. Here she was, dating the strongest man in the world. A man that could lift pillars, toss horses, and crush stones with his bare hands. A warrior. A gladiator. But in the presence of Delilah, this mighty soldier was as gentle as a lamb. He became comfortable. And as soon as he became comfortable, he lowered his guard and next thing he knew: snip snip, hair gone. He was conquered. The strongest man in the world will become the weakest man in the world in the arms of the right woman."

"I've got it!! I've got it! I've got it!" Gail screamed, nearly waking any sleeping passengers. "I've got it!"

"Well then, can you share it?!" Sam asked.

"All these guys fly a lot, right?"

"Yeah. And?" I was clueless to where she was going.

"Well, Montana, you are going to 'coincidentally' bump into each of the five men during a flight on their way home. And after you 'coincidentally' bump into these men, because you will be looking incredible, they will each request your company for an evening, which will give you the opportunity to what? Snip snip, hair gone," Gail explained, smiling from ear to ear.

"And how, pray tell, do you expect her to 'coincidentally' accomplish this near-impossible feat? Should she hang out in the airports masquerading as a homeless woman, then as soon as she spots one of the five men, like Clark Kent, dash into a phone booth and change?"

"No," Gail said, raising her eyebrows. "She won't have to do that, because she'll *know* in advance when each will be traveling."

"How?"

"Yeah, how?" At this point, even I was intrigued.

"The Passenger Information List! The same way I find out about my male prospects is the way we'll find out about yours. Since they all have frequent flyer accounts, I'll just get my agent hookup to punch in their names, pull up their frequent flyer numbers, and we'll know the next time they will be flying the friendly skies! Then, we'll swap flights, switch routes . . . do whatever we have to to make sure you are on the flight, and then voilá! Snip snip, hair gone!"

Suddenly, what seemed impossible became almost probable. It was a shot. A long shot, but a shot nonetheless.

"Again, I hate to admit it," Sam begrudgingly added, "I really, really, really hate to admit it, but she's got another good point."

"But I've dated all these guys before and I'm not engaged now. Why would this time be any different?"

"'Cause this time *you* will be different," Sam said with confidence. "When they see you this time, they won't just see the woman that they remember, looking the way they remember. This time, they'll see a new and improved Montana. Poised. Confident. Self-assured and self-aware. The woman of their dreams. A woman that makes them believe they can fly. And to be different and expect a different outcome, you have to first change your actions. Same actions, same outcome. New actions, new outcome. First thing is—and this might be one of the hardest—when you see these men, all of which you've probably had sex with, under no circumstances, no matter how hard it gets and no matter how hot and bothered you become, will you engage in any sexual activity."

"How about if she just—"

"No."

"But what if she just—"

"No!"

"You mean she can't even—"

"No! No high heels, no hot pants, and no sex!"

Feeling the need to bring my earlier indiscretions to Sam's attention, I offered, "Uh Sam, I hate to tell you this but—"

"Girl, I already know, but read my lips: same actions, same outcome. New actions, new outcome. Consider it a fast. A sex fast. Think of it as your candy machine having a broken quarter slot. The candy will still be fresh, protected, and visible to the naked eye, just temporarily unattainable. It's more intoxicating that way, anyway. We all want what we can't have, agreed?"

First looking at Gail, who was rolling her eyes, then back at Sam. "Agreed."

"Rule number two, no matter how tempting the choices may get, you can't make a decision until after you have spent time with *all* five. That means you can't do like you usually do—"

"And what's that?"

"Let yourself get all caught up, swept away, let him fill you with a thousand pounds of helium until you're floating at an altitude higher than this airplane. Then, as all of your past men have done, once he sees you floating, he'll pull out a needle and pop a hole in your bubble, sending you spiraling, spiraling, *splat!* Face cracked, shattered on the ground."

"Thanks, Sam."

"Girl, that hurt me more than it hurt you. No matter how alluring, how exciting, how tempting each one may be, you *must* keep your two feet firmly planted on the ground and your legs closed in their locked position. Then . . . if everything goes as planned and with a little luck, in three weeks . . . you'll have a husband. So, are you in?" Sam was first to extend his hand like the Three Musketeers. Gail was next, placing her hand on top of Sam's. I sighed for a moment, then slowly, I extended my arm, placing my hand on top of theirs.

"I'm in."

"First thing when we land, we're taking you to get a makeover, 'cause the Mary Poppins look? Hate it!" He scrunched up his face.

"He's right, girl."

"You got to get fly, girlfriend. Attitude has to be fierce, hair has to be whipped, clothes have to be tailored, and scissors have to be sharpened. Why?"

Sam eyed both Gail and me down, flailing his arms, snapping his fingers, "Snip snip, hair gone!"

As the plane made its final decent, I was ready to hit the ground running headfirst into my most daring adventure yet. A three-week, nearly thirty-thousand-mile hunt for a husband. My latest mantra: same actions, same outcome—new actions, new outcome. In other words, snip snip, hair gone.

We landed, taxied to the gate, unloaded the passengers, and dashed through the airport like an Olympic 400-meter relay team. We each had our mission. Sam hit the lounge to find three eternally layed-over flight attendants and beg them to swap trips, giving us our needed free time and them more desired flight time. I checked the gates for the next available Transcontinental flight back to Baltimore. If there weren't any available on our particular carrier, then possibly a sister airline would allow us to hitch a ride. Gail used her feminine wiles to seduce a male ticketing agent into giving her access to the frequent flyer accounts of our five male finalists. We were off. Begging, pleading, punching in numbers, bringing up codes, we were off. Almost exactly as planned, within an hour we were back at the gate. Trips traded, doubts faded, and mission accomplished.

"Welcome aboard Transcontinental Flight 862 with non-stop service to Baltimore's BWI airport." We made it, whew.

With our hands full of magazines, we ripped and laughed, slashed and argued our way from one magazine to the next. Sam wanted me to look like Barbra Streisand and Gail wanted me to look like Mary J. Blige. We barely served coffee and I don't think we poured one drink for one passenger. We were too focused.

Before we knew it we were back in Baltimore and still debating which end of the fashion spectrum I would choose. We raced through the terminal, hopped the shuttle, reached my brick-covered apartment building, and raced up the stairs to apartment 2C. We took a quick minute to catch a breath.

"Okay, so we only have twenty days," proclaimed Gail. "We have to make each moment count."

"First stop, the closet," Sam shouted, grabbing Gail, rushing into my room, and sliding the mirrored closet door open.

"Aaaah!!!!!" they both exclaimed, standing in front of my closet, eyes wide like they'd seen a ghost. Then calmly, with his voice slightly above a whisper, Sam cautiously said, "Montana, hand me your telephone."

"Sure," I said, innocently handing him the phone.

He slowly put the phone to his ear and began speaking. "Hello, Homicide? I need to report a murder. Chile, somebody done killed fashion! Her name is Montana Moore. Hurry, before she strikes again!" They laughed and howled as I snatched the phone back. Then like Judge Joe Brown, Sam delivered my sentence.

"Montana Moore, you are being charged with two counts of wrong color combinations, three counts of cheap material, eight counts of shopping from the Sears and JCPenney catalogs, and twelve counts of how-in-the-hell did this jump off the rack and into my closet!!"

"Come on, guys," I whined, trying to salvage a few threads of my wardrobe. "It can't be that bad. I mean this works, this is nice right?" I pleaded, holding up my favorite ensemble. Their faces were expressionless. "Okay . . ." rummaging again through the closet. "This. Now I *know* this is nice." Again, no reaction.

"Girl, absolutely nothing in your closet works," Gail offered, sliding my closet door shut. "Not a scarf, a hat, a sock, nothing! And not only that, Montana, you've got to do something about your appearance."

"The black Barbie look has long since been played. Your hair is a mess and your makeup is all wrong," Gail softly added.

"Well if I was that bad, how come nobody said anything?"

"Girl, my daddy always told me if they're sleeping, don't wake 'em up," Sam said.

"Was I sleeping that much?"

"Girl, you were in a coma! This situation is desperate," Gail said as she paced the floor, heavy in thought. "And as much as I love Baltimore, Baltimore ain't gonna do it for you. You are in a drastic state, and drastic times call for drastic measures. Sam, are you going where I'm going?" Gail asked.

"Girl, I've been there and back," Sam responded and broke into song. "Start spreading the news." Gail joined in, "We're leaving today . . ."

"Montana," Gail said, holding my hand, "we are headed to New York!"

Grabbing our bags, again, we were off. Catching a cab, running down trams, dodging vendors, flashing passes, begging agents until finally we boarded an air shuttle headed to Manhattan. We hit the ground in New York's LaGuardia Airport, smack dab in the middle of afternoon rush hour traffic.

After two hours, we made it to Elizabeth Arden's Red Door salon and spa for a massage, facial, and derma scrub.

"If you want to look good, you've got to first feel good," Gail explained. "I'll handle the feel good. Sam, you handle the look good!"

Sam took my purse, flung open my wallet, pulled out my credit cards, kissed me on the cheek, and went skipping and hopping away.

An hour later I'd been seared, tugged, rubbed, pulled, and smacked by what seemed like a thousand hands on a million body parts, then pittered and pattered, splittered and splattered by what seemed like a thousand pounds of warm wet mud.

When my session was over, Gail was waiting. She had a message on her phone that Sam was waiting for us at Thirty-Seventh Street and Fifth Avenue with Oscar—Oscar James, one of New York's top hair stylists who does all the fly cuts for all the big stars and soon-to-be stars. I couldn't believe it.

"Girl, you know you would never *ever* get in here on just a day's notice," Sam said. "But a couple of months ago, Oscar's travel agent messed up his ticket and sat him in coach. I recognized him and moved him up to first class. He said whenever I was in town, he would hook me up. You know I *got* to love you for this."

We entered the salon, a rustic two-story loft, with vibrant-colored paintings by Charles Bibbs and William Tolliver covering the walls.

"Welcome. We've been expecting you," rumbled the voice of a man, dark skinned and dreadlocked. He offered his hand and we walked to the bowl for my wash and rinse. "Do you believe in Heaven?" he asked as he lowered my head into the basin. Steam swirled from the bowl.

"Of course," I replied, unsure of his question.

"Have you ever *been* to Heaven?"

"Not yet, but hopefully someday."

"Today is your someday," he affirmed, tilting my head, soaking my scalp, then applying shampoo, the good shampoo. Not that cheap stuff the ghetto stylists pour into the expensive containers to make you think it's the real thing.

Then, he glided and moved, slided and grooved his hands through my scalp like the amazing human scrubbing bubble. This brotha must belong to some space-age pampering coalition.

Lulled into a tranquil daze, I began quoting the Beatitudes as he scrubbed. Through the gospels of Mathew, Mark, Luke, John, and a few more folks I can't remember, he scrubbed. The clouds opened, and the light shone through, and there was Jesus descending from the clouds, touching my arm, lifting me higher and higher and higher and ...

"All done," he whispered, knowing exactly what he had done. "Like I said," he continued, smiling while wringing his towel, "sometimes, you can have heaven on earth."

I rose from the bowl and saw Oscar standing proudly, dressed in black, flared, no pleat slacks and a tight-fitting, canary-colored top.

He was peering down from the top of the hardwood staircase that led to the second level of the loft. Oscar was the man, holding his shears like a Japanese samurai warrior. A black Zorro, an ebony Edward Scissorhands. I ascended the stairs and eased into his chair.

"You know, I was thinking maybe—"

"Silence!" he roared. The whole shop grew still. Even the shampoo god had to pause.

He swung me around in the chair like a graceful black raven sizing up its wounded prey. Spinning me once, he glared. Spinning me twice, he stared. Then he snapped on his cloak and began.

"Scissors!" he yelled. "Trimmers!" he shouted.

He began with a snip, then a stare. Then a cut and a glare. "Color!" he yelled. "Toner!" he shouted, while several assistants hurried and scurried about, fulfilling every command.

Almost two hours later, out of the daze of the hair-covered haze, there was Oscar, finished—a glass of riesling in his hand and a smirk of satisfaction on his face. Hair was his sex, style was his orgasm. Sam stood in the corner and I noticed a tear of adulation falling from his eye.

Gail was also standing nearby, looking as if she too had just made a connection. Then a hand slowly moved from her hip, up her waist to her face, past her lips. It was the shampoo god. Knowing Gail, she *had* just had sex.

"Can I take a look?" I humbly requested. Shaking his head with a smile, he calmly protested.

He stepped aside, revealing a light-skinned man. He was well built, smiling wide, obviously proud of how much his momma had spent on regularly scheduled trips to the dentist.

"The name is Fine. Sam Fine." It was Sam Fine, the makeup guru. The man responsible for the faces of Vanessa Williams, Mary J. Blige, and supermodels like Tyra Banks and Naomi Campbell. Glancing at Gail, he winked. This was obviously her hook up.

While the sun fell and the moon rose, like Picasso, he painted. My face was his canvas. Using his small brush, light brush, black brush, white brush, he painted. When the moon had illuminated the night and the cold winds blew gently through the crack in the window, fine Sam Fine announced that he was finished.

Finally I was allowed to look in the mirror. My hair was a smartly cut bob with honey-colored highlights. I began to see the reflection of a face more beautiful and elegant than before. The face of a woman of means, a woman of class, a woman of sophistication. Surely my eyes were playing tricks on me. Surely the reflection I saw couldn't possibly be me.

Turning to Sam, then looking at Oscar, I was speechless. Common as it may be, the only phrase I could find to express my emotions was "Thank you."

Over their shoulders I noticed *my* Sam toting bags full of clothes. Oscar and Sam stepped aside, letting him through. Taking my arm, he led me to the back room where I could change.

"Try this on first," he said, unwrapping one outfit after another.

"Next, this. Next, this. And next, this." Outfit after outfit, shoe after shoe, until finally, we agreed on a look. He nodded, Gail applauded. I was a goddess in a painted-on, body-gripping, red strapless gown by Valentino, accented with Gucci diamond studded earrings. Nude strappy sandals by Miu Miu, a buttery leather asymmetrical bag by Hermès, and the scent of Donna Karan's Cashmere Mist completed the ensemble.

Looking at Sam then turning to Gail, once again I offered a soft and sincere "Thank you." I was overwhelmed.

Nearly breathless, like the ballerina on my childhood musical jewelry box, I twirled out of the salon. The entire way home to Baltimore, I twirled. Alone in my bedroom, I basked in the glow of the new me and twirled some more. As the bedroom I rounded, and the music box chimes sounded, and my neighbors down below me pounded, I twirled. I was a black ballerina and no thing or no one could cause me to descend from my cloud.

"Montana, what the hell are you doing?"

Except for my mother.

"Meoowww!"

It was as if the music box exploded, catapulting the ballerina headfirst into the ceiling, snapping her body in half.

"And why are you all dressed up, spinning around, staring in the mirror looking retarded?" she asked.

Talk about being smacked back into the present.

"And what in the world happened to all of your beautiful hair? Why did you cut your hair? God made man for *His* glory. He made woman for *man's* glory. And a woman's hair is *her* glory." Still I was speechless. "I'm talking to you, Montana," she stated, eyes wide, awaiting my response.

"Which question would you like me to answer first, Momma?" I replied.

"All of them. You make the call."

Wait a second. Okay, now she is really trippin'. I am not on the witness stand. She's in *my* house, the apartment that *I* pay for with the money that *I* work hard for. I don't come over to *her* house unannounced, stick my key in *her* door, walk up *her* stairs, stand in *her* hallway like a Peeping Tom asking her a million questions. Why can't she give me that same respect? Suddenly the words "Same actions, same outcome. New actions, new outcome" rang through my head. It was time I stood up to my mother. Time I let her know what a nagging, prying, boil on my butt she had become. Time to let her know that because of her, I've become a crazed, love-torn, husband-chasing fool that's on a three-week hunt for a fiancé. My mother needed a wake-up call and I was the one to dial it. So, lifting my brow, squaring my shoulders, I looked directly into her eyes and I told her exactly what was on my mind.

"This is Gail's dress," I lied, buckling from the pressure. But wait, the lying got worse.

"Why are you wearing Gail's dress?"

"'Cause she bought it for a birthday party and uh . . . well, she got caught up on a flight, and uh . . . didn't have time to try it on, so she asked if I could try it on for her and uh . . . that's what I'm doing, trying it on. I mean, it's not something I would personally wear, but . . ." I was spinning, weaving, getting tangled in my own web of deceit. The sweat rolled down my face and she could sense I was sinking.

"Mmm hmm. And what about the hair? Why is your hair so short?"

"Uh . . . it's a new regulation. Transcontinental came up with this stupid policy that all flight attendants have to wear their hair closer to shoulder length. You know, no more than ten centimeters lower than their ear. Yep . . . Stupid, huh?" I said with a lopsided grin, sprinkling my lie with canned laughter.

"Yes, very."

Finally, she let me off the hook. "Well, anyway, I'm here to talk to you about your sister Sheree." Whew. I sighed to myself, glad that the focus had shifted from me.

"Sheree? What's wrong with Sheree?"

"Well, I had a conversation with her after Thanksgiving dinner and for some reason, all of a sudden she's confused. All of a sudden she's thinking that she doesn't love her fiancé, and because she doesn't love him, she thinks they shouldn't get married. I don't know where she would get such a stupid thought. I need you to talk to her."

"Me?"

"Yes you. We've made too many plans, and have already ordered the flowers and invitations. Half of the family has already made travel arrangements to be there. I need you to talk some sense into your sister. For some strange reason, she listens to you. God only knows why. I mean, what advice about marriage could you possibly give her?" she said, leaving the last half of her snide remark implied but unspoken.

Wow, I thought. What a skill she has. The power to build you up and at the same time tear you down. But then, I don't recall her ever building me up. She always just tears me down. And now she wants me to talk my little sister into making one of the worst mistakes of her life? No, Momma, I'm sorry. This time you've gone too far. There is no way in hell I will become an accessory to a crime when I know in my heart it's wrong. And right now, Momma, you are wrong. Okay? You are wrong, wrong, *wrong!*

"Okay, I'll talk to her," I said with a sugar-coated smile.

"Good, I knew you would. Tomorrow and not a day later. Goodnight. Oh, and uh, take off that dress, you look ridiculous. Now give me a good-night kiss, baby."

She kissed me, I kissed back, she was gone. Sighing deeply, I thought, God, I am part of the most jacked-up family on the face of the earth. I was sure that the strength I needed to face my mother would arrive one day. Just not today. And who cares anyway? Tonight, it's about me. I'm the focus. Tonight, I loved myself. Better yet, I *liked* myself, which was amazing because, as I'm thinking, I can't really remember the last time I felt that way. Same actions, same outcome. New actions, new outcome.

"RRRRing!!" Startled, I ran to the phone. Who in the world would be calling me this late?

"Hello?"

"Girl. It's me, Gail. You ready?"

"Ready for what?"

"Girl, Damon Diesel, come on down! You're the first contestant on the flight is right!" she laughed, amused with herself. "Girl, my hook up came through. Damon's on a flight from Houston to New York this Friday afternoon!"

Friday afternoon, I thought to myself. That's day after tomorrow! "But Gail, I . . ."

"No buts, your flight's been confirmed. Call me when you get to Houston! And remember girl, no sex, no sex, NO SEX! Girl, I got to go, that's Charles at my door."

"At one o'clock in the morning? What are y'all about to do?"

"What else? Have sex! C-ya!" She hung up.

Prayed over and made over, I was headed back to New York thinking no sex, no sex, no sex. How ironic, considering "diesel" represented more than just Damon's last name. Danger, Will Robinson. Danger!

## Chapter 7

My alarm clock buzzed. It was 6:30 a.m. on the sixth of December, exactly 18 days before Sheree's engagement party. I opened my eyes, hoisted my legs from the bed, opened the window, and inhaled the unseasonably warm breeze flowing gently through the tree outside my bedroom window. Aaaah. Air never smelled so nice.

I turned on the radio. On 92.Q they were playing Maxwell, then Angie Stone, then a host of other neo-soul trying to be original-soul but lacking any real-soul artists. But it didn't matter, they all sounded good today. Aaaah, air never smelled so clean.

The stage was set for an extraordinary day. Like my first day in high school or college, I was excited and scared at the same time. I had a set of new clothes, new shoes, a fresh hairdo, and more important, a new me. Aaaah, the air never smelled so fresh.

I went into the bathroom and looked in the mirror. Was yesterday's makeover only a dream? Whew! I smiled. I wasn't dreaming, I really had been transformed. Still looking good. Hair still whipped and eyes still bright. I brushed my teeth, washed my face, and stepped into the shower. To the rhythm of the music, I washed and scrubbed with soft-scented apple gel, lathering myself from neck to toe. After I rinsed off, I wrapped myself in a soft, thick, white cotton towel and stood in front of the mirror.

Slowly I lowered my towel and stood naked. It's been a long time since I actually dared to look at my body completely naked. I sighed. I liked what I saw. I actually liked the image staring back at me. Eyeing my curves, embracing my swerves. I was God's most beautiful creation. From my hips to my lips, I wasn't perfect, but finally, I felt perfect for me.

I applied some face moisturizer. Then face vitalizer, neutralizer, and sanitizer. If men only knew the ridiculous lengths a woman goes just to walk out of the house, they wouldn't complain about waiting for us so long. They'd be grateful we made it at all.

I sprayed my new fragrance once, twice, three squirts in the air, and then walked through the mist so that my whole body was covered from head to toe. I pulled out the step-by-step makeup manual for reconstructing my look and gently, very gently, calm, and collected, I repainted the painting. Like I was da Vinci and my face was the *Mona Lisa,* I painted. Thanks to Sam Fine, I didn't do too badly for my first try.

I was smelling good, looking good, and feeling good. Now for the underwear. This time, I reached into the stash I saved for special occasions. You know, the ones you wear when you've already made up in your mind that you're gonna give him some. I pulled out those. I wanted to feel sexy. Even on the plane, I wanted to feel sexy. Even though I wasn't *supposed* to give him some, I still wanted to feel sexy. I reached in my closet and pulled out my uniform. It was Transcontinental's standard blue, which was never intended to make a fashion statement. But after Sam got finished, it looked like Armani tailored and designed it himself. Fitting like a glove, it was painted on. Sam had hooked me up. And the shoes: a pair of blue Prada pumps set the whole suit off. I threw the Guccis in my ears and I was ready, my new look complete.

"What do you think, Muggly?"

"Meooww."

Good. She approved. Pulling my overstuffed rolling bag behind me, I gave Muggly a hug, locked up the house, and left.

Outside I waved and whistled, shouted and yelled, trying to flag down a cab. All were full, off duty, or just not interested in stopping. Time was ticking, and any minute I would be dangerously close to missing my flight, which would cause me to miss my connection, which would cause me to miss Damon. I fanned myself to avoid sweating. It seemed like the louder I whistled, the faster they sped past. I looked at my watch, still fanning my face. I heard a honk.

"Need a lift?" It was William. Thank you, God.

"Yes, I'm running late to the airport. Do you have time to take me?" I asked.

"Sure."

William hopped out of his aged family truck with the words "When It's Wright, It's Right" painted on the side. He lifted my bag into the back, opened my door as he always had, and we rushed to the airport.

"You know, I almost didn't recognize you. You look totally different."

"Well, some of us like to update our image every decade or so," I said, looking around at the van that his daddy's daddy's daddy probably bought from Henry Ford himself.

"I know, I know. I've been meaning to get a new van for the past year or so. I guess I just never got around to it."

"Uh, yeah," I said playfully as we both laughed. "So, you like it?" I said, showing off my new do. From the sparkle in his eye I knew that he liked it, but a woman can never get enough positive feedback.

"Yeah, it's cool. What's the occasion?"

"I'm the occasion. I'm meeting a friend in Houston, and then he and I are flying to New York together."

"Oh, that kind of friend. Why would your *friend* have you meet him in Houston when New York's only an hour away?"

"Well, he's not exactly meeting me there."

"So, why are you going to Houston to meet somebody who's not exactly meeting you?"

"It's a long story," I said, shrugging my shoulders, hoping he'd drop it.

"Montana, what are you up to now?"

William knew me sometimes better than I knew myself. For years he's seen my plans range from the incredible to the unbelievable. He was fishing.

"Montana, what's going on?" Now he was cutting his eyes, shooting a glance.

"Nothing is going on."

When he was fishing, he usually stayed quiet for a few minutes, knowing that it was only a matter of time before I offered whatever information he requested.

"I'm meeting my husband in Houston, okay? At least one of them. Then I'm moving on to Detroit, Atlanta, Los Angeles, and D.C.," I said, sounding ridiculous even to myself.

"You have husbands in all of those cities?"

"Potential ones, yes."

"Montana, this wouldn't have anything to do with your little sister's engagement party, would it?"

"How do you know about the party?"

"Montana, if your mom knows, the whole world knows."

"Well, no, this doesn't have anything to do with Sheree."

"Montana . . ."

"It doesn't!"

"Montana . . ." Raising the pitch of his voice and the height of his eyebrows.

"Okay, so what if it does? Is there anything wrong with me wanting to show up to my baby sister's engagement party with an engagement announcement of my own? If I don't, I'll be the last Moore family female past puberty that hasn't been married at least once."

"Montana, there's no magic to getting married. The magic is in *staying* married. Most couples plan for the wedding and never think about the marriage. Take my mother and father, for example. They stayed married for almost fifty years before he passed away. He worked the same business, drove the same van, and stayed in love with the same woman. Every night at six o'clock, there was an oven-cooked meal sitting on the table."

"The same one?"

William cut his eyes while he continued driving.

"No, I know. I get it. But William, everybody isn't like your family, certainly not my family, that's for sure. Some of us don't have the luxury of having our food or our relationships oven-baked."

"Yeah, then you can't complain when it doesn't taste as good or stay heated as long," he responded.

"Yeah, but if you ask someone who's starving, I guarantee you they won't mind if it's a little bland or a little cold, as long as it's filling."

"Maybe. But there's a big difference between filling and fulfilling."

Ouch, I thought to myself. Once again William's commonsense banter hit the bull's-eye. I had to give him props.

We finally reached the Transcontinental terminal. "Well, thanks for the ride," I said, grabbing my bag from the backseat as I closed the door and stepped to the curb.

"Good luck. And *bon appétit*." William smiled as he drove off.

I entered the airport, strutting down the aisle like Naomi Campbell working a runway. The cameras flashed, and the buyers cheered. I was Mahogany, and BWI airport had transformed itself into Fashion Week at the famed Prêt-à-Porter. I was a hit. Head high, hips switching, bob bouncing, I could see the vendors whispering to their homies, "Damn, she's fly!"

Ticket agents nearly broke their necks wondering who it was they were seeing. "Who is that?" they whispered, leaving a line of anxious passengers angry and restless. Even female flight attendants from other airlines were staring. Hating. Glaring. Wondering why their uniforms didn't fit like mine. "Who does she think she is?" they muttered, bitter and jealous.

I don't think, I *know* who I am. The new and improved Montana Moore, I affirmed to myself, as I acted like I dropped something. I turned around, and walked past them again, this time giving them even more drama. Switching harder, bob bouncing, highlights reflecting off the airport light, I was giving them drama. While they were player hating, I was celebrating. With a devilish grin, I smiled, knowing they wished they could be me. Finally I arrived at my gate.

While passengers boarded the plane, heads turned. Coffee and tea spilled as I worked the plane, strutting up and down the aisle giving them drama. From first class, to business, to coach, I wasn't stingy. I was more than happy to share with the entire plane who and what I had transformed myself into. I even peeked into the cockpit to speak to the captain.

"Good morning!" I eased through my MAC lip-glossed lips.

"Good morning," the captain responded, barely believing his eyes. As I closed the cockpit doors, all I heard were the sounds of high fives and whistles. I was even giving the captains drama.

And it didn't stop there.

"Would you like sugar or cream with your coffee?" I asked an older gentleman obviously pleased with my look.

"Neither," he responded. "Just stick your finger in the cup and that'll be all the sweet I need," he said, winking.

"That wouldn't be sweet. That would be diabetes," I said, returning his wink.

Finally, we arrived in Houston. The moment of truth was only seconds away. I quickly boarded Flight 702 with non-stop service to New York. Since Damon always flew first class, I made sure I worked coach, wanting to catch him off-guard.

One by one the passengers continued boarding the plane and one by one heads turned, catching a glance, stealing a look. Five minutes before the doors were closed, still no Damon. I was getting nervous. Maybe Gail made an error in her calculations. Maybe Damon had changed his plans and had booked himself on another flight.

I kept looking at my watch and kept getting nervous. Then finally, rounding the corner and boarding the plane was a pair of unscuffed, fresh out the box, camel-colored Timberland boots. It had to be Damon, and it was.

He was sporting a thick, cream-colored, wool turtleneck sweater and chocolate-brown loose-fitting jeans. The latest Sean John bomber with fur trim hung from his wide-framed shoulders and a cream-colored fitted scully framed his head. In one hand was a leather Louis Vuitton briefcase. In the other, he held the latest technological toy, part two-way pager and part cell phone. He was mid-conversation, talking via the earpiece with the microphone dangling from his ear. On his pinky was a platinum ring with the diamond-encrusted initials DD. On his wrist hung a diamond-bezeled Rolex and around his neck, jewelry by Jacob. He had just enough bling to let folks on the street know that he was no regular brother.

Damon was young, at least younger than me. Chocolate, chiseled, and fly, just like I remembered. Licking his lips, moving like a panther, shoulders shifting, legs lifting, he oozed the grittiness of the New York streets. But he had class. The brother had style, flair . . . he was somebody special. A young Puffy in the making. A big baller, a shot caller. The CEO of Platinum Entertainment, his motto being "Make the green scream and the dolla holla!"

I took a deep breath and adorned myself with an air of pleasantness, making my way row by row until I reached his seat. "I got this one," I whispered in the first class attendant's ear. Then, addressing Damon's shoulder, I spoke, "Excuse me, can I help you with your coat?"

"Naw, baby girl, I got this. You can help me with something else, though." He smiled, licking his lips, not yet realizing who I was. Then suddenly it hit him. "Montana? Is that you?"

His eyes canvassed my entire body, working their way down from my highlights, to my eyes, down my lips and to my breasts, where he paused in awe, looking at me like I was the last sparerib on the Fourth of July. Clearly impressed, his eyes continued past my hips, past my calves, and on down to my designer shoes. Then slowly he worked his way back up, licking his lips. Oh yeah, he was definitely impressed.

"Girl, I almost didn't recognize you. Give me a hug!"

Grabbing my arm and pulling me close, we embraced. As I felt the growing stiffness on my thigh, it was obvious he was very happy to see me. And he definitely wanted me to know; pulling me closer, hugging me tighter, making an even stronger statement and an even firmer imprint that had now grown from my thigh up past my waist. Oh yeah, he was definitely happy to see me.

Damon was an overnight bag with duffel bag tendencies. A frequent-flying layover with a history of non-stop flights that were almost guaranteed to make multiple connections. A coach class carry-on with first class aspirations. When we met, I was in between relationships and he was a welcome distraction. You know the kind: When you start thinking about how much your current man's hurting you, you call Damon. When you start thinking about how much time, money, and emotion you've invested and ultimately wasted, you call Damon. Not that you have that much in common. On paper you really aren't that compatible. But in bed, you fit like hand in glove, like yin and yang, like Ashford and Simpson. Damon's lovin' was solid . . . solid as a rock. That's why you call Damon. All of a sudden, before you even realize it, you're calling Damon just because you want to call Damon. You're addicted, destined for the rehab.

Finally we released each other. "Girl, you look good. You shoulda emailed a brother a head shot or built you a website. Something! We coulda hooked up a lot sooner."

"You don't look so bad yourself, Damon. You still making music?"

"Making music, making moves, making money, and making time for you if you're not busy when we get to the city." Full of game, and full of lines, Damon could sell water to a river. Standing there watching him licking his lips, I was relieved. Gail's plan had worked and Sam's look was a hit. Damon had bit. Bit hard.

The plane landed, and the games began. He quickly wrapped his arm tight around my waist as we walked through the airport. That was his way of staking his claim. Men say women are territorial, but it's funny because they're the same way. Damon was making sure all the young players knew that I was with him.

A few minutes later, we were in his tricked-out Hummer, heading over the Triboro Bridge into Manhattan. His Hummer had buttery soft leather seats, rims dipped in chrome, and the sweet smell of honey-scented incense filling the air. The sounds were pumping. It was Biggie, Tupac, Method Man . . . somebody rapping. Admittedly,

I'm past the hip-hop age, so to me they all sounded alike. But whoever it was and whatever they were saying sounded good.

In the past, he would always listen to the radio, hoping to hear a song from one of the artists he was producing like Murder Clan, the Homicide Posse, or MC Electric Chair. I've forgotten their names. I was curious as to why now he was listening to CDs.

Barely able to hear my own thoughts, I shouted, "What happened to the radio? Don't you want to know if the stations are playing your artists?"

Calmly, almost without breaking from the rhythmic bounce of whatever hip-hop artist we were listening to, he responded, "Only fake producers listen to the radio. I get SoundScan emailed to me every week. I see my money before my money sees me. Money is like a tree, when you watch it, it never grows." He had obviously stepped up his game. "Puffy don't watch his money. Russell either. That's why it grows. I'm next. Double D. BK to the future, hittin' switches, pumping through clubs, rolling on dubs, we doin' it, baby! We for real with it! Making the green scream and the dolla *holla!*"

Most of the time, he talked only in slang. It didn't matter that I didn't know what the hell he was saying half the time. He was a street poet, a producer; his finger on the pulse. Whatever was hot in the streets, he'd use for his beats.

"You hungry?"

"Sure."

"I'm taking you to Justin's. That's where the ballers hang out. And if you want to be a baller, you gotta do what the ballers do. Eat what the ballers eat. If you want to be like them, you gotta *become* them."

"I should probably change."

"For what? What you got on is ill. Sistahs ain't hip to that look. That's what makes you fly. You can't get that shit at Macy's. Anytime you shopping at Macy's you at least six months behind what's hot. Stick to the streets, baby. The streets don't lie. The streets gon' always tell you what's hot *and* what's not. Trust. What you got on is blazin', sis. No doubt."

Damn he was sexy. There's something very very sexy about a

brotha from the streets wearing Timbs telling a sistah what she should wear. There's something about a man with a dream that's intoxicating. Not that I have anything against a man with a nine to five, but I have to give it up for a man who's not scared to take chances, a man who's willing to go against the norm. And Damon was definitely that kind of man.

At Justin's there was a line of folks dressed to the nines eager to get in. I heard the security telling a couple that it would be at least a half hour before they could be seated. Justin's was obviously the spot.

The valet grabbed Damon's keys. "Watch the rims," he shouted, "they cost more than you make in a year!"

He led me to the front of the line. He whispered in the ear of the front door security and instantly we were allowed inside. He had pull. I'm glad, 'cause I was starving. Justin's was upscale. Soft lighting, hardwood floors, cozy light-tan booths, and soothing music completed the atmosphere.

"What up, D?"

"Yo, D, what's up?!"

"D-Nice, what's good!"

"Double D! I see you, baby!"

Damon nodded, high-fived his way through the crowd. He was obviously the man.

"If folks don't recognize you, you ain't doing your thang. Even if you ain't doing your thang, you got to play like you are," he said as we glided through the room, making our way to a prime location.

Damon loved working the room. All the ladies were looking. The waitresses smiled, pretentious, fake, and eyed my outfit up and down. That was cool, I knew I was doing my thing and was more than happy for them to look. When you're confident, you welcome the attention. This time, and this trip to New York, rolling with this young baller, I was very confident.

Finally, we made it to our table, where we sat down, locked eyes, and had our first real conversation free of pumps, bumps, or beats. Just as he was about to speak, his phone rang. Then his two-way went off. Then his other phone rang. Though put off at first, I reminded myself of one of his more popular sayings and primary reason for not having a home phone yet carrying two cell phones: "If folks can reach you at home, you ain't working. And if you ain't working, you ain't making no dollars. And if you ain't making the dolla holla, then you sho' in hell ain't making the green scream."

"One second, Boo." With his eyes still locked in on mine, he answered his phone. "Yo, it's D, you gotta hit me later. I'm busy right now. One." And then without even blinking, into the other phone, "This D, whatever it is, it can wait. Aiight." I was impressed. Very impressed. He had chosen me over his business. The waiter approached the table.

"Can I get you something to drink?"

"Sure, two glasses of red wine. A port. Between '79 and '83," Damon responded. "Those were the good years." He winked. Again, I was impressed. He had definitely stepped up his game from the Cisco he usually drank. "So, how you been?" he asked.

"Fine. Working. Living. Trying to be the best me possible."

"From what I see, you ain't trying, you doing." He licked his lips even more. "No doubt, you definitely doing it."

"How about you?"

"I'm doing my thang, you know. Pimping this record game. Trying to do it to them, before they do it to me." Taking a pause, his eyes became pointed, as he seemed to direct all of his attention toward me. "It's no coincidence that we bumped into each other at the airport." I smiled to myself, knowing what he didn't.

"No, for real. I'm starting to think things happen for a reason. You know, like maybe bumping into you was a sign. Like maybe we was meant to be."

Looking into his eyes, it didn't matter that his subject verb agreement was always wrong. Or that port is a dessert wine to be sipped after the dinner and not before. What mattered to me was that he was real. And, from the look in his eyes, he was sincere.

"On the real, the streets ain't like they once was. All the players got a woman, one woman. Russell got Kimora. Puffy had J-Lo. Master P., Uncle L., Dr. Dre, Snoop, they all married. Days of being solo are done. Brothers are locking down, trading in their player cards for models and movie stars."

"Yeah, but Jennifer Lopez is Hispanic, and Kimora is Asian. So that means that you would need an international woman, right?"

"Naw, that's them. I like having a woman that looks like my momma. I don't want to be hanging out with the in-laws for Thanksgiving and they serving enchiladas, or shrimp fried rice. I want some ham, some collard greens, and some corn pudding. You know what I'm saying?!"

We laughed. Damon could always make me laugh. He was fun. He was young. And he was real. For a second I wondered what it was that had torn us apart in the first place.

"Hello, Damon. Didn't you get my two-way?"

Okay, now I remember. Standing over our table was a beautiful woman, her hair in a fly twisted up-do, dressed in tan leather boots and a body-hugging wool dress. She flashed her eyes over me, looking as if I had something that belonged to her that she was now ready to claim. Then she locked firmly on Damon, waiting for his response.

Yeah, now it's coming back to me. Damon was a ladies' man, and there was always some woman approaching us like a chef, seasoning and ladle in hand, all too eager to stir up some drama. Drama that eventually led to me being upset, him getting upset, and both of us promising to never call each other again. Though for a while our promises were empty, the last time they were honored. We just stopped calling each other. I thought maybe years later, things might have been different. Unfortunately I was wrong.

"Montana, meet Janine. Janine, meet Montana, the woman that I had hoped would one day become my one, my wife."

"Well, call me when you get a minute. Nice to meet you, Montana," she said insincerely, rolling her eyes and walking away.

Wait, what just happened? She was supposed to get stank, he was supposed to get loud, and I was supposed to react by getting up from the table, still very hungry, grabbing my coat and leaving. Either he had seriously changed, or he had stepped up his game to the point where the sistahs wouldn't dare give him grief in public for fear of his backlash in private. Either way, it didn't matter, she was gone, leaving no residue, and stirring no drama.

"Janine works with the label."

"A port, 1981." It was the waiter pouring just a taste in Damon's glass.

Damon, taking the glass and swishing it around, put the glass to his nose, inhaled, and then sipped. After Damon's nod, the waiter poured the wine and he ordered our meal.

"For the lady, the baby lamb chops with a salad. I'll have the farm-raised catfish, blackened. For an appetizer could you bring us both a bowl of the Louisiana seafood gumbo?" What . . . no buffalo wings? Wow, Damon had matured. He had grown more sophisticated. Still with an edge, but with class.

We drank, and we ate, sharing dreams, losing ourselves in the "what ifs"or "what could have beens." The evening was going better than I had imagined.

"No dessert, thank you, I'm stuffed," I said, having eaten way too much. Well, really, not too much, but you know how it is when you're really hungry and you wait too long to eat.

"So when was the last time you got your party on? Shook your booty, got hot and sweaty like we used to?" he asked.

"It's been a while."

"You ain't forgot how, have you? I know you all grown up and all. You still remember how to get down?"

"I remember how to get down."

"You know, they ain't doing the Freddy Krueger no more."

"I know that. But, they're still doing the Inspector Gadget, right?"

"Nooooo! I ain't taking you nowhere with me if you gon' be doing the Inspector Gadget!!" We cracked up.

Damon was fun. He had jokes. The check came, he pulled out a Louis Vuitton leather billfold lined with a sea of multi-colored credit cards. Scanning for the proper one, he pulled out the American Express Platinum. Well, all right! Damon had game and cash.

"Did you pack anything for the club?"

"I got a little something."

We hopped in his truck and pulled up to what looked to be a medium-rise office building. "Yo, my studio's inside, you can change there. Be careful, though, I got cameras all over. I don't want you to pop up on the internet or something like that."

"In that case, I'll take my time. If I'm gonna be on the 'net anyway, we might as well make it worth the download."

"Oooh, you got a little freak in you. Maybe you should change in the bathroom with the pole." He smiled, licking his lips, looking even more eager to not only see what I had planned to put on, but later how he planned to remove it.

I was being a little bad, I'll admit, but I was feeling good . . . and he was looking good. But I still knew the rules. No sex. No sex. No sex.

Reaching in my bag, I freshened up, took off my tailored uniform and transformed into my Lil' Kim look: a short jeans skirt and a shirt so tight it looked painted on. Actually, I was too covered up for Lil' Kim. More like Mary J. I walked out of the bathroom, and he was in shock.

"Okay, so you was like, when in Rome, do as the Romans, right?" he said, looking pleased and eyeing me up and down. "I'm taking you to Cheetahs. It's one the hottest spots in NY."

Badu's hypnotic grooves filled the air as we drove. By now, the sun had set and the bright lights of New York were aglow. He started patting his own leg, then mine, and then touched my thigh. Just testing the waters, as men often do. I didn't stop him. I figured a little touch was harmless. I know. I know. No sex. No sex. No sex.

The club was packed. There were stages, lights, and rooms that led to rooms that led to more rooms, that led to even more rooms. We made our way through. One room went crazy as the D.J. spun a new tune. A track I had never heard before.

"You know who that is, don't you? That's my artist." He was proud as the crowd went wild. It was his night. We bumped into Latrell Sprewell from the Knicks.

"Spree, this is my one, Montana. Montana, Spree." The basketball player and I greeted each other, then Damon and I kept making our way through the crowd, my hand in his. He had called me his one.

Once on the floor, things got heated as we danced. Teasing and rubbing, brushing against bodies, acting like we weren't trying to arouse each other, but we knew what we were doing. The waitress came by and Damon ordered one drink after another. Finally, my drinks from dinner started calling me.

"I'll be right back. I have to use the ladies room."

It was a single-room restroom with a freestanding toilet and sink. It took a while but my turn came and I made it in. It was dark. Black walls, black seat, black sink, lit by a soft lavender light. I locked the door. At least I thought I had. Slowly the door opened. It was Damon.

"What are you doing in here?"

"I have to wash my hands. Don't mind me." He stood at the sink, taking his time, rubbing the soap in his hands.

"Could you hurry up, I have to use the restroom."

"I said don't mind me, girl, I'm just making sure my hands are clean."

I couldn't wait any longer. I lined the seat with as much tissue paper as I could find, unzipped my skirt, pulled down my panties, and sat. As quietly as I could I eased out the more than three tall glasses of wine from my system. I could notice his eyes in the mirror watching me, his hands still covered with soap. Fortunately the water from the sink drowned out the sound of the water being dispensed from my body. I was finished. I wiped, stood up, turned around, first pulling up my panties, then my skirt. It was stuck. For some reason my skirt was stuck. It was Damon's hand keeping it from moving up.

"What are you doing?"

"I'm being a gentleman. I'm helping you get dressed. See, that's the problem with you sistahs. You don't appreciate a brother helping you out." As he talked, his fingers entered my panties, slowly working their way down.

"That's not helping me get dressed."

"Your panties were stuck in your butt, I was just trying to help you out. See, that's what I'm talking about. Instead of saying 'Thank you, Damon, for pulling my *draws* out my ass,' you're complaining."

Slowly my panties started to glide down my waist and down my thigh. No sex, Montana. No sex. No sex. No sex. His pecs rubbed against my back, his hands glided under my top and over my breasts, grazing my nipples, making me almost explode with excitement.

Outside, they were banging on the door. Inside, I was leaning over the seat, holding on to the wall. He was gliding and moving, holding my shoulder with his one hand, gently touching my breasts, stroking my back, arms and neck with the other.

I wished I could blame my freakiness on the alcohol or some other brain-numbing intoxicant, but I couldn't. I was in full thought, full mind, and fortunately for Damon, in full heat. The banging, pounding noises on the door intensified.

"Okay, Damon, that's enough. I'm not giving you none in the bathroom."

Pulling up my panties and zipping my skirt, I turned, gathering myself as he was back in the mirror, washing his hands.

"See what I'm talking about? A brotha can't even wash his hands without getting molested in the bathroom." Like I said, he had jokes.

We exited the bathroom to a long line of angry women made even more angry now that they knew exactly what had taken us so long. Damon took my hand and we continued through the crowd. Finally making it outside, we began walking toward his truck.

"So you had a good time, right?"

"It was cool."

"What time is your flight out in the morning?"

"Around eleven."

"Not until eleven?"

"No, not until eleven."

"Oh, so you can hang, that is if you're not sleepy. I know you all mature and everything. Mature folks like to get their sleep on."

"I'm cool, but you know, if *you* got a curfew, I'll understand. The streetlights came on three hours ago. I don't want your momma running in the street chasing you with a broomstick."

"Oh snap, you got jokes. That's funny. I want to take you by my crib. Let you see how I'm living. A lot's changed, Boo. We can hang out there for a minute and then I'll take you to the hotel."

Who did he think he was foolin'? I knew that as soon as I get to this brother's apartment he's going to be all over me like white on rice. I was adventurous. I was alive. I could handle it. And besides, in my mind I had already sinned. If I was going to have to repent anyway, I might as well make it worth the wear and tear on my knees.

We pulled up to his place, a brownstone off Seventieth and Park, the good part of Manhattan. It was quiet. Damon took my hand and lifted my bag. Wait . . . my bag?

"Damon . . . why do you have my bag?" I asked, knowing his intentions.

"I was just being a gentleman. You might need something in there. You know, like a change of socks, a toothbrush, some pajamas for when you spend the night."

"I'm not spending the night."

"I know. But you might want to change into the pajamas under your clothes so that all you have to do is jump in the bed when you get back to the hotel. Why you tripping?" He smiled. He was good. Always making me laugh. That was his way.

We entered his apartment, which was dark. He hit one button and dimmers softly lit the entire room. Another button and the sounds of old school Jodeci rang through the apartment. One more button and naked abstract art appeared, illuminated by a single pin light providing ambience. In the living room were cream-colored custom-made leather couches, bordered by thick, cozy cream-colored rugs that hugged the newly polished wood floor. He had obviously studied Eddie Murphy's character in *Boomerang*.

"You like?"

"Yeah, it's all right."

"All right? That's it? Oh, you're not impressed, huh? Well, let me show you the bedroom."

Leading me to the back, we entered his room. Black granite-tiled floors sparkled beneath the mirrored ceiling. A gold-covered chaise, draped with a chenille throw and leopard print pillows, sat by the bed. A platinum champagne bucket had also been placed by the bed, which faced a built-in, fifty-inch plasma screen. Over the headboard hung more naked abstract art. It was laid.

In the bathroom, a seven-foot sunken Jacuzzi tub was lined with candles and incense. Next to that, a beveled glass-covered shower, and across from the tub, you guessed it, naked abstract art. He was leaving nothing to the imagination.

Reaching down into the Jacuzzi, he began filling the tub. The water flowed like a waterfall, and like a waterfall, I too was flowing. But there was no way I was getting into that Jacuzzi. That big, spacious, hot-water-filled Jacuzzi. No way. Absolutely not. Out of the question. No sex, no sex, no sex.

Sensing my hesitation, he slowly began undressing, raising his sweater over his head. My God, I had forgotten how sexy he was. His body had more ripples than the Atlantic. Damn, he was fine. Then slowly, he eased out of his jeans. By now I had enough water in my own jeans to fill the entire Jacuzzi myself. Slowly his jeans went past his rippled thighs, past his knees, one leg out. I began twitching with anticipation. Then the other leg was off and finally he stood only in his boxer-briefs. The elastic was barely able to withstand the pressure from within. Then slowly, they lowered. I almost collapsed with dizziness. The earth moved with each step he took toward me.

He reached for my top, lifting it slowly over my head. No sex. Unzipping my skirt lower and lower. No sex. Soon after, my panties dropped and we both stood naked, looking at the tub. No sex, no sex, no . . . Oh, to hell with Sam, I was getting some tonight! And regardless of how I was going to feel in the morning, I wanted him just as much as he wanted me. He was again a diversion and again, I was his layover. Not a booty call but a booty fly by.

As we sank into the tub, I made sure my hairline stayed dry. The steam was bad enough, but water would surely make my European-looking hair revert back to its tribal African roots. I didn't want to go in looking like Halle Berry and come out looking like Kizzy Kinte.

From across the tub, Damon began an underwater massage of my feet, working his way to my calves, then slowly moving up my thighs, taking his thumbs and massaging the innermost curve of my leg. He softly approached my lips, kissing once, twice, his tongue filling every crevice of my mouth. Then slowly, with one long stroke, he licked me from my face down to my neck, past my breasts and over my stomach. With a big breath, like an Olympic diver, underwater he went.

Taking a moment to breathe, he inhaled and went under again, this time for minutes, hours, days he went down. Single-handedly shattering two myths: one, that black people don't swim and two, that black men don't go down. He was part human, part dolphin. Like *Finding Nemo* he went down. Like he was reading a good book. Like he was headed to the Australian Outback. Like Mike Tyson in the Lennox Lewis fight. Like Cuba Gooding in *Men of Honor*, Damon was one bad motha—shut your mouth.

In one motion he stood, taking my hand. As I stood up, he lifted my dripping wet body, wrapping me in a warm towel that had been heated by his chrome-covered towel warmer. He carried me into his bedroom as if I were a gift. Jodeci followed us as he slowly lowered me onto his bed and with his hands, gently suggested I roll onto my stomach. I was in for a massage.

He started kissing me at the nape of my neck then went down my spine. This feels good, just a little foreplay and teaser, warming me up for the kill. Vertebrae by vertebrae, into the small of my back he kissed. Wow, this is different, he's never gone that low. Still kissing and licking and lower and lower, kissing and licking. Wooooo! I was like Julie Andrews in *The Sound of Music* as I sang, "The hills are alive with the sound of Oooooo!" Then I became Patti LaBelle with my arms flapping, "Somewhere over the rainbow, way up high. Birds fly over the rainbow, why can't Ooooo!" "Oooh woo woo." I started sounding like Jeffrey Osborne as I woo woo wooed until he gently motioned for me to roll back over. Right about now, I was about to *give* this brother anything. Everything he was about to get he had *earned*.

He slipped on a condom from his end table without missing a beat. Holding me by the small of my back, slowly he began to enter me. Throbbing, working his waist. My eyes opened slightly and I could see, through the reflection in the mirror, his back muscles flexing as he sent chills through my body with every motion. It felt like he went deeper and deeper until I could no longer tell where he started or where I ended. He went so deep, he was penetrating places that had long since been untapped. By now I was unconscious with eroticism. The room was floating. He had altered my equilibrium as our positions flipped. Damon made my body do things that I never thought it could. Damn, he was good. Having landed, refueled, changed planes, and made multiple connections, I lay wrapped in his arms, intense in the moment.

"Damon," I whispered huskily in a Toni Braxton baritone. "Damon," involuntarily escaped from my lips. And again, "Damon, Damon . . ."

"Damon, I know you're in there!!" came the high-pitched shrill voice, piercing through the front door. Not now. Oh God, please not now. Not in the midst of my *Guinness Book of World Record*–breaking multiple connection marathon.

"Damon!!!" The voice was followed by pounding, banging, knocking, and the continuous ringing of the doorbell.

"Oh, shit," Damon said as his eyes sprang open.

"Damon, I know you can hear me!!" The pounding intensified.

"Who is that?"

"Janine," he said, disgusted, shaking his head.

"Janine? The girl at the restaurant?"

"Yep." Instantly, we had a sudden loss in cabin pressure.

"Damon, I know you in there. Is that my Jodeci CD? I know you ain't playing *my* Jodeci CD!!?" Damon slowly pulled out as he grabbed his robe, looking disheveled.

"I thought she worked at the label."

"She does. Well, sort of. She owns the label."

"Owning the label and working at the label are not sort of the same. Tell her you have company. This is your apartment!"

"I can't tell her that."

"Why not?"

"'Cause it's her apartment. I can't afford all this shit."

"You can afford a Hummer. You got a platinum American Express card!"

"Them shits is hers too."

Imagine my head making a 360-degree turn.

"Damon, don't make me break this door down." She continued yelling, now kicking the door, hoping to break the frame or pop the latch from its chain.

"But, she had a ring on her finger. I thought she was married."

"She is. I'm her booty call."

"Damon, I know you ain't got some ho up in there!"

"Who she calling a ho?"

"You! Shhh."

"Shhh? I ain't shhh'ing nothing! And how you gonna be some-body's booty call?"

"I was your booty call. Why you trippin'?"

"Damon, I'ma have the police put a boot on that Hummer if you don't open up this door!"

"Wrap the sheets around you and get down," he whispered, pour-ing with sweat.

"Get down? For what?"

"Please, baby, if she catches us together she's gonna take all my credit cards. I'll be ruined!"

"Don't call me baby."

"All right. Just get down. She can see inside from the street."

"Damon, I cannot believe this is happening."

"Shhh!"

"I'm not gonna shhh."

"You better shhh. She's crazy, she might shoot you!"

"Why would she shoot me? She should shoot you."

"She ain't gon' shoot me."

"Why not?"

"I'm her booty call. A good booty call is hard to find."

"Obviously."

"Shhhh!"

"Damon!!!!"

So there I was, crawling around the apartment wrapped in a wet sheet while Jodeci played and some crazy woman screamed and walked around the brownstone peering into the windows determined to get a glance. We crawled around for the next half hour like snipers were surrounding us. Finally, the yelling ceased. She was gone.

"Whew! That was close," he said. "You think the water in the Jacuzzi is still hot?"

Not willing to justify the lunacy of his question with a response, I quickly put on my clothes, thinking to myself, Wow. Could he be that stupid? Actually the bigger question was could *I* be that stupid. Our non-stop flight had abruptly made a crash landing. In doing so, I had learned a valuable lesson: once a frequent flying layover, always a frequent flying layover. One down, and four more to go.

## Chapter 8

**2:57 A.M. EST**
**SATURDAY, DECEMBER 7TH**

**17 DAYS, 17 HOURS, 3 MINUTES TO "E-DAY"**

At my hotel, I showered, picked up the phone, and ordered one big mug of hot chocolate, a warm slice of carrot cake, and three extra pillows. The hot chocolate was to erase the taste of Damon, the carrot cake was to fill my now empty feeling inside, and the three pillows were because I never trust the hotel's first set.

I began flipping through the On-Demand channels searching for an escape. Preferably a romantic movie. Not that I'm masochistic, but I always found that the best way to escape thoughts of your own failed romance is to lose yourself in someone else's successful one.

Flipping through the action-adventure films, the comedies, and the more than one hundred adult channels, finally I landed on a Meg Ryan movie. She was my favorite. Watching her movies always gave me hope. No matter what the obstacles were, no matter how great the opposition, no matter how ridiculous the lengths to which she had to go, by the end of the movie Meg always ended up with her man. Whether it was Billy Crystal, Kevin Kline, or Tom Hanks, they always walked off into the sunset hand-in-hand, blissfully in love. I could relate to Meg.

In too many other films the female leads were bitter and angry, either slicing clothes in a fit of rage or lighting them on fire. And if they weren't bitter, they were trying to steal a man from a woman who herself would soon be bitter. But not Meg. Meg was my girl. At least she *was* my girl. Wait—a movie with Meg and Denzel? Not Denzel! Tom Hanks and Kevin Kline you can have. Billy Crystal you can *really* have. But not Denzel. Denzel was holy, pure, set aside like the last swig of Kool-Aid or the last piece of grandma's sweet potato pie. Denzel was sacred. Denzel was *ours.* Ya'll already have Brad Pitt, George Clooney, even Sean Connery (who, I might add, is still one fine ponytail-wearing white man). But let us keep Denzel. You can't have him.

He's the soul stud of the ghetto. The black prince of the silver screen. Our generation's Sidney Poitier. I mean, I'm down with a colorblind society, but Meg and Denzel together on screen getting it on was keeping too much hope alive! We wouldn't see Angela Bassett and Brad Pitt together in a love scene. 'Cause trust me, they know. Once Brad goes black, Jennifer Aniston will never ever get him back.

A movie with Meg and Denzel I *had* to see for myself. I sat up in the bed, poised, ready to scream in protest. Picket signs standing by. Half an hour went by, nothing. An hour, nothing. The movie started and ended and there was nothing. They weren't even on the screen at the same time. I sighed. I was relieved. He was still pure, sacred, and undefiled.

I called for a 9 a.m. wake up call and dozed off watching another movie. The next morning I headed to the airport for my 11 a.m. flight to St. Louis. My Saturday was pretty routine except for an irate passenger in first class. The situation with Damon kept popping into my head, as well as Sam's words. Same actions, same outcome. New actions, new outcome. I realized my same action with Damon had led me to my same outcome but I kept trying to push it out of my mind.

That night, back at my hotel in St. Louis, I looked forward to my flight home in the morning, when I could relax and regroup. It seemed as if I had just fallen asleep and was in the middle of a dream date with Denzel when—

"RRRrrring!!!"

I had forgotten to turn my phone off. I hoped it wasn't the airline telling me that my flight home had been delayed. I glanced at the clock and it was 4:15 in the morning, four and a half hours before my flight was scheduled to leave.

"Hello?"

"Hey, girl, it's me. Did y'all do it?" It was Gail, a day late and a dollar short. As usual, she wanted a play by play. This time I was neither eager nor willing to provide one.

"Gail, it's four o'clock in the morning."

"And?"

"And I don't want to talk about it. It's a long story."

"Good. 'Cause I don't have time to hear it anyway, and neither do you. Put your clothes on. I booked you on a flight that leaves out in forty-five minutes. You gotta fly to Cleveland for contestant number two!"

I know she didn't mean any harm. She was only doing what I had asked. But I really wasn't in the mood to see anybody or travel anywhere but home. Emotionally I was drained. Mentally I was exhausted. And physically I was still recovering from one of the single most satisfying sexual experiences of my life.

"Gail, I'm sorry. Forty-five minutes is impossible. It's four o'clock in the morning, I'm exhausted, my coochie is still quivering, and besides, I was in the middle of a romantic evening with Denzel."

"Is Denzel going to escort you to Sheree's engagement party? If not, you tell Denzel you have a plane to catch. And what is your coochie quivering for? Girl, did you—"

"Bye, Gail!" I hung up the phone. I can't stand Gail. But she's right. Okay, Montana, pull it together. Pull it together.

Releasing my customary three pillows, I dragged myself from the bed, quickly dressed, repacked, and was off. Bye bye, Denzel.

I quickly checked out, jumped in a cab, and was on my way to Lambert–St. Louis International airport.

"Please, if you could get me there in twenty minutes, I'll be eternally grateful."

"Eternity is nice, but twenty dollars in the here and now will get you there in twenty minutes," the driver responded.

"Deal!"

I nearly fell out of the back of the cab as the driver sped his way down the overcrowded expressway honking, bobbing, weaving, honking some more, and breaking every law from speeding to tailgating to reckless disregard for human life.

I was headed for a quick hop to Cleveland with an early morning connection to Atlanta. I was now sixteen days, nineteen hours, and seventeen minutes away from Sheree's engagement party. Sixteen days, nineteen hours, and seventeen minutes away from my crowning moment where I would unveil to the world the man of my dreams. My husband-to-be. My future baby daddy. Flaunting him like a pedigreed poodle at a dog show. He'd be on a leash and I would take him, table by table, to greet each bitter Moore family woman. One jaded Moore family woman after another would seethe with rage because my man would look better, walk taller, and smell nicer than any other man in the room. Reaching the airport, I paid my fare, tipped the driver, and sprinted through the airport to hop on Flight 210 to Cleveland. Once in Cleveland, during my brief layover I prepared my mind for contestant number two, Reverend Curtis P. Merewether, pastor and founder of Greater House of Deliverance Tabernacle of Prayer, Worship, and Miracles. His church was one of the biggest Pentecostal churches in the whole state of Georgia.

Being greatly in need of forgiveness for my most recent transgressions, I was more than pleased to know that he was my next contestant. Curtis was a man of morals. A man of honor. A man of God. Like a hard-edged executive bag, Curtis was steadfast. He was unmovable, and always abounding in the work of the Lord. Three parts carry-on mixed with five parts curbside check-in, Curtis was caught in the matrix between not-too-good-looking but not-so-bad-looking either. He was a good old country man, the kind that says "Yes ma'am" and "No ma'am." Healthy and corn fed, raised on collard greens, spareribs, and homemade biscuits, Curtis was at least a size 40. Sturdy and tangible. The kind of man you can hold on to in case of an earthquake, tornado, or any other instant natural disaster. A few jiggles in the midsection, but not enough to make him unattractive, just enough to give him character.

After I heard him speak at the C.O.G.I.C. women's conference during one of my layovers in Philadelphia, he quickly became one of my favorite speakers. Every chance I got, especially when he was in Baltimore, I would find time to hear him preach. Having seen me at several revivals, prophetic conferences, demon purgings, street meetings, and tarry services, his interest was sparked and we soon began dating. Unfortunately, though, what had at first appeared to be the possibility of a long-term, long-distance relationship soon fizzled into short-term, very infrequent long-distance calls. So for me, this was the perfect opportunity to not only be preached to, but possibly proposed to as well. Curtis was a welcome change of pace from my experience with Damon.

Oh my God, that's right. I just had sex with Damon and I was going to see Curtis. What if he could tell what I had done? What if he called on one of the prophetic gifts of the spirits? Like Mary Magdalene, the woman with the issue of blood, or Tammy Faye Bakker, I would be outcast, shamed. The entire visit ruined. I had to do something fast.

Fearing that I might still carry the scent of sin, I slipped into the airport's ladies room, pulled my perfume out of my rolling bag, and squirted Chanel No. 5 on my neck, my arms, under my arms, my calves, and yes girls, sadly enough, I squirted there too. Owwwwch! My God, that stung.

While heading toward the gate for Flight 986 with non-stop service to Atlanta, I fanned my perfume hoping I hadn't over-sprayed in my haste. I boarded, gathered myself, and walked slowly down the aisle.

"Hello, welcome aboard. Welcome aboard, hello." Even though I wasn't working the flight, it was in my blood to serve and since I was bumming a ride, I figured it was the least I could do.

Still turning heads, I was working the aisle, wearing a Donna Karan two-piece caramel-colored skirt set, with a cream-colored top showing just enough cleavage, and the skirt just enough leg. It was the perfect outfit for the very conservative Curtis.

Scanning, scanning, walking, scanning—Bingo. There he was. Seated in 10C. Wearing a dark blue narrow-brimmed hat, a navy blue suit with powder blue pinstripes, a crisp baby blue shirt, powder blue silk handkerchief, a powder blue tie, powder blue crocodile belt, and matching powder blue gators. A graduate of the Steve Harvey school of fashion, Curtis was Midwest sharp with a hint of Southern charm. The outfit wasn't exactly suited for my Northern tastes, but fashion was something that could be easily fixed, no doubt *after* the engagement.

Silently, I recited the Twenty-Third Psalm and what few disconnected passages of inspiration I still remembered. I wanted to at least appear to be in a state of Holy Communion.

"Excuse me, would you like me to help you with your coat?"

"Yes ma'am, I most certainly . . ."

For a moment, Curtis was at a loss for words. His eyes lit up like a Christmas tree as his glasses lowered, his Bible closed shut, and softly, calmly he spoke as the spirit of God gave utterance.

"Eyes have not seen, ears have not heard, neither has it entered into the hearts of man, the good things that God has in store for them that love Him."

He panned my body from head to toe and then he continued.

"Oh taste and see, that the Lord, He is good, and His mercy endureth forever." Then, pulling out his silk powder blue handkerchief, which was folded with precision, creased with perfection, he snapped the handkerchief open and wiped the corner of his mouth. "Sister Montana. My, my, my, looking sweeter than a Georgia peach and prettier than the Rose of Sharon. The Bible says we must greet one another with a holy kiss."

Rising to his feet, Curtis held my face while he kissed me once on one cheek. "Ain't He good?" Shifting my face, he kissed me twice on the other cheek. "And the answer would be Yes Lord! Yessss Lord!!!" Breaking out into a brief holy dance, he quickly returned to his state of calm.

"Pastor Merewether, what a coincidence to see you here."

"Sister Montana, what man calls coincidence is just God's way of remaining anonymous. For the Bible says for everything there is a season, and a time to every purpose under the heavens. Please, Sister, call me Curtis. Although I am a man of God, I am *still* a man. Born in sin, shaped in iniquity."

Unable to remove his eyes from mine, he continued, very focused, ever intent on keeping all possible distractions at bay. "I pray God has kept you in His perfect peace."

"Yes, thank you. I've been fine." My cleavage, like a magnet, irresistibly drew his attention.

"Fine as cat hairs, that's what I can see. And drinking a hearty supply of milk. Can the church say amen? Amen! And again, Amen! Whooo, Glory!"

"And how about you, Pastor—Curtis. You're looking . . . bright."

"Sister Montana, I'll put it like this. I've had some good days and I've had some hills to climb. I've had some lonely days and some sleepless nights. But when I look around . . . Oh, I don't think ya heard me. I said when I look around, and I start to think things over, all of my good days outweigh my bad days, and I won't complain! God has been good to me. Oh, I wish I had a praying church; He has been good to me!"

Breaking out into an a cappella version of the gospel classic "I Won't Complain," Curtis quickly transformed the business class to business pews, converting a Muslim in coach, a Buddhist in first class, and a row full of Spanish-speaking passengers who appeared to be speaking in other tongues. Though it could have quite possibly been their neighboring tongue, so I wasn't sure. At any rate, it was Curtis at his best. Lifting spirits, spreading joy, and not ever breaking a sweat.

We chatted through our short flight and when we landed, Curtis asked me to accompany him to his church for Sunday morning service. Everything was going according to plan. At the passenger pickup, two oversized bodyguards and one overzealous personal assistant greeted us. The assistant wore coke-bottle glasses, standard missionary drag, and sported a perm badly in need of a touch-up.

"Praise the Lord, Pastor! We prayed that God would extend His traveling mercies while you were on your trip. That the anointing filled the room, breaking yokes, freeing captives, making the lame to walk, causing the dumb to—"

"Sister Shonda, Sister Shonda," Curtis cut her off, as he was obviously used to her long, drawn-out greetings. "Zip it up? Amen. I preach. You assist. Me preacher, you assistant. Blessed is he who gets in where he fits in, amen?"

"Amen, Pastor."

"*Amen* then. I'm sorry, Montana, you have to forgive Sister Shonda. She was sent to us from the Sam I Am Christian Academy for the Academically Challenged. But God doesn't discriminate and neither do we." He turned his attention back to Shonda. "Sister Shonda, meet Sister Montana. She's a dear friend, and by the Grace of God, we have been reunited. Reunited and it feels so good. Reunited and we understood. Sister Shonda, I want you to have a driver take Sister Montana to her hotel so she can freshen up and then immediately back to the House of Deliverance for Sunday morning service, amen?"

"Amen, Pastor."

"Sister Montana, may the Lord watch over thee and me, until soon we meet again. And the church said . . . amen? Amen. And again, amen."

One hour later the town car pulled up to my hotel and off we went. With a sign in the car that said "Clergy," we raced down the expressway, exited on Peachtree Avenue, turned right on Peachtree Drive, and took a quick left on Peachtree Lane where almost a mile away you could hear the hand-clapping, foot-stomping, knee-slapping sounds of an old-fashioned Sunday morning throwdown.

Suddenly the driver's lead foot hit the gas as the town car sped forward, kicking up dust. Apparently I wasn't the only one feeling a tug from the spirit and eager for a Pentecostal praise party. Being in the air as much as I am, it was a long time since I'd been to a good service, especially a good *Southern* praise and worship service.

Upon reaching the church, the driver opened my door and I hopped out of the car, one hand on my oversized church hat that I had quickly grabbed from the hotel gift shop, the other hand on my flowing flowery sundress that barely reached my knees. I hadn't packed anything longer, so I figured the least I could do was keep it from flaring up and revealing God's good handiwork that lay beneath.

Suddenly the large wood and stained glass–lined doors swung open to reveal the main sanctuary, and what a sanctuary it was. Just as I had envisioned, tambourines were clanging, church hats were waving, Jheri Curl juice was slinging, and the very foundation of the church seemed to be shaking. The congregation was swaying, the bass was thumping, the musicians were jumping, and the choir loft was rocking from the strain of what seemed to be a thousand extremely overweight choir members waving and flailing their bright red and gold church robes.

They were having what we used to call "sho nuff chuuuch." It was the kind of church that made you wonder why you ever stopped going to church. The kind of church that made you want to rush out to purchase a James Cleveland or Walter Hawkins or Mighty Clouds of Joy CD. It was a Holy Ghost induced, spirit-of-God back-flipping produced, shout hallelujah seduced, cartwheeling, triple somersault down the aisle kind of throwdown.

The church building was immaculate. Mosaic murals celebrating the black experience lined the walls. Rich crimson-colored velvet lined the pews. The rug was a deep gold with deep imprints from hours of indentions caused by high-heeled shouters. Over the pulpit was a thick wooden cross backlit with flashing lights that illuminated the entire church. In any minute I expected Jesus Himself to leap from the cross to cut a Hallelujah dance of His own. It wasn't church—it was *chuuuuuuch!*

After nearly fifteen minutes of non-stop praise and worship, lead guitar solos, and folks falling out, the music calmed and a sharply dressed woman approached the podium and spoke.

"And the word of God said, 'How can you hear the word without a preacher and how can he preach unless he be sent?' At this time, I'd like to ask you to stand as I introduce to some and present to others, my pastor, your pastor, the pastor and founder of The Greater House of Deliverance Tabernacle of Praise, Worship, and Miracles, Dr. Curtis P. Merewether. Are you ready for a miracle? I said, are you ready for a miracle?!"

"Yes!!" the congregation exclaimed as the entire church erupted.

Like James Brown at the Apollo Theater, Curtis entered from behind a flowing burgundy velvet curtain to thunderous cheers and a standing ovation. With calm, poise, and humility, he waved the congregation to their seats. Dressed in a loose-fitting, custom-made, black silk preacher's robe trimmed with an African print, he looked regal. Kingly. And though it was probably not an appropriate emotion, I was getting a little excited. It was something about a man in a uniform that was sexy, especially a man in God's uniform.

The bass and drums gave way to the soothing sounds of the organ as Curtis began setting the mood for a life-changing, sin-snatching, spiritual breakthrough. Curtis was a very gifted speaker in his own right. Like Bishop Noel Jones or T. D. Jakes, Curtis possessed more than the typical whoop and holler, quote a lot of clichés and then rely on the organ to bail you out, old school style of preaching. Curtis had substance. He had a way of making you feel that in a church full of people, you were the only one he was speaking to. You may be in a five-thousand-seat megachurch, but you still felt as if you were sitting in the storefront church where you grew up.

His raspy voice filled the room, sounding like a cross between David Ruffin, Gerald Levert, and Teddy Pendergrass.

"Praise the Lord."

"Praise the Lord," the church responded.

"We're so happy to be coming before you this morning. But before we get started with thus saith the Lord, I'd like to take a moment for thus saith your pastor." The church erupted in laughter, as they were obviously used to his sidebars.

"Church, how many of you know that God has a way of taking you up when you want to go down. Making you go right when you want to go left. Pulling you in when you want to go out. I like to think of God as the Great Paradigm Shifter. Touch your neighbor and say 'paradigm.' Touch another neighbor and say 'shifter.' That means He has the ability to instantly, and almost effortlessly, change a course of actions, a routine, or a pattern from one direction to another.

"Church, today, my paradigm was shifted. On a plane returning from Cleveland, I had the good fortune of running into an old friend. One I had assumed was out of my life, but we all know what happens when you assume. Amen? Come on now, y'all saw the episode of *The Odd Couple*. Amen? She's a dear friend and she's here with us this morning. I'd like her to stand. Sister Montana Moore, congregation. Congregation, Sister Montana Moore. Greet her with a hearty amen."

I wasn't expecting to be outed. Slowly, with one hand on my hat, and the other on my too-short sundress, I stood. The whole church clapped. Well, almost the whole church. I noticed a few jealous sisters in the choir who obviously had their eyes on Curtis. But I was hardly going to let them ruin my moment.

Then, lowering his reading glasses, he adjusted his posture, opened his Bible, and began speaking. "Now, turn with me, if you will, to the book of Galatians."

Quickly I opened the Bible I had borrowed from the hotel. The sister next to me stared, recognizing that my Bible was generic. I smiled, then cut my eyes, thinking to myself, don't hate on my Bible just 'cause your pastor called me out.

"Today's subject will be the lust of the flesh."

Suddenly the church became dead silent. Fans stopped waving, hands stopped clapping. Even the amen corner ran out of amens. The sister next to me who was hating lifted up her index finger and tipped out the back of the church. This was obviously a topic that was hitting way too close to home for most of the members.

"Come on now, y'all, don't get quiet on me. Just a minute ago when the music was playing and the choir was singing, it was like Super Bowl Sunday up in here. Now, it's like somebody ran over your dog. I said, today we will be talking about the lust of the flesh. Turn to your neighbor and say 'lust.' Say it again, 'lust.'" The synchronized responses nearly shook the room. "Now, turn to another neighbor and say, '*my* lust.' One more time, '*my* lust.'" The congregation once again found his words amusing. "See, you got to make lust personal. That's the problem with most of us. The only time we make lust personal is when we're in the act of being lustful, and once we've acted upon our lust, we find every excuse in the world to make lust like a distant cousin at a family reunion that you only see once a year, whose name you can never remember. Turn to that same neighbor, look him in the eyes and say it again—'*my* lust.' All right, now turn to the last neighbor and say 'of the flesh.' If I'm driving down your street, don't say a word, just tap on the horn and say honkety honk honk!" Again the congregation was amused as, in his own special way, Curtis knew exactly how to loosen the crowd, and then pounce on them with a lesson.

"How many of you know that lust of the flesh is only a manifestation of loneliness? I once heard a songwriter say, 'Do me wrong, do me right, tell me lies, but hold me tight—just don't let me be lonely tonight.' Come on, now. Y'all know the record. It was the Isley Brothers, 1973, the *Three Plus Three* album. We weren't saved all our lives, amen?

"Lust is a demon. And it ain't no small demon. It's a great big ole Jurassic Park–sized, monkey-on-your-back demon. Lust will make you stay longer than you wanted to stay, and cost you more than you were willing to pay." The laughter quickly turned into moans and groans as Curtis hit a little too close to home.

"And how many of you know that lust is just love unrequited. Turn to your neighbor and say 'unrequited.' And most of us search to find the love in others that we are really seeking in ourselves. If I'm hitting your bell, just say clang-a-lang-a-lang." What seemed like the entire church, including me, shouted "Clang-a-lang-a-lang!"

"'Cause most of us not only don't love ourselves, but we don't even *like* ourselves. Amen? 'Cause if you really liked yourself, you would be comfortable *with* yourself, and if you were comfortable with yourself, you wouldn't need anybody *but* yourself. I'm on the line, don't hang up!"

Slowly, I began reflecting on Damon as visions of my prior evening's lustful escapades raced through my head faster than a speeding bullet and the guilt grew more powerful than a locomotive.

"Loneliness is a web, amen? A web that traps you in a snare of sexual indiscretion. It baptizes you in a fountain of fornication. Lathers you in a sea of sin. It rocks your boat, and it docks your hope." The organ rumbled, accompanying his words.

I felt myself tearing up. Getting emotional. Maybe this was a sign. A sign that there was a greater purpose in my coming to Atlanta to look for a husband. Maybe Atlanta was my healing.

He continued, "And the sex may be good. Not just good but like a bowl of Campbell soup, um um good. Like Maxwell House, good to the last drop. But I don't care how good it is, the feeling never lasts. Lust without love is a quick fix. Like crack. A manufactured, man-made upper, full of extremes, loaded with imbalance, and ultimately void of fulfillment. But how many of you want to experience a high that will build you up and never let you down?"

"Yes, Lord!" I shouted, by now totally caught up in the spirit. "Thank ya, Lord!" I cheered, as emotions went riveting through my body.

Suddenly an older church mother grabbed my hand and off we went. Rounding pews, hopping over little children, we were off. Hands waving, tears rolling, church hat flying, bob bouncing, still with one hand on my too-short sundress, we were off. We ran and we ran. Through the offering we ran. Through three baptisms, we ran. For the next three services we ran. Until finally the benediction was spoken, and the last choir's song was sung. Finally we stopped running. And though I probably should have been exhausted, I was renewed, refreshed, reinvigorated and ready. I hugged the old mother, and she hugged me back with a grandma-gon'-make-every-thing-feel-better kind of hug. I felt a tap on my shoulder.

"Sister Montana, the pastor would like to see you in his study." It was his assistant, Shonda. "Nobody goes back to the pastor's study after evening service. You must be very special."

I left the main sanctuary and followed Shonda. Down a long

winding hall we walked. For what seemed like a mile we walked. She was silent; I was still on a high. Finally we arrived at the pastor's study.

Shonda knocked twice quickly, then three times slowly, then once, pause, and then once more, pause, then twice more very quickly. After several seconds the door slowly swung open. Shonda stepped aside, motioned her arm for me to enter.

"Aren't you coming inside?" I asked.

"Oh no. Nobody ever enters the pastor's study after evening service. You must be very special." She smiled, turned, and then quickly walked down the hall.

She was acting a little strange but it didn't matter. I was still drunk in the spirit, still high from what had added up to a little over six and a half hours of non-stop preaching, praising, and purification. Yes, I was special and Curtis was the man. He was God's man. And I was God's man's first lady. I had just taken the liberty of personally upgrading Curtis from business to first class.

I paused before entering the study. For a moment, I made believe that the doorsill was a threshold, and after stepping into the study I would appear in a long, flowing, winter-white lace gown and Curtis would be dressed in a three-quarter-length black tuxedo with his signature powder blue bowtie. First, we would pray together. Next, we would make passionate love together. Spiritual love. The kind of lovemaking that no ordinary man could provide. The kind of lovemaking that would last through this lifetime and the next. The kind of lovemaking that would make the earth move. Suddenly Curtis looked better than Denzel. His body more chiseled than 50 Cent's.

I stepped carefully into the room, and there he was, just as I had expected. Looking heavenly. Illuminated, almost as if a light outlined his body. This was heavy. This was holy.

"Sister Montana. I'm so glad you could make it. You being here caused quite a stir in the congregation. Whether you know it or not, I've been looking for a first lady for quite some time now, and though I have a church full of single women, God spoke to me and told me that my wife wouldn't come from inside the church. Not even from inside the state. God told me to get my house in order. For my bride would come without warning, without notice. She would appear like a thief in the night. My heart she would steal, the empty spaces in my life she would fill."

Suddenly I felt like I was in a Harlequin Romance novel. His words couldn't have been sweeter. I heard strings from a violin. I felt the gentle touch of a concert pianist. This evening couldn't have gone any better if I had planned it myself. Okay, maybe I did plan some of it. But not this part. This part was inspired. Surely the next words from his mouth would be a proposal. Be still my beating heart. Be still.

"Sister Montana, I believe in my heart that you would make a mighty fine first lady. Mighty fine." His words were by far the closest thing to a proposal I'd had since William had asked me to marry him in the third grade. "But there is one challenge. One little mountain must be removed. But how many of you know that if you have faith the size of a mustard seed . . . oh, I don't think ya heard me. I said if you have faith the size of a mustard seed, you can say to that mountain 'Be ye removed!' and it *shall* be removed! Do you have faith?"

Even in his challenge, Curtis was inspirational. Once again I felt like I was in the pew, being ministered to. Being motivated. Being made better. Whatever the challenge, whatever the mountain, I knew in my heart it could be and it would be removed.

"Yes, Curtis, I have faith."

"Why don't you take a seat, Montana?" Uh oh. Suddenly the mountain started to grow rocks. There was the cabin pressure again, shifting.

"Sister Montana, you are well aware that we are in the South. The deep South. People in the South are traditional. Old fashioned. Set in their ways, if you will. The missionary board had a few concerns about your sundress. For their taste, it wasn't appropriate for a potential first lady. I hope I haven't offended you."

"No," I responded. "Not at all. Actually, I'm relieved. I thought it was something big. The sundress is no problem at all. Actually, I would have worn something else, but it's the only thing I had with me. That's not a mountain, Curtis. That's more like a molehill. The sundress is gone. Is that it?"

"No, not quite."

"Oh. What else?"

"The earrings. They said you reminded them of Jezebel. I don't know if you're familiar with the Bible, but Jezebel was a harlot."

"They called me a harlot?"

"Actually, they called you a ho. I thought harlot sounded nicer. Oh, and the hair. Too much bouncing and not enough behaving. And the makeup too. They said you looked like you were about to audition for the Universal Soul Circus." Reaching in his pocket, he pulled out a piece of paper and began to read from the list. Clearing his throat, he continued.

"The glossy lipstick, the fingernail polish, the open toe shoes, the toe polish, and the hotel Bible. In your defense I told them you weren't expecting to come to church and that's why you had a hotel Bible, but they didn't buy it. They said if you were saved, you would have been traveling with one of your own. They had a pretty good point, so we kept that one on the list. Lastly, they wanted the first lady to look a little more first lady–ish."

"What is first lady–ish, exactly?"

"Like a gospel singer. One of the ones they play on the radio all the time."

Now, I was really confused and needed some clarification. "Like Mary Mary?"

"Oh no. Mary Mary is scary scary. One of the more spiritually mature gospel singers."

"Yolanda Adams?"

"Not quite mature enough. You know, they play her on the secular stations."

"CeCe Winans?"

"No. They haven't forgiven her for breaking up with her brother BeBe."

"How spiritually mature do they want me to be?"

"They were thinking more like Shirley Caesar mature. Albertina

Walker mature. Mahalia Jackson mature. But that's only until they warm up to you. You know, the first few months or so. You know, like a year . . . or four. Again, I hope I'm not offending you."

The violins had stopped playing and the concert pianist started hitting all the wrong notes. Make that a seismic shift in cabin pressure. I paused for a moment to exhale. I stared into his eyes. I could still sense his sincerity. His eyes made me feel that what the missionaries requested was going to be harder on him than it was on me. Suddenly his request didn't seem so bad. A Shirley Caesar makeover was a small thing to deny a man that was willing to make me his first lady. I mean, what did I really have to lose?

With boldness and confidence I looked him in the eyes and replied, "Curtis P. Merewether, if the missionaries want a makeover, then a makeover they shall have!"

Curtis grabbed me, picking me up, turning me around, then placing my feet on solid ground. Suddenly the concert pianist was once again on-key.

"Sister Montana, you have made me the happiest man in the whole state of Georgia. The only thing left before we can get married is for you to get saved." The violin strings popped.

"That means being in church Monday night for prayer meeting, Tuesday night for Bible class, Wednesday for Missionary service, Friday for Young People night. And once you've tarried for the Holy Ghost, spoken in at least two tongues, rolled under the pews at least three times . . ." The piano was again poorly out of tune and the ground rushed to meet Curtis and me for yet another crash landing.

". . . after you take the right hand of fellowship, that's when we'll start you off on the usher board. That's for backsliders and new converts. Then the hospitality committee. Then you can help raise money for the building fund, you know, by selling cakes, pies, and chicken sandwiches in the basement. Then you can move on to work in the prison ministry, join the junior missionaries, then the senior missionaries. You can sing in the choir, teach Sunday school, become a deaconess . . ." His muffled voice began sounding like Charlie Brown's teacher as he rattled off one committee after another, one obligation after another. His eyes becoming brighter and brighter with each one. Mine growing dimmer and dimmer. I'm not even sure he knew when I stepped out of the study and into the awaiting town car. I crawled into the hotel for a good night's rest, still without a clear choice for a husband. And since I couldn't say amen, I simply whispered *ouch*.

Chapter 9

RRrrring!"
     "RRRrrring!"
     "RRRrrring!"
I was determined not to answer the phone for fear that it was Gail. I still needed to find a husband, but I was tired and taking a much-needed and highly relaxing hot bath inside my hotel bathroom. And since the phone number on my phone was blocked, I really wasn't trying to answer.

"RRRrrring!"

But what if it was an emergency? What if someone in my family had been hit by a bus and needed a quart of my blood to save their life? But then again, Sheree and I have the same blood type, so they could call her. Perfect. I'm not answering it.

"RRRrrring!"

But what if it was Curtis? What if he had had a change of heart? What if he had suddenly resigned from pastoring The Greater House of Deliverance Tabernacle of Praise, Worship, and Miracles and decided to start a new church? A more accepting and less judgmental church. A church where things like the way you dressed and the way you looked weren't nearly as important as your soul. No, it's not Curtis. And I'm not answering the phone. It can ring till Jesus returns. I'm not answering it.

"RRRrrring!"

It's probably Gail and if it is Gail, she's not going to stop calling until I answer, so I might as well answer.

"Hello, Gail."

"How'd you know it was me? I thought I blocked my number."

"You did."

"So, girl, tell me for real . . . y'all doin' it, ain't you? I know ya'll doing it. Y'all back in the study doing it, huh? Girl, I read in *Jet* magazine that this one preacher in Birmingham got three women pregnant in the pastor's study. You pregnant?"

Gail had just catapulted the absurd to a whole new level. "No, I'm not pregnant!"

"Why? 'Cause you on the pill?"

"No!"

"Oh, he wore a condom, then?"

"No, he didn't wear a condom."

"And you ain't pregnant? I'm really confused. If ya'll did it in the back study, and you ain't on the pill, and he didn't have on a condom, how come you ain't pregnant?"

"Who said we did it in the back study?"

"*Jet* magazine!"

Suddenly I felt like I was Abbott and Gail was Costello and we were in the middle of playing Who's On First. Talking to Gail was always a workout and I was already much too tired for clever banter.

"Gail, listen to me very closely. I am not pregnant. Not because I'm not on the pill. Not because Curtis didn't wear a condom. I'm not pregnant because we didn't have sex. The only thing we did in the pastor's study was talk about what he wanted in a wife and why it unfortunately couldn't be me."

"Oh. Why didn't you just say so in the first place instead of getting me all worked up? And why couldn't it be you? Because of the other three women he had already gotten pregnant?"

"Gail, Curtis didn't get anybody pregnant. It wouldn't work out because Curtis doesn't want to marry me. Curtis wants to marry Mahalia Jackson."

"Mahalia Jackson? Ain't she dead?"

"Yes. Mahalia Jackson is dead."

"Then why would he want to marry her?"

"Not *literally* Mahalia Jackson."

"But that's what you said. You said he wanted to marry Mahalia Jackson."

"Gail, please, okay?! I meant someone *like* Mahalia Jackson. And as great a catch as he is, and as tempted as I am to move to Atlanta to get far away from my mother, I am not Mahalia and have never had the desire to *be* Mahalia."

"So, that's all he wanted? For you to be like Mahalia?"

"Yeah."

"Montana, answer me this, have you ever met Mahalia Jackson?"

"No."

"Then you don't know what Mahalia Jackson was really like, do you? Like, I know she was a famous gospel singer and all, but who knows, shoot, after she got finished singing about the Upper Room, she mighta locked the doors, turned off the lights, and turned into a straight freak! Right up in the Upper Room."

"Girl, you are tripping."

"No girl, *you* are tripping. Shoot, if that's all he wanted I coulda worked that one myself. I would've given him Mahalia on Sunday and Lil' Kim Monday through Saturday. By the time I finished with Curtis, he'd a preached the shortest sermon ever—first Sunday woulda been 'Stop sinning, amen!' Next Sunday, 'Trust God, amen.' Next Sunday, 'Jesus saves, amen.' Next Sunday woulda just been 'Amen.' Whoo girl, I think I need a cigarette!"

Together we laughed as I momentarily lost focus on the severity of my situation.

"Well, girl, I just wanted to check on you. I'm stuck in Idaho but I'll be back home in the morning just in time to do some Christmas shopping. You know, Christmas has changed, girl. It ain't like it used to be. Last year I spent all my money on a bunch of gifts and I didn't get shit. Not this year. This year, I'm buying gifts, wrapping them, and leaving them in the trunk of my car. When I get a gift, they get a gift."

"Yeah, that's the holiday spirit, Gail. I'll be back tomorrow, too. I get in around three o' clock and I can't wait to get home. All this husband-hunting on top of working has worn a sistah out."

"Well at least it's for a worthy cause, right? All right, well, get some rest tonight. Call me tomorrow when you get in, I'll come by and we can hang."

"I will, good-night."

"Good-night, girl."

I fell into my bed exhausted. I slept through the night and went out window-shopping in the late morning to kill some time until my 1 p.m. flight. Once again the ringing of my cell phone interrupted my plans.

"RRRrrring!!!"

"Girl, you can't go home just yet."

"Gail, what are you talking about?"

"What I'm talking about is you have a flight in one hour."

"Gail, I can't. I'm tired, I'm worn out, and I'm—"

"I'm single. Say that. I'm pathetic, say that too. And I'm desperately in search of anything hairy with a heartbeat to showcase to my crazy family in less than fourteen days, say that. Girl, don't start with me. You've got to get to Richmond to meet Langston, who's on his way to D.C. So sharpen your shears, girl. Snip snip, hair gone. Good-bye."

"Gail. Gail. Gail!" She had hung up.

She was right. It was now fourteen days, ten hours, fourteen minutes and counting until Sheree's engagement party. I had no time to spare, and no time to argue with Gail. Besides, she had already hung up anyway.

I sprinted through the airport like O. J. Simpson in a Hertz commercial, hopped on trams like Edwin Moses, and weaved through the crowds like the Jamaican Olympic bobsled team, this time headed for Transcontinental Flight 812 with non-stop service to Boston. I had to go from Boston to Richmond just so I could get to

D.C. It was ridiculous, but with time ticking away I had no choice. With less than ten seconds to spare, as the doors of the plane were just about to close, I shouted, "Wait for me!!!" Thank God it was a friend working the flight. I made it.

"Flight attendants, prepare your doors for departure."

I slipped into the lavatory to change. Thankfully Sam had purchased more than enough outfits. I was prepared. Prepared and in flight, headed for my next planned chance encounter and an evening with Langston. Langston Jefferson Battle III, super attorney turned city councilman, and now running for United States Congress.

A chunk of Tavis Smiley, lumps of Larry Elder, a dash of Clarence Thomas, and a sprinkle of Jesse Jackson, Langston was a political gumbo. Sharp. So articulate you'd think he was born with a silver dictionary in his mouth. Very opinionated and outspoken. He didn't believe in gray areas. People were either good or bad, for you or against you. Langston was born a third-generation Republican but defected to the even more extremist right wing Libertarian party.

Langston hated the idea of reparations. He often said the only winner in the fight for reparations would be the Cadillac dealerships. Affirmative action crippled the black man, making him lazy, complacent, and dependent upon handouts. In Langston's opinion, the Million Man March was more about selling bootleg T-shirts, bean pies, and pictures of Farrakhan than it was providing a platform for economic empowerment.

Langston was definitely a piece of work. We met at a political rally at Temple. He was there lecturing about how Blacks needed to be more politically savvy and more involved in the laws that shape their communities. Looking good, standing tall. I felt like Diana Ross in *Mahogany* yelling "I want my man back!"

After he'd finished speaking, Sheree forced me to introduce myself. Actually, she didn't have to force me at all. I was planning on doing it anyway. But her prodding made it look less intentional. We locked eyes, exchanged numbers, and began dating shortly thereafter.

Langston was educated at the finest schools. The kind of man that knows the difference between a fish fork and a salad fork. As far as looks were concerned, Langston was no doubt a first class carry-on. Always on time, and if for some reason he was running late, he always called ahead to let me know. He was considerate but very precise. Like I said before, with Langston, there was no gray area. He liked what he liked, wanted what he wanted, and he was used to *getting* what he liked and *having* what he wanted. He always insisted on my look being clean, sharp, and precise. He didn't like ruffles, loud colors, or lots of jewelry. So, I'm thinking maybe I'll go for the Lynn Whitfield look. Elegant, sexy, and smart. Dressed in my custom-tailored Transcontinental blues, I simply replaced my comfortable shoes with Jimmy Choo.

Everything with Langston was about image and perception. But as important as his public image was, his private image could not have been more drastically different. Like most men, Langston liked a woman to look like a lady in public, and be able to transform into a Penthouse Playmate in private. He held no fewer standards for himself.

Langston wasn't as freaky as he was kinky. He liked to be tied up and spanked. He had a pair of steel handcuffs he kept locked up under his bed for special occasions. It was new to me, but if he liked it, I loved it.

What was also new to me was that Langston really didn't like intercourse. Langston liked giving oral sex, and boy could he go. After our first couple of sexual encounters I nicknamed him Pac Man. You could stick a quarter in Langston's neck and he could go all night long. Sometimes, when he was on a roll, he'd score an extra man, which made him go into bonus minutes. Chomping, chomping, chomping. Head bobbing up and down like a plastic bobble-head doll. Chomping, chomping, chomping. Bouncing, bouncing, bouncing. That little head would be out of control.

One time he got dizzy and passed out. I splashed some cold water on his face. He came to and like a trouper hit it again. Pleasing me pleased him. He always said when I was happy, he was happy. And trust me, I was happy. Very happy.

After a couple of months, he became very busy with his position on the city council and we just faded apart. He always said that when and if the time ever became right, I would be his choice for a wife. Maybe this was the right time.

"Welcome to Logan International Airport. Flight attendants, prepare for descent."

The plane landed, passengers exited, the cabin was cleaned, and passengers traveling from Richmond to D.C. entered the plane. And there, first on the plane as usual, was Langston, refusing to be second to anyone in anything.

He was still looking good, refined. High yellow, tall, and handsome. A black Ken doll. Not a black wavy hair out of place. The perfect smile. Not by birth, but by caps. He arrived at his first class bulkhead seat, removed his dark gray wool coat and flipped it inside out, folding it once vertically, sleeves folded once horizontally. It was his ritual. Everything was perfect and in order.

I stayed out of sight, waiting for the perfect opportunity to reacquaint.

"The captain has turned off the seatbelt sign, you are now free to move about the cabin."

Langston rose from his seat and appeared to be headed toward the lavatory, but the first class lavatory was already occupied. Excellent. Langston would have to use the lavatory in coach. Slowly he made his way up the aisle.

"Excuse me." As he passed passengers one by one.

"Excuse me." He said politely, passing more. Five, four, three, two . . .

"Excuse me."

"Sure, no pro—Langston?!"

He paused, startled, but instantly recognizing me, he exclaimed, "Oh my God, Montana Moore. Look at you! What a coincidence!" Eyeing me up and down, he was hooked. His eyes never left me as we sat and talked for the next hour.

The plane landed, the cabin doors flung open, and soon after, we were off. He invited me to a dinner that night with a multi-millionaire building contractor interested in contributing to his campaign fund.

I accepted of course, and the race began. After retrieving his luggage, we reached the garage and the *beep beep* car alarm sounded on his brand-new 720 BMW with personalized license plates that read LJB III. He popped open his trunk. It was pristine. Showroom clean. He laid flat his garment bag, closed the trunk, walked over to *his* side, opened *his* door, hopped in the car, and rolled down his window.

"We don't want to be late. Dinner is in an hour and a half."

No, this brother didn't sit his beige ass in his car and not even open my door or offer to put my bag in his trunk. Okay, maybe he has a lot on his mind with the approaching election and this dinner tonight. I'll give him the benefit of the doubt. He wasn't expecting me, and maybe it's going to take a few moments for chivalry to kick in. I exhaled, straightened my face, and like a lady asked, "Langston?"

"Yes?" he responded, glancing at his watch.

"Aren't you forgetting something?"

He paused for a second looking uncharacteristically dumfounded. Raising my brow, I guided his eyes with my eyes to the trunk.

"Oh." He looked remorseful. "I'm sorry, forgive me." Pressing a button on his console, the trunk door flew open. "Try not to wrinkle my suit. It's virgin wool."

I hoisted my bag up and laid it in the trunk, making sure it smashed every inch of his suit. Then I closed the trunk, opened my *own* door, and hopped in the car.

"Montana, I can't tell you how good it is to see you!"

Zooming off, we jumped on the 295 and headed to his townhouse in Georgetown. On the way we listened to the *Larry Elder Show*.

"Do you believe that, Montana? See, that's what I mean about the political parties. They've got the wrong idea. So what Colin Powell is black? The day-oh day-oh guy was right. Colin Powell *is* a house slave but then the day-oh guy is a field slave. What's the difference? They're both slaves. See, that's where we go wrong. Personally, I don't aspire to be a field slave *or* a house slave. I aspire to own the house and the plantation that the house sits on and hire *them* to be the slaves. That's how we win. That's how we rise."

The car zoomed and Langston fumed as he debated with call-in guests, one after another. Finally, we arrived at his townhouse.

"I'll get your bags."

"Thank you." Thinking to myself, You should have done that in the first place, Duke man. We made our way up the pristinely manicured walkway leading to his house, where we paused before entering.

"Montana, it's perfect that you're here, especially since my date Stephanie cancelled at the last minute because her mother was in a car accident. She *knew* how important this evening was and after the dinner, she would have had plenty of time to make it to the intensive care ward. Well, she cancelled on me, so now"—pulling out his electronic Rolodex, scanning through the names—"I'm cancelling her. Delete. You know Montana, funding is the only thing standing between me and my seat in the United States Congress. Montana, I've realized good family men make good congressmen. It's no coincidence you're here. Out of all the woman that I know, and trust me, I do know many, I couldn't think of anyone who would represent the potential of family more than you."

Suddenly I felt bad for all the nasty things I had called him in my head. He had just killed two birds with one stone. A double shot— potential and family, both were music to my ears. Like a Vegas slot machine, my heart skipped a beat as the rattling sounds of coins began clanging in my ear.

His front door opened. Running to his legs, panting, licking, obviously full of affection, was the cutest little toy poodle. And what looked like the perfect play buddy for my Muggly.

"Hey there, Juicy. Yeah, girl. Come here, Juicy." Awww, Langston had a dog. A cute little warm and fuzzy dog. This was a side I hadn't seen from Langston. He was caring. Cuddly. "Yeah, girl. I missed you too." He cooed, petting and stroking the toy poodle.

It was like a scene on a Hallmark card. The successful D.C. politician enters his home with his loving wife, and their loyal and loving toy poodle greets them both. The only thing missing was the snow falling, the smell of eggnog, and the sounds of Nat King Cole singing

"White Christmas." This was definitely a scene I could get used to, and Langston was looking more like the kind of man I could settle down with.

"Montana, this is Juicy. Arguably the only consistent female in my life. Juicy, this is Montana, arguably the only female who I wished had never stopped being the only consistent female in my life." At that moment, I wanted to jump into his arms so I could be petted and stroked like Juicy.

"Can I pet her?" I asked, wanting to receive some of the love that she was obviously receiving. Juicy looked so sweet. So loving. So calm and affectionate. The kind of dog anyone would instantly fall in love with.

"Of course," Langston responded. "Of course."

I reached out to pet her. "Grrrrrrrrrrr!!!" Barking and snarling, Juicy's little teeth dripped with saliva as she transformed herself from shy sweet puppy poodle into Cujo the killer dog, nearly biting my entire hand off.

"Juicy, stop! Stop, Juicy! Juicy, sit!" He put her down on the floor, "Sit, Juicy! Don't mind Juicy, she gets a little protective. She's just marking her territory. Like most women, she wants you to know that *she* is the woman of the house."

"Grrrrrrrr!"

"It's all right, Juicy. She doesn't mean any harm."

Leaning down, he pulled out a doggie treat from his pocket and hand fed it to her. After a moment, she calmed down.

"What I've learned is that Juicy responds favorably to continuous positive verbal reinforcement. I missed you today, Juicy." He spoke while petting his dog. "Juicy loves affection. Constant stroking, petting, and rubbing. Quite an interesting case study. Look at how pretty you are, Juicy," he said, still stroking. "Then once you've fulfilled their need for attention, you are free to go about your day and attend to whatever needs attending to. Just like with a woman. The similarities in characteristics are frightening."

Uh oh. Reverse my earlier reversal of the nasty things I had called him in my head. Langston man was at it again. Right about now, I wasn't sure if his canine comparisons to women and his obsession with Juicy were cute or if they were sick. So I inquired, seeking the deeper meaning to his recent fascination with a toy poodle.

"Langston, I would have never pictured you with a dog. I mean, with your schedule as hectic as it is, it just seems odd," I said, hoping not to offend.

"Oh, it's really no problem at all," he said with no offense taken. "Actually, I like having a bitch in the house. Especially one that has been trained to obey."

My jaw dropped through the floor. Did he just say bitch? I know he didn't just say bitch. No, this educated, well-read, well-traveled man did not just stoop to the lowest levels of street gutter slang. This articulate, expressive, personification of oratorical genius must have somehow tangled his thoughts, twisted his words, and once asked, surely will offer a fitting retraction.

I used all of my might to restrain myself from slapping the grease that had dripped down onto his forehead. I cleared my throat and asked, "Uh, Langston . . . did you just say 'A bitch in the house that has been trained to obey'?"

"Yes." He looked pointed, unaffected, and unapologetic. "Webster defines bitch as being a female dog. Look it up. The fact that some less articulate and uneducated men have chosen to use the word dichotomously and interchangeably both to endear and to degrade is of no consequence to me. Now, we have exactly thirty-one minutes before we're late. And I'm never late. Towels are in the master bathroom. You can shower first because I wouldn't want us to get, how can I say this, distracted." He winked, looking pompous and full of himself.

I wanted to wrap my overstuffed bag around his neck, but not wanting it soiled with gobs of petroleum goop from his hair, I decided to chill. The evening was still young, and I didn't want to make any rash decisions. Maybe he would redeem himself. I didn't see how, but stranger things could happen.

"By the way, I called my assistant from the plane and had her pick you up a dress for tonight. It's hanging up in the bathroom. Shoes, accessories, and stockings."

"You had your assistant pick up an outfit?"

"Yes. Montana, tonight is *very* important. Certain colors have certain connotations. Red means power. Blue means stately. Green means festive. I want everything to be just right."

"Langston, how do you know that what I already have isn't just right?"

"I don't know and since I've supplied your outfit, I don't need to."

"But Langston—"

"Grrrrrrrr!"

"Juicy, stop. Quiet, Juicy. Come, Juicy. It's time to go pee. Pee, Juicy." This was obviously going to be a very very long night.

The walls in his living room were lined with framed articles of himself, plaques honoring himself, head shots with politicians and himself, and an oversized portrait of . . . you guessed it, himself. Down the hallways were more framed articles, through the bedroom and into the bathroom, more pictures, plaques, and articles all high-lighting his hero, his idol, his self.

Quickly I showered, dried off, and pulled on the dress his assistant had selected. This wasn't just a dress, this was a gown. A long, flowing, black gown. I have to say, his assistant had good taste. It's not what I would have chosen, but it was classy, and elegant, and even more sur-prising, it fit me to a T. I had forgotten that it was Langston's nature to know every nuance of the woman he was dating. I remember on our first date he made me fill out a questionnaire. My shoe size, dress size, mother's maiden name, favorite color, social security number, and the like. He said it was part of a routine security clearance, but as I can tell, the information came in handy for purposes other than security. For-tunately, my measurements had remained the same.

The restaurant was located inside one of the most lavish hotels in Georgetown. As we arrived, tall white men wearing thick wool coats and thick-laced hats opened our doors.

"Good evening, Councilman Battle."

Exiting the car in my long flowing gown, I was turning heads and making a statement. Langston pulled me gently by the arm and whispered into my ear, "Follow my lead."

We entered the hotel. The chandelier hanging from the ceiling alone looked like it cost a million dollars. Rich burgundy wood lined the room. Thick golden curtains cascaded from the windows. This was opulent and exclusive. Very exclusive, upper-six-figure-salary exclusive.

When we arrived at the table, we were greeted by an older white man who had a striking resemblance to Colonel Sanders. Very white, and obviously very rich. Any minute I was expecting him to offer me a three-piece meal. His wife looked barely alive. Very pale, very life-less. She brightened up briefly when we were introduced, and then drifted back into her state of lifelessness.

"As always, Langston, you are right on time." Colonel Sanders eyed his watch and smiled. "And with two minutes to spare." Giving Langston a pat on the back, he turned directly my way. "And, who might this beautiful young lady be? She's much too pretty to be your date." He laughed in obvious self-amusement. What a flatterer. Maybe he didn't look so much like Colonel Sanders after all.

"This is Montana Moore. Montana, this is Howard Donaldson, owner and founder of Donaldson Steel, the largest contractor in the Washington Metropolitan area."

"My pleasure." I greeted him again with a bright smile.

"The pleasure is all mine, young lady," he replied.

"She's much more than a date," Langston offered. "Montana is my very significant other who was gracious enough to fly into town to have dinner with us tonight."

"Well, I'm impressed, Langston. And you say significant? Exactly how significant?" he asked.

I was asking myself the same question. Significant? I hadn't seen or spoken to him in almost a year.

"Very significant."

"You sly fox, you. You've done a good job hiding her. The press loves to snoop, you know. Montana, I hope you're prepared to han-dle the heat that this upcoming election is bound to bring."

"She'll be fine, sir. Montana comes from a lineage of strong, durable, and flame-retardant women. She'll be just fine."

Almost as soon as we were seated, an Italaian waiter, thin mustached, with a light accent and charm to match, approached the table.

"Hello, welcome to Il Tiramisù. My name is Luigi. May I start either of the ladies off with a cocktail?"

"My wife will have a Shirley Temple and I'll have a scotch. Very dry. Straight up with a twist of lime."

"And for the lady in black?" the waiter asked.

Wow. I felt so international. The lady in black. Scanning the drink menu, I had finally figured it out. "The lady in black would like to have—"

"A Shirley Temple as well," Langston interrupted. "And I'll have a glass of scotch as well. Only make mine wet."

I looked at Langston like he was crazy. I hate Shirley Temples. I started to order again. "No, actually, I'd like a—"

"She'd like a Shirley Temple. Thank you. We'll be ready to order dinner in a few minutes. Mr. Donaldson, would you excuse us. I'd like to show Montana the breathtaking view from the atrium." Langston grabbed my hand and we smiled as he led me around the corner out of sight of the table.

"What are you doing?!" Langston was furious as steam oozed from his nostrils like he was a bull in a bullfight. "You're about to blow my contribution."

I was confused. The only thing I had done was smile and attempt to order a glass of Sprite.

"Langston, what are you talking about? How am *I* going to possibly blow your contribution?"

"What I'm talking about is let *me* order the food. The food, the drinks, and the dessert. Trust me, I know what I'm doing, okay? And if you hate the dinner, as soon as we leave, I'll take you anywhere you want to go and you can order whatever you want. Can you trust me?"

I stood watching him stare at me with a look of passion and desperation and decided that now wasn't the time to argue.

"Okay, Langston, you can order the dinner, the dessert, and the drinks."

"Thank you."

Back at the table it was take two. The conversation started off light enough. Automobiles, weather, and then oddly enough, things got steamy when the conversation shifted to sports.

"Langston, I can't tell you how excited I am that you're running for Congress," Mr. Donaldson said as he buttered his bread. "And it's no secret that I will pledge my support, both moral and financial. I met with the board and we've decided to donate a very generous amount."

"How generous?"

"Let's just say, if for some reason you're not elected into Congress, it won't be for lack of finances."

"Thank you, sir." He sat almost teary eyed, in a state of manufactured emotion.

"You're welcome! I think it's time the halls of Congress became more diversified. More integrated. Langston, I see you as a trendsetter. Like Tiger Woods and the Williams sisters. When you're elected, you'll have an opportunity to make your people very proud."

"If you're referring to the American people, I have every intention of making the American people, of which I am one, very proud," Langston responded.

Uh oh. I could tell his response was the calm before the storm. Hopefully for the sake of his election, Mr. Donaldson would leave the subject alone.

"Right. But I was speaking about black people specifically." I had feared as much. Mr. Donaldson wasn't going to leave it alone. "Not only can you do for politics what Tiger Woods and the Williams sisters have done for golf and tennis respectively, you can give your community something to cheer about."

"I live in Georgetown," Langston offered, not once blinking an eye, shifting in his seat, gearing up for the debate. "Georgetown represents my community. Tiger Woods lives in a Bel Air estate and represents that community, Bel Air. The Williams sisters, who keep a residence in Compton, represent their community."

At this time I was silently praying to myself, asking God to end this debate and return peace and tranquility to our table.

"So are you saying that because of Tiger Woods' social or economic status that he is no longer relevant to those of like skin color?" Mr. Donaldson asked. I could see him become more noticeably and curiously perched in his seat. Prayer denied.

"Well, first you have to determine Tiger Woods' true color."

Now I was really confused. I always thought Tiger Woods was black. He had big lips, big teeth, and pimp-walked around the green like Iceberg Slim at the Players Ball. So, he *must* be black.

"What makes Tiger Woods black . . ." Langston continued, ". . . would it be his passion for things that directly pertain to the condition, the consciousness, and the upward mobility of the Black race as a whole."

Amused at the absurdity of his statement, I offered my own response, hoping to lighten the mood. "What would make Tiger Woods black is that plate of collard greens and neck bones his grandmama cooks on Thanksgiving."

Mr. Donaldson immediately broke into laughter. Overly tickled, tears of laughter ran down his face. Even his wife came alive. She too found my comments funny. Unfortunately Langston wasn't laughing quite as hard. Shortly thereafter we were once again around the corner in a heated sidebar.

"What in the hell was that?!"

"That was a joke."

"Collard greens?! Neck bones?!!! Montana, you just took our entire race back five hundred years. It wasn't funny."

"Mr. Donaldson thought it was funny. He was laughing."

"Yes, he was. But he wasn't laughing with you, he was laughing at you. Laughing as he reminisced over our ancestors serving his ancestors, while we waited for the scraps, the leftovers to be served from Massa's table. Think about that next time you want to coon at my expense. Okay, Stepin' Fetchit!"

Cooning at his expense? Okay, he was just a little too uptight for me. So much so that it was starting to make me uptight. Uptight and very annoyed. Taking the advice of my aunt, who said when you get overwhelmed and upset you should count to ten, I began counting.

One, two, three—pull it in, Montana. Four, five, six—hold it together, girl. Seven, eight, nine. This is *his* night, Montana. Ten. Exhale, breathe, and exhale.

"Langston, I apologize."

"Good." We headed back to the table for round three.

"Hello, I hope everyone has had a chance to look at the menu." It was Luis, returning to take our order for dinner. "Might I recommend the osso bucco, the seared ahi, or our three-pound lobster topped with chilled mango sauce. For the ladies?"

Mr. Donaldson ordered for himself and his wife. "My wife likes to keep it simple. She'd like the grilled salmon. I'll have baked chicken with the garlic mashed potatoes."

"And for the lady?" The waiter stood, awaiting my reply. I paused, looking at Langston, allowing him the lead.

"The lady would like the osso bucco." Osso bucco? I didn't even know what that was.

"Are you sure you want osso bucco?" Mr. Donaldson asked. "It sounds good, but it's not exactly the best tasting dish in the world. You look more like us, Montana. Our taste buds aren't quite as refined as Langston's."

"Actually, Montana loves osso bucco. She orders it almost everywhere we go. Not only is she classy, but might I also add, very expensive. After dinner I might need you to contribute to more than my campaign fund." He laughed a phony laugh. I returned an even phonier laugh, snarling within.

"So, Madam, how would you like your osso bucco prepared?"

Langston quickly started to respond, "Prepare it—"

Cutting him off, Mr. Donaldson quickly interjected. "Now, Langston, wait a minute. If your constituency knew you were a chauvinist it would take more than a campaign donation from me to get you elected. Prove to me and the rest of the voting public that you're not. Since the lady orders it all the time, I'm sure she knows how she likes it." I could tell Langston was boiling. But Mr. Donaldson was rich and offering quite a lot of cash. "Don't mind us men, little lady, we have to sometimes be reminded that it's always a woman's prerogative to have her osso bucco prepared however she likes it."

The waiter asked again. "So, Madam, how would you like your osso bucco prepared?"

Now, the pressure was really on. Not only did I have no idea how it should be prepared, I didn't even know what kind of meat it was. Glancing at the menu, I tried to peek and find what category it was under, but my napkin covered the menu. Okay, osso bucco. Is it a fish? Is it poultry? Is it beef? Okay . . . if it's fish, it could be seared, smoked or grilled. If it's poultry it could be baked, roasted, or fried. If it's beef it could be rare, medium, or well. It's beef. Yep, it's beef. No. It's chicken. I'm sure it's chicken. No, fish. It's fish.

"Luis, I'd like you to smoke the osso bucco."

The table fell silent. Then after a moment, Mr. Donaldson broke out in laughter. Luis followed. Mrs. Donaldson came alive. I joined in. But again, Langston was in no way amused.

On the ride home, you could hear a pin drop. Turns out osso bucco is shanks of lamb in a stew. We exited the car, entered the townhouse as Juicy rushed to his ankles, panting, licking, barking with joy.

"Good, Juicy. Sit, Juicy."

I could no longer take the silence. I had to break it with what I thought would ease the tension.

"Langston, I really apologize for ruining your evening."

"Ruining my evening? Ruining my evening?" he said, as his tone grew higher. "You did anything but ruin my evening. Mr. Donaldson *doubled* his contribution. The collard greens and the smoked osso bucco jokes were the highlight of his evening."

"Well, you have to admit, it was sort of funny," I said, feeling in a way vindicated.

"No, what I have to admit is that if you are to indeed accompany me to public places, you must first learn the proper etiquette and conduct becoming of a lady, *my* lady."

"Etiquette, becoming of a lady? Langston, now come on. Don't you think you're taking this a bit far? I mean, just because I made a few jokes doesn't mean I'm not a lady. Langston, honestly, sometimes I don't think you realize who you're talking to."

"Grrrrrrrrr!"

"Juicy stop. Sit, Juicy! I don't *think* I'm talking to anybody; I am unequivocally and without question talking to you."

"Grrrrrrrr!"

"Juicy, go pee. Pee, Juicy! Montana, I have worked very hard to get where I am and I'm not going to let you just pop up out of nowhere and tear down what has taken me ten years to build."

"Grrrrrrrr!"

"Juicy, sit. Sit, Juicy!"

"How am I trying to tear down what you've built up?"

"Grrrrrrrrr!"

"Langston, all I did was make a joke."

"Grrrrrrrrr!"

"A joke, a simple little joke. And you got twice as much money because of my joke."

"Grrrrrrrr!"

"This is not about the money."

"Grrrrrrrrr!"

"Then what is it about, Langston?"

"I'll tell you what this is about, Juicy, this is about—" He froze. Caught up in the moment, he had done the unthinkable.

Barely able to utter the words, I asked, "Whhh . . . whhh . . . what did you just say?"

"What did I just say?" Langston countered, attempting to downplay his blunder.

"You just called me Juicy."

"I did?"

"Yes, you did."

"Then I apologize, but again, you have to admit, at times the similarities are overwhelming."

No he didn't. Yes he did. One, two, three, four, five and all the way up to ten times ten times ten to the tenth power I counted. And then I spoke. "Langston?"

"Yes."

"I think I should go."

"Why? We haven't even spent any time together."

"And I don't think we will."

"Why?"

"Because, Langston, you're an asshole," I said calmly. "You're a greasy-headed, pompous, pale, pomade flinging ass. You're a freak, a bigot, and if it were not for your Eveready battery–operated tongue, you would have absolutely no earthly value," I said, still calm, never once raising my voice above a whisper. "It's late. I've got an early flight first thing in the morning; I probably should be headed back to the hotel. If you don't mind, I'll mail you the dress."

"Keep it. Your performance tonight earned it."

I grabbed my coat, lifted the handle of my overstuffed rolling bag, and walked to the door. Pausing, I looked in his eyes. For all his shortcomings, which were many, he was still single, successful, articulate, and good looking in a world where the women outnumbered the men, thirteen to one. If not me, I'm sure Langston would have no problem finding twelve other bitches that would learn to obey.

## Chapter 10

While riding in a cab headed to Reagan National Airport, I had some time to reflect on Langston. I know Langston's momma didn't raise him like that, so I can't blame it on his upbringing. His behavior was obviously learned. There was some woman in the past or recent present that, instead of slapping the taste out of his mouth, giggled and smiled at his actions, believing that the road of least resistance was the pathway to the altar. That had to be the only explanation. Otherwise his words couldn't have oozed so comfortably from his mouth like Aunt Jemima syrup on a stack of buttermilk pancakes.

Is it that bad out here that some women would actually put up with Langston's antics? Are the pickings *that* slim, the choices *that* narrow, the competition *that* great? Are there actually women in the world so needy, desperate, and eager that they would actually consider being with such a man? But then again, look at me; I'm out here trying to find a husband in what has now dwindled down to two weeks, so I guess the answer to that question would be a resounding yes, it is that bad out here.

But I still have two more candidates to go, so now is not the time to RSVP as the guest of honor at my own pity party. I need to hun-

142

ker down and dig my heels in the dirt. Time to focus, concentrate. Like that little old ant that believed he could move that rubber tree plant, I've got to keep my hopes high. Like Gloria Gaynor, I will survive. Just as long as I know how to love, I know I'll stay alive. I will survive! I will survive! Hey, hey!

"Sorry, ma'am, the shuttle's shut down for the evening," were the words of the skycap at the Transcontinental terminal.

On the heels of my verbally affirmed moment of seventies' soul inspiration, those were the last words I wanted to hear. I was so close to home, yet so far. I slumped back into the cab. The cab driver, who badly needed a shave and a shower, offered a half-hearted solution.

"So what do you want to do? I could drive you into Baltimore, but I wouldn't advise it."

"Why not?"

"Because for what it will cost you, you could put a down payment on a house."

"Is there any way I could get a discount? Can I just pay a flat rate?"

"Yes, there are ways you could get a discount, but for a decent-looking lady such as yourself, again, I wouldn't advise it. "

I noticed the cab driver was staring at me through his rearview mirror like I was a biscuit. His breath smelled like roasted garbage. I quickly reached into my purse, pulled out some cash, paid the fare, and exited the cab.

"Have a nice evening," he said as I slammed my door closed.

Slowly he pulled off, waving. He was a pig and his cab was his pen. Surely he wasn't raised as a pig. I suspect he was once a well-mannered, Catholic school–educated, decent and respectable kid. So I prove my point once again, his behavior was learned. Somewhere, at some time, he discovered some woman willing to let down her hair for a break in her fare. Langston I could see, but the rotten-toothed cab driver?

Wow. It *is* that bad out here. But again, I'm not going to succumb to the negativity. Expectations of success are still alive and well. Like James Cleveland, I don't feel no ways tired. Nobody told me that the road would be easy, but I don't believe God brought me this far to leave me. Now I know using God and the Bible for what has nothing to do with God or the Bible is somewhat inappropriate, but being that I was raised in church, you'll have to indulge me. Organ, please.

Yes, brothers and sisters, God has a plan. God has a man. Better yet, God has a man with a plan. A man, who like Abraham's ram in the bush, will present himself as a living sacrifice, holy and acceptable unto God, which is his reasonable service. And please, God, forgive me for just having flipped and flopped the scriptures like they were a stack of pancakes. Whew! I feel much better now.

Okay, so it's after eleven o'clock and I'm an hour away from home. There's no shuttle, a cab ride will cost a thousand dollars, and there's *no* way I'm spending the night anywhere close to Langston or D.C. Okay, Montana, who are you going to call? There must be somebody ready, willing, and able to leave their warm and comfortable home at almost midnight to drive an hour one way just to bring you home. For all you've done, all the investments you made, there must be somebody. Someone who in the past had no problem imposing on you and in the spirit of reciprocity should have no problem being imposed on. Got it! I'll call my mother, sounds like a great idea to me!

Dialing. Dialing. Dialing. Yeah, I'll call my mother so that I can be trapped in a car like Houdini, bound and gagged like King Tut, or probed and prodded like Mark Fuhrman at the O. J. trial. CLICK!

I've got an even better idea. I'll call Sheree! My little sister Sheree. Dialing. Dialing. Dialing. The one who has now become public enemy number one. The one who violated my love and trust and who, because of her weakness, has caused me to expend most of my time and all of my energy looking for a husband of my own to masquerade around a room of overweight and overbittered women living an underwhelming life with someone who they themselves were pressured into marrying. CLICK! Wait, I know who I can call. William! I'll call William. I'd do it for him. I even did it *to* him. That's gotta count for something. And besides, William would jump through hoops of fire wearing gasoline drawers if I asked. Dialing. Dialing. Dialing. And since now we're platonic friends, it's like calling my brother from another mother. The brother that I never had and always wanted. I just hope he isn't asleep. He likes watching old movies all night, so he's probably up. Yeah, he's up. And since he's up, I won't feel as bad asking him to drive an hour away.

"Hello?" Uh oh. He's not up. He's got that I-was-having-some-good-sleep voice. "Hello?"

"Yeah, hey! William, it's me!"

"Me who?" Obviously still groggy.

"You know. Me, silly!"

"Me who?"

"Montana."

"Montana, do you know what time it is?"

"Yeah, it's uh, around nine or something, right?"

"Try the 'or something.' It's almost eleven-thirty."

"Right, right. I thought you'd be up watching a movie or something."

"I am. It's a movie starring over a hundred sheep. Here's the plot. I'm counting them."

"Oh, so you're not watching a movie right now?"

"No."

"Do you want to watch a movie right now?"

"I hadn't thought about it, but I suppose I could."

"Great. There's a twenty-four-hour video store right around the corner from my apartment. Let's pick up a movie there."

"I suppose you want me to come pick you up too?"

"Yeah, if that's not a problem."

"Oh no, I'll get out of my warm bed, throw some ice-cold water on my face, and race to my car as the arctic inner harbor air needles through my bones."

"Cool."

"I'll see you in about fifteen minutes. Bye."

"Wait."

"What?"

"I'm not at home."

"Where are you, downtown? Over your mother's?"

"No. But you're getting warmer. I'm at the airport."

"You're at BWI?"

"No, but you're getting warmer. I'm at Reagan National. Hello? Hello?" I swear I'm going to get a new cell phone company. I've got entirely too much drop out. Dialing. Dialing. Dialing.

"Hello?"

"William. I'm sorry. I was calling you from my cell phone. I had drop out. Hello? Hello?" Now, this is ridiculous. Somebody's going to have to adjust my bill this month. Dialing. Dialing. Dialing. "William? I'm sorry, I had drop out again."

"It wasn't drop out. I hung up on you."

"You did?"

"Yeah."

"Oh. Of course you did. I'm sorry for calling you so late. That was insensitive of me. Rude, and just way out of line. I was tripping, thinking that an almost thirty-year relationship gave me some right to call you this late. William, I apologize. So, why don't I let you get back to sleep, okay.—No, stop! Please, leave me alone, I don't have any money!" I yelled away from the phone.

"Montana, what was that?!"

"Nothing. Just a pack of gypsies, tramps, and thieves walking to and fro seeking out who they might devour."

I hear William chuckle to himself. He knew exactly what I was doing. "You're good, Montana."

"I know. That's why you love me. I'm in the downstairs terminal. Look for the gorgeous bombshell with the honey black bob."

"So, I'm picking up Sheree?"

"Ha ha."

Like clockwork, it was almost exactly an hour and fifteen minutes later when the Fred Sanford–looking Wright family van pulled up. Hopping out of the van, looking obviously worn, was William. Such the gentleman, it was never too late, his body never too weary for chivalry. That's what I loved about him. Just like a business class E-ticket, William was always hassle free.

"William! Hey!"

"Hey!" Hoisting my bag into the van, I hopped inside and we pulled off, headed down the Baltimore-Washington Parkway.

"Montana, you know you're wrong for calling me this late. What if I had been in the middle of something?"

"Something like what?" He just looked at me. "Oh *that* something. Then you wouldn't have answered the phone."

"Of course I would have. Anyone that calls after eleven has to be calling for some kind of emergency."

"Well, were you doing something?"

"That would be none of your business."

"Well, if you were, it couldn't have been all that good."

"How would you know?"

"Because you sounded like you were asleep."

"You're still wrong for calling. You really think you got it like that."

"Don't I?"

"Well if you do, you won't always."

"I'm cool with that as long as always never comes. Besides, who else was I going to call?" I smiled, shooting him my *$25,000 Pyramid* gold medal champion smile.

"Your family, maybe. Your mother or Sheree. Or better yet, your new husband. I'm sure by now you've found him."

"Not yet. But I've got two weeks and two more finalists to go." Before I could barely get the words out of my mouth, William broke out in laughter.

"What are you laughing at?"

"Nothing."

"No, it was something."

Knowing William, those little laughs usually meant he had more to say but because he knew my level of sensitivity, he dared not say anything for fear it would hurt my feelings. This time, I wasn't letting him off the hook that easily.

"No, William, for real. What are you laughing at? I know my three-week trek seems silly to you, but it's because you're a man. You're on the opposite end of the ratio. Try being on my end and it wouldn't be so silly. Finding an eligible man is like looking for a needle in a haystack. And at thirty-five, I have consumed enough hay to qualify for the Kentucky Derby. So laugh on. I should've stayed and got mugged by the gypsies, tramps, and thieves. At least they weren't laughing."

"Come on, Montana, don't be so sensitive. I'm not laughing because it's silly. I'm laughing because it's ironic."

"What's ironic?"

"You. You're a flight attendant, yet you carry around so much baggage all the time. I mean, you're traveling around the country looking for someone that you claim will help you carry your baggage, but each time I see you, with each different relationship all you do is accumulate *more* baggage. Have you ever thought that maybe the secret to getting rid of some of your baggage is to stop adding new pieces to the set? Or better yet, when you check the baggage that you have, stop claiming it. Just let it revolve on the carousel until security comes to pick it up."

"That's crazy. Why would I want somebody else walking around with my baggage?"

"It doesn't seem to be doing you any good. I mean, think about it. The first thing people do before they travel is what? We pack things we need but mostly things we don't need but think we do. We stuff and cram, we shove and jam. Then we're off to the airport, excited and ready to fly. We reach the ticket counter and check our baggage. We check our baggage because we've been told that in order to fly, we have to be free of the extra weight. Then we board the plane, find our seat, fasten our belts, and we fly. Nearly touching the clouds, we soar. Then, after landing, what's the first thing we do? We rush to the baggage claim area. Everyone stands, jockeying for position, almost coming to blows, dead set on making sure that no one else claims *their* baggage. Some customized, some personalized, but all hand-picked to fit their specific tastes and individual needs. We fight to claim the very thing that weighed us down and prevented us from flying in the first place. If that's not irony, then what is? But what do I know, I'm just a dusty old contractor. You want to stop and get something to eat?"

"No, thank you. I think I've just been fed. Fed and read. You must have been reading one of those popular self-help books. I didn't know dusty old contractors could read."

"We can't. I saw it on *Oprah*." He paused to look up through the front windshield. "Would you look at that? It's snowing."

I took my attention off William for a moment to look out of the window. "It is, isn't it? A little early, but it's nice. A little snow falling, a nice big cozy van . . . you wouldn't be trying to set a mood, would you?"

"With you? No, you got way too much baggage for me."

Ouch. "Thanks."

"I tell you what, why don't you just relax? Lean the seat back and take a nap. I'll get us home safely."

As I leaned back, I thought about what William had said. He made a lot of sense. Probably more sense than ever. In a Dr. Phil kind of way, his words were sexy. Don't get me wrong; I'm in no way suggesting that Dr. Phil is sexy, but having answers to the issues that plague the feminine race, and presenting them in the way that he does, causes a certain tingle of eroticism.

The snow fell and the night faded into eternity. I felt the constant gentle flow of warmth pumping from the van's oversized vents across my face. My ears were caressed by the mellow sounds of Magic 102.3. I was very relaxed. More at peace than actually tired.

William's presence was comforting, warm, and reassuring. His words made me feel like somebody was listening to me. Not only listening, but caring. Before I knew it I had drifted into a state of unconscious rest.

In what seemed like only seconds later, the van stopped. Thank God, I was home. I couldn't wait to get inside my warm cozy bed. Slowly opening my eyes, I realized I wasn't at home. I was around the corner from my home in front of the twenty-four-hour video store.

"Where are we?" I looked at my watch, acting as if I had just awakened from a crust-in-your-eyes, slobber-on-the-corners-of-your-mouth, pouring-down-rain-the-day-after-Sears-installed-a-new-water-heater kind of sleep. Surely if William believed I was that sleepy he would have mercy on me and not make me follow through with what he knew were insincere movie-watching intentions.

"We're in front of the twenty-four-hour video store," he answered. "We're renting a movie. Remember?"

Using my groggy voice, and with squinted eyes, I responded, "This late?"

"Montana . . ."

"Yeah. William, is that you still talking?"

"Yeah, it's still me, you're not hallucinating. And don't even try the 'I'm sleepy' voice. And stop squinting. You can see me. You forget, I know you. You got me out of my bed at almost midnight. Either you're going to be watching the movie or the movie is going to be watching you. Either way, something is getting watched tonight." We stared each other down. Waiting to see who would blink first. Unfortunately it was me.

"Ha! You blinked!"

We hopped out of the van, ventured into the video store, and argued over which movie to watch, finally deciding on *Like Water for Chocolate.* "But it's got subtitles . . ."

"And? Do you have something against subtitles?"

"No. I would just prefer to hear what the actors are saying instead of having to read it."

"You'll be able to hear it. You just won't understand it." I had forgotten William was a smart mouth. I hated it, because I was the same way.

We hopped back in the van and off we went, passing my apartment—bye-bye apartment. Bye-bye nice warm apartment with my nice warm bed and piping hot water destined to flow into my oval-shaped porcelain tub. Bye-bye Muggly.

Soon we arrived at his house. I loved William's house. It was the house he grew up in and where I'd spent most of my time growing up as well. It was a cozy, detached, two-story red brick house built in the early forties, with the biggest fireplace I had ever seen. As kids we would always watch movies in the family room in front of the fireplace, waiting for his parents to go to sleep so we could play Doctor, which later turned into Hide and Go Get It, which later turned into just plain ole It's Right Here, Now Take It. We entered the house.

"Make yourself comfortable, you know where everything is." It was just like I had remembered it. The clock with the broken second hand was still broken, and the plastic that we had ripped as kids was still ripped and covering the same couch.

"You want something to drink?"

"Sure? What do you have?"

"Milk and orange juice. Oh, and some Kool-Aid."

"Kool-Aid? What flavor?"

"There's only one flavor for black folks, Montana, red."

"Red is not a flavor. It's a color."

"In the ghetto, red is a flavor *and* a color."

"Do you really have Kool-Aid?"

"No, but I wish I did. Oh, I know what. I have just the thing. It's the perfect occasion."

"What's the occasion?"

"Just a minute." Rushing out of the room, trying to surprise me, it was William at his usual best. Fun-loving. Playful. Still a kid at heart.

"You better hurry up. I don't have all night, you know."

"First, let me take a little chill out of the air." William entered the family room looking like Paul Bunyon with an armful of logs.

"You could have just turned the heater on, you know."

"I could have. But it's broken. I've been meaning to go get a new one, I just haven't gotten around to it yet."

"You're a contractor and you don't have a heater that works?"

"Yeah. Just like dentists have the worst teeth. And mechanics have the worst cars. And flight attendants have the most baggage."

"Touché!"

William started the fire with the skill of a Boy Scout. Fanning the flames, flipping the logs, poking and prodding until like one of the Fantastic Four he yelled—"Flame on! Perfect. Warm. Toasty. Just like when we were growing up. And next, a little something to wet the whistle." William pulled from inside the tall wooden buffet a bottle of champagne that looked like Chicken George himself had fermented it. It was covered with dust as thick as cotton, which, after he stopped himself from choking to death, William quickly wiped off.

"This bottle was a gift from my father to my mother in 1982."

"Don't you mean 1882?"

"Ha ha. It was 1982, to celebrate their twenty-fifth wedding anniversary. And since of course my mother, like your mother, believes drinking is a sin and an abomination before God, she never opened it. Their loss is our gain." Handing me a glass, he started to open the bottle.

"But it's for a celebration," I said. "We have to have something to celebrate if we open it."

"We do. We'll celebrate you finding Mr. Right. That's right with an R, not a W," he said winking, and popping the cork. The champagne erupted from the bottle and after he poured, we clinked glasses and slowly sipped. It was good. Sweet, just like I like it.

"Okay, so now I'm wide awake. This movie better be good."

"Why don't you grab it and put it in the VCR while I add a couple of logs to the fire." As I slipped the videotape into the machine, I noticed our old high school yearbook inside the glass cabinet in the entertainment center.

"William, is this what I think it is?" I pulled it out. "Is this our yearbook? Oh my God. I haven't seen this in ages."

"Neither have I."

"Ha, look at your bowtie! It's almost as big as your head. And your hair. You had a Jheri Curl?"

"I didn't have a Jheri Curl. I had a texturizer."

"Same thing."

"No, it's not. My gel didn't drip. Shall we flip to your picture? 'Cause I wasn't the only one using gel." He grabbed the book and flipped to my page.

"And here we are. Montana Moore, also known as Baby Hair! Looking like ghetto Elvis."

"I don't know what you're talking about; baby hair was in back then."

"Not for an eighteen year old, it wasn't. I coulda killed you when

I went to brush my teeth and my brand-new toothbrush was covered with brown gook."

"That wasn't gook. That was the good gel that kept the baby hair in place. Man, those were the days!"

"Yeah they were. Remember the poem you wrote in the back of my book?" He flipped to the back of the book and pointed out the poem I had written.

> *So fresh and so ill.*
> *So cool and so chill.*
> *Come day or come night.*
> *You're my rapper's delight.*

"I did not write that!"

"Yes, you did! And you signed it. Look, see there? 'Love. Baby Hair.'"

"You better stop calling me Baby Hair, looking like Oh Sheila. 'Oh . . . Oh Sheila, Oh-oh-oh-oh, Oh Sheila.' You weren't just Ready For The World, you were ready for the entire galaxy!'" I said, as we both started cracking up.

"Okay, you got me. That was good. Ready for the galaxy. That was good. But for real, after all these years, I still can't figure out what the poem meant."

"What it meant was since the song was the hottest rap song of all time, I was saying that you were the hottest young brother of all time."

"Oh, like Ali. Right, I shook up the world!"

"There you go!"

As the pages turned, and the fire logs burned, we laughed and reminisced, never once watching the movie, and never once caring. It was like we were back in high school. Carefree. Responsibility free. A time when the only thing that mattered was what time the street-lights came on and who said she said he said about who.

"Guess what I found the other day? You're going to really trip out on this," he said, disappearing into the hallway and returning with a stethoscope.

"No, that isn't that raggedy ole stethoscope you used to play Doctor."

"Raggedy? Please, this thing saved your life. If it wasn't for this here stethoscope you wouldn't have known whether your heart was beating or not."

"You couldn't hear my heart beating because you used to put it on my butt all the time."

"What's wrong with that? The booty has a heartbeat."

"No, it doesn't, stupid."

"Yes, it does. Hold up. Let me listen one more time. Let me see what I hear."

"You are so stupid."

In his usual playful way, he put the stethoscope in his ears, kneeled down, and pressed it against my butt.

"You are so silly."

"Shh. I'm trying to listen. Hold up, let me move it to the other cheek. Nothing. Now let me check your heart. I gotta make sure you're still alive."

"William, would you stop acting so stupid?"

"I'm not acting stupid; I'm trying to save your life!" Placing the stethoscope over the outside of my shirt, over my heart, he listened closely.

"What do you hear?"

"Wait. There it is. It's beating. Looks like you're going to live. See that? Good thing you know a doctor who makes house calls."

"Is that the only thing you make?" Uh oh. Obviously the alcohol had started writing checks that my body would soon be obligated to cash. Even so, I was happy I had asked. And I was even happier that I could blame it on the alcohol.

"Actually it's not. Every so often I've been known to make a few other things."

"Like what?" Damned alcohol. Now it wasn't just a check, it was a cashier's check.

"Well you know, things like fire."

"How do you do that?" It was now a direct deposit. Montana, what are you doing?

"You start by putting in a couple of logs and waiting for a spark. After the spark, there's usually some smoke, and where there's smoke there's fire."

"Okay, so you make house calls, and fire. Is that it?"

"Now that you asked, no, that's not all I make. I can also make love."

"How do you do that?"

"Well, you start with two people. Two people that are attracted to each other. That trust each other. That want each other. Love each other."

"And what do you do after you've found these people?"

"You usually put them together in a room. Stand them close to one another. One starts off with looking into the other's eyes, touching their hands, holding their face, and kissing their lips. Something like this." Suddenly, just like he had described, looking intently into my eyes, with one hand holding my hand, and the other hand holding my face, he leaned in and slowly began kissing my lips. Softly. Gently. Effortlessly. It was like being kissed for the first time. Gentle like a breeze, soft like a feather, and warm like the sun. I should've known what I was getting myself into. Doctor always led to further examinations. This was probably a good time to end our evening.

"William," I said, still gazing into his eyes, "I think I've had a little too much to drink."

"I know you've had too much to drink."

"So, that means whatever happens tonight I can blame on the alcohol?"

"If that'll make you feel better."

"It will."

"Then let's blame it on the alcohol."

His hands released my face and moved to my waist, pulling me closer, then gently against my backside. Slowly my hand moved up against his thigh, up past his backside, and up to his rock solid chest. Then up to his neck, grabbing his head. The examination had begun.

With skillful hands like a surgeon's, he lay me down on the floor in front of the fireplace. I could feel the buttons of my blouse coming undone, freeing my already toasted body. Then my bra. Soon the flames' reflection danced across my breasts, their warmth slowly erecting my nipples. Slowly he moved to my pants, then my panties. I was soon lying naked. Like a marshmallow, I was hot. Toasted on the outside, melted on the inside. Then William leaned in to my ear and began undressing my mind. Whispering softly, little sweet nothings quickly converting to bigger sweet somethings. They were words coming from the lips of someone who cared. Still, after all these years, he cared.

He slowly removed his clothes. Damn, construction does a body good. Looking all cut up, chiseled, like a bronze statue of David, the Mandingo version, William was packing, and not just a set of tools if you know what I mean. With the hammer he was carrying, my house didn't stand a chance.

As I stared into the soft flickering glow of love's dancing flames, the crackling sounds of popping fire melted into the panting sounds of desire as we made love and made light. It was right. Right with the W.

His propellers roared. William was a non-stop flight and I was headed for my first connection. Holding his waist, pulling him close, my body shivered. My soul quivered. As the pouring sweat raced down the sides of my face, he made another connection. And then another. Calling my name, we connected. And we connected some more.

"Montana."

"Oh, William."

"Montana."

"Oh, William."

"Montana, we're here." We sure are, I thought to myself.

"Montana, wake up! Wake up! We're here."

Wake up? What is he talking about? Oh no, wait. Please don't tell me . . . It can't be. Squinting my eyes, it was. I had been hoodwinked, bamboozled, led astray, run amok. I had been dreaming. I checked my watch; it had been exactly an hour and fifteen minutes and we were in front of my apartment building.

"You were sleeping like a baby."

"I was sleeping, but not like a baby. Trust me, that was some grown-up woman sleep."

"What?"

"Nothing. Thanks for the ride."

"No problem. You still want to get a movie?"

Movie? Damn the movie! I wanted him to bring his chocolate chiseled power drill upstairs for some home improvement. Oooh Montana, be good now. It's too close to Christmas to be a holiday ho ho ho. I stood grasping at moral straws, searching for an ever-fleeting strand of restraint.

"No. It's pretty late. Can I give you a raincheck?"

"Sure."

As usual, William hopped out of the van and handed me my overstuffed rolling bag.

"Okay, well, I'll talk to you soon."

"Right."

"Good-night."

"Good-night."

He made sure I had entered my building before hopping back in his van. I waved from my glass front door. As he pulled off, the thought raced through my mind—that was the some of the best loving that I had never had. With any luck, tonight I could pick up in my dreams where my reality had just left off.

Now I know exactly what Dr. King must have been going through: Keeping the dream alive is no simple task. It's been five nights of dream deprivation. No William. No wine. No power tools. No nothing. Just me and Muggly, wrapped in my quilted down comforter, slurping mug after mug of instant hot cocoa and eating spoon after spoon of coffee-flavored Häagen-Dazs ice cream. The moment had obviously passed.

Always looking for the bright side, at least I had an opportunity to catch up on some much-needed rest. Especially after trekking around the country on my wild grooms chase. Now I have only ten days left before my hopes and dreams shrivel and dry up like a raisin in the sun.

Shortly after the episode with Langston, Gail called to say that contestant #4 was disqualified. He died. Which of course left me one man short and one man left before being forced to make my one final decision. A decision that as of right now had no clear front-runner, just a string of underachievers. Bottom dwellers. Like crabs at the bottom of the ocean. Not one of them had risen to the occasion. However, among these bottom-dwelling crustaceans, one can also find oysters. Oysters with pearls. Precious pearls. Sacred gems. I was determined to find a bright side, a silver lining, and a light at the end of the tunnel.

Making my list and checking it twice, my hopes were alive and my spirits were high. It was the holiday season, my favorite time of the year. Full of stars that twinkled and bells that jingled. It was the holidays. I had to believe that something good was destined to happen. I could feel it in the air.

Ensconced in my sheets, suspended in the gray area between unconsciousness and cognizance, I could almost smell Christmas; the aroma of eggnog sprinkled with cinnamon, just the way my mother would always make it, and the scent of freshly cut mistletoe. I remember when I was a kid, my mother would sneak into our rooms, wave a sprig of mistletoe under our noses, and wait for our eyes to open so she could yell "Kissy kissy!"

I tossed and turned, reaching for those last good moments of sleep. I could almost hear Momma's voice . . .

"Kissy kissy! Kissy kissy! Kissy kissy!"

I opened my eyes. I realized I really was smelling the *actual* aroma of my mother's eggnog flowing from my kitchen and into my bedroom, and the fragrance of freshly cut mistletoe was *actually* her standing over my bed waving that mistletoe less than an inch from my nose.

"Kissy kissy!" she repeated, while in her usual tradition, she leaned down and kissed both my cheeks, shifting side to side.

"Wake up little Boo bear! Momma's here."

"Momma," I said looking at her with contempt. "How long have you been here?"

"Oh, not too long, just a couple hours. I let myself in. Muggly and I had a good ole time, didn't we, Muggly?"

"Meoowwww." Muggly had obviously been paid off as she cleaned chicken gizzard juice from her whiskers.

"And since you were sleeping so peacefully," she continued, "I thought I'd make use of the time and straighten up around your apartment. As usual it was a mess. Dust and papers everywhere, but not anymore. Then after that, I went into the kitchen and you know you had your plates in the wrong cabinet, so I moved them for you.

And your silverware had spots on them so I hand washed all of the pieces, towel dried them, and put them away. They were in the wrong place too, but not anymore. And your pots, I moved them too. You know, the way a woman keeps her kitchen says a lot about the way she'll keep her man. That is, of course, if she *had* a man."

"Meoowww!"

It was just like Momma to sling mud around the same apartment she claimed she had just cleaned.

"But look on the bright side," she continued. "At least you've got a kitchen. That's a start. Anyway, I left a note on the counter so you can find everything when you get ready."

My first thought was to stab her with the spoon from my bowl of melted coffee-flavored Häagen-Dazs ice cream. The second thought was to find where she had moved my pots, and then hoist one upside the back of her crooked wig. But instead I counted to ten and, like Terry McMillan, I exhaled. I wasn't going to let her get into my already crowded emotional space.

"Thank you, Momma. That was so nice of you."

"You're welcome!" she answered gleefully. Uh oh, there's a twitch in her lip. That twitch usually meant there was a frown beneath that smile. Something was on her mind and it was only a matter of time before she would force me to inquire. But not today, Momma. Today I refuse to be drawn into your web of drama.

"So how are you today, Montana?" This was a trick. Ask me how I'm doing so I'll be forced to ask her the same.

"I'm fine."

"That's good. That's good. That's good . . ." After at least ten more "That's good"s, she realized she had hit a dead end. I was not playing her game.

"God knows I always want my children to do fine. Every mother wants her children to do fine. Not just *do* fine, but *be* fine. That's a mother's prayer, that their children are fine. Regardless of what state a mother is in, she just prays to God that her children are fine."

Oh, so now she's thrown God in the conversation. Heavy artillery. But, I'm still not falling for it.

"Till my knees would fill with fluid I would pray. You know, one time the doctor said he was going to have to give me an artificial kneecap from all the praying I was doing? Sure did. Told me to stop praying. But I kept on praying. As God is my witness, I prayed. A prosthetic kneecap was a small sacrifice for my children."

I was still doing fine. But then she started singing Shirley Caesar's "No Charge."

"For the nine months I carried you . . ."

"Meoowww."

"Growing inside of me . . ."

"Meoowww."

"No charge."

By now even Muggly began singing along. Still I stayed strong.

After three more verses, two more choruses, one refrain, and a key change, I could stand it no more. I had reached my breaking point. Bracing myself for an hour of holiday-draining conversation, I asked the question she had worked so hard for. "So Momma, how are you doing?"

"Who me?" Oh shoot. Make that two hours. Even Muggly ran out the room. Anytime she answers with the "Who me?" it's serious.

"Yes Momma, you. How are *you* doing?"

"Oh, I'm doing fine. Everybody's excited about next week. The whole family is flying in, you know. Sheree is happy. Her fiancé is excited. Everybody's in a wonderful mood. You know how much marriage means to the whole family . . . well, almost the whole family." She paused, clearing her throat again, having thrown yet another dagger into my heart.

"Yeah, everybody's excited. Everybody except . . . except . . ."—after a deep sigh—"Except Mitchell. Yeah, I've never seen him like this. After all these years."

All what years? They just got married!

"I can't say I've ever seen him like this," she continued. "Never seen him so down."

Mitchell? I wasn't expecting a conversation about Mitchell. For all her issues, which are many, I sincerely hoped she wasn't headed for yet another divorce. I hated to ask the next most obvious question, but it's my mother, I am duty bound. Faking concern, fixing my face, I asked, "Is something wrong with you two?"

"Oh no. Everything is fine between us. It's not me that's the problem . . ."

I was relieved. Maybe this wasn't as serious as I thought. Maybe it was just business or health or something that was easily solved.

"Is there something wrong with Mitchell?"

"No."

"Then what is the problem?"

"It's not what. It's who."

"Oh, well then who?"

"You."

"Me?"

"You." Picture my head, once again, making a 360-degree turn.

"Me? Momma, what the *hell* are you talking about?"

"Don't you cuss at me."

"I'm sorry, but how could *I* be the problem? I haven't even been around Mitchell long enough for there to be a problem. At least not with me."

"That's just it."

"What's just it?"

"Mitchell thinks you don't love him."

"Momma, I *don't* love him. I barely even know him."

"So, he's right."

"Right about what?"

"That you hate him."

"I didn't say I hate him."

"You just said you didn't love him . . ."

"But that doesn't mean that I hate him."

"Then what does it mean?"

"It means that I don't know him enough to have developed any specific feelings one way or the other."

"But he's your daddy."

"No, he's not my daddy. He's your husband."

"Well he's your step-daddy. Maybe you should try and get to know him."

"No, maybe *you* should get to know him. Maybe then you'll keep him. Or he'll keep you. Either way somebody'll be kept."

"Meoowww."

Muggly had obviously been standing by the door eavesdropping. Uh oh. I had done it now. Momma was standing there huffing and puffing as I saw my words in slow motion leaving my mouth and hitting her ears. Oh yeah. I had really done it now. Her face turned beet red. That meant the gloves were on. So long, holiday cheer, prepare for the Thrilla in Manilla, the brawl for it all, the rumble in the jungle. It was on. My mother was no easy win. A formidable opponent, a master magician, the queen of flipping the script, twisting the truth, and spreading the guilt thicker than a McDonald's milkshake. But this time I wasn't in the mood. It was too early, too close to Christmas, and too close to the engagement party for me to care. At this point I had nothing to lose. Bring it on, Momma, bring it on! Let's get ready to Ruuuumbbble!

Perching her neck like an ostrich, spreading her arms like a peacock, she was enraged, but this time I was poised for battle. I was ready for her. Ding ding ding!

"Oh, so I guess you're the expert on love now, Ms. Never Been Married."

"No. You are, Ms. Never *Stay* Married."

"Meoowww!" Muggly was obviously impressed by my retort. Momma was against the ropes, her knees buckling.

"Oh, okay, so it's like that, huh? I come over here to bring you some holiday cheer and this is how I'm treated? I clean your little nasty kitchen, kept poor Muggly from choking to death from dust inhalation from your little nasty living room, and this is the thanks I get? To be attacked and disrespected like this? After I spent seventy-two and a half hours in labor, tearing up my body, struggling to give your little bitter manless self some life. This is the thanks I get? Well, you're welcome! And I'm leaving!" she said, grabbing her purse, preparing to go. "I'm not going to let you ruin my good mood, especially a week before my youngest child celebrates the happiest day of *her* life. Do me a favor, Pigpen; try not to bring your little funky attitude to an otherwise festive occasion, 'cause we don't need it!" she said, reaching the door.

"First of all, I'm not bringing a funky attitude because I'm not going to *have* a funky attitude."

"I don't see how not. If I had been a spectator at as many weddings and engagement parties as you have, I might be a little musty."

"Well, maybe this time I won't be a spectator because this time I'll have a fiancé of my own. How 'bout that? Whatcha think about that? Huh? Huh, Momma? I don't hear you, don't hear you! Say somthin'!" Caught in celebrating my own verbal lashing, shuffling like Ali and believing I had won, it suddenly occurred to me that I had just handed to her on a silver platter the platinum nail she would use to seal my coffin. Uh oh. "Momma?" I said, taking it down several notches.

It was too late. Immediately her mood and expression changed from anger to joy. She began shouting, dancing, and speaking in tongues.

"You have a fiancé? Oh thank you, Jesus! The prayers of the righteous availeth much! What's his name? Where's he from? What's his denomination? Is he a Pentecostal, Baptist, Southern Baptist, Church of God in Christ—?"

"Momma, slow down a second."

"Slow down? I've been waiting thirty-five years to hear this. Forgive me if I'm a bit overwhelmed. What's his name?"

"His name is . . . is . . . I'll tell you at the engagement party. It's a surprise."

"He's coming with you, isn't he? I mean, this would be the perfect opportunity to introduce him to the family. They'll *all* be there."

"Yes, he's coming. But, Momma, it's a surprise. Please. Please. Please, do not tell a soul. Read my lips, Momma, do *not* tell a soul!"

"Your secret is safe with Momma."

Noticing at least a thousand winks from her eyes, with her hands, legs, arms, fingers, and toes crossed, I knew that within moments the entire planet would know my plans for engagement.

Holding my arms, looking at me intently, tearing up, she said, "Montana, this moment is worth every second of those seventy-two and a half hours I labored with you, the thirty-five years I've been the laughingstock of this family having given birth to the only Moore family girl, post-slavery, ever to eclipse twenty-five, then thirty, then thirty-five and not be married. Montana, this moment is worth all the disrespectful, hateful, spiteful, vicious things that you've ever said to me, including the ugly, undeserved, mean, and despicable things you said to me this morning. Montana, this moment was worth it all. Like Dr. King, I had a dream, Montana. The dream was that one day . . ."

As she continued to recite the entire "I Have a Dream" speech, it suddenly occurred to me that my dream was alive, and that it had quickly turned into a nightmare. After she was done with Dr. King, she moved on to Jesse Jackson's 1984 "Keep Hope Alive" speech, then on to Al Sharpton's "No Justice No Peace," then on to Farrakhan's 1995 "Million Man March" speech, until finally, grabbing her purse and wiping her eyes, she left.

The look on Muggly's face said it all. Montana Christina Moore, you've stepped in it now.

"Meoowww!"

Y ou told your momma what?! Girl, are you out of your mind?! It was supposed to be a surprise!" Gail blasted me as we both welcomed passengers onto a short hop from Baltimore to Chicago. "Happy holidays. Welcome aboard. Good morning."

"I know. But it was early. I was half asleep and she started attacking me, throwing up the fact that she had been married five times to my none. Welcome aboard! Then she started talking about Sheree and *her* engagement, and how happy and excited the whole family was for *her* and how badly they were all feeling for *me,* and I just couldn't take it anymore. I had to say something to get her off my back. Happy holidays! And that's exactly what I did. I said something. And it worked. Because now, she's off my back. Good morning, happy holidays, welcome aboard."

"Yeah, it worked all right. She got off your back, and a ten-thousand-pound gorilla hopped on. Good morning. Welcome aboard!"

"I know."

"I know you know. Girl, you stepped in it now."

"I know."

"I know you know. A bird in the hand, Montana. How many

times do I have to tell you that? A bird in the hand. You never *ever* send out the press release that you've captured the bird until you've got it locked up safely in the cage."

"I know."

"I know you know!"

"Well, it's too late now. The bird has left the cage and is headed south for the winter."

"Does anyone else in the family know?"

"*Do* they? Please. My answering machine started smoking from recording so many messages. I've received telegrams, sing-a-grams, flowers, wedding catalogs, honeymoon packages, fertility packages . . . I even got a call from the producers of *Ricki Lake* wanting me to be a guest on one of her shows called 'Happy to be hitched.' Good morning, happy holidays. Good morning."

"If you thought the pressure was on before, now you can multiply it by ten. But look on the bright side. It takes pressure to make a diamond. Girl, you got to drill deep to hit oil, and sift through a lot of fool's gold before you find real gold."

"Yeah, but how much sifting before you find it? How much drilling before you strike it? And how much pressure ruins a good stone that could have been an even better diamond?"

"Come on now, Montana, now is not the time to get yourself down. Next week, maybe, but not now. You still have seven days left and you've already seen three out of the five. There *had* to have been *something* good about *somebody*. They all couldn't have been a hundred percent bad." I looked at Gail and rolled my eyes. "Come on now, girl, they can't be all that bad. Try looking through my Rolodex. Trust me, you'll gain a much greater appreciation for the word 'bad.' Happy holidays, welcome aboard."

"Okay, so maybe they're not *all* bad. But mostly bad."

"What about the guy in New York? He was cool, right?"

"Yeah, he's cool. He's fun. He's ambitious. But there are two things you're guaranteed to have with Damon. One is a whole lot of drama."

"How much drama?"

"Emmy Award–winning drama. Number one–rated drama. *ER* and *The West Wing* kind of drama. In my twenties, I could've handled it, but right about now, I don't have the time or the energy."

"I hear you. Well, what's the second thing?"

"Oh, the other thing is sex. With Damon you can always count on some sex. Not just sex, but great sex."

"How great?"

"Like Tony the Tiger—*grrrrreeeeaaaat!*"

"Ooh, girl, like that?"

"*All* that. Actually, Damon is probably going to make some woman a good husband one day. Unfortunately, not one day soon. And certainly not in one week."

"Okay, how about the brother in D.C. The congressman? You know, D.C. got it going on when it comes to brothers."

"They do. Their only problem is that they know they have it going on, and they let every woman in town know that they know. On paper Langston is perfect. He's successful. Articulate. Upwardly mobile. He's in demand. He's in the mix. But unfortunately, he's in love."

"With who?"

"Himself. Oh, and Juicy."

"Juicy? Who's that?"

"His other woman. A woman who has been trained to obey."

"What kind of name is Juicy for a woman?"

"It's not a name for a woman. Juicy is Langston's dog that he treats like his woman. If I could only get rid of the dog, we might have a chance."

"Girl, that's easy."

"You have to see them together to understand what I mean. Trust me, it's not."

"No, girl, trust *me*, it is. I'd put up with the dog through the courtship, the engagement, and through the honeymoon. I'd act like I was in love with the dog. But then, we'd get home from our trip, walk in the house, and I'd be like, 'Baby, why don't you pour us some wine so we can pick up where we left off?' He'd rush to the kitchen to pour the wine thinking he was about to get some and there I'd be. Finally left alone with Juicy. 'Here Juicy! Come here, girl! Did you have a nice time on our honeymoon? Yeah, girl, I know you did, barkin' all damn night, shittin' on the carpet, peeing on the comforter. Yeah, here you go, Juicy. Momma brought you back a gift. A nice big bag of cyanide-flavored milk bones. That's a good girl, that's right, eat up, you greedy little bastard. Eat all you want. Here, have another one. That's a good girl. Oh, Juicy? What's wrong, Juicy? Look at your eyes rolling around in your head. And your tongue, what's wrong with your tongue? It's changed three different shades already, from pink to red to black. And you're not breathing . . . Awwwww.' See? No more Juicy!"

"If it were only that easy."

"It is. I got a cousin who works at a chemical supply company. We can get all the cyanide we want."

"Thanks, but no thanks. Lastly, there's the Right Reverend Doctor Bishop Pastor Curtis P. Merewether."

"Ooooh, that's the one I like. The upper room."

"You like him because you haven't met him. Him or his staff of missionaries that do more blocking than the entire offensive line of the Dallas Cowboys."

"No, I like him because I listened to that cassette you gave me of his church service. Girl, he can preach. And anybody that can take you there spiritually can damn sure take you there sexually. Say what you want, Curtis is a catch."

"He might be a catch, but you've gotta avoid the rush long enough to throw the pass."

"Have you forgotten that I was a Raiderette for three years? I learned a thing or two about avoiding a rush."

"Yeah, well then consider him a free agent, 'cause I don't want him."

"Is that restricted or unrestricted?"

"Both." Laughing, we continued boarding the passengers until it was almost time for take-off.

Looking at her watch, Gail's mood suddenly changed. "Girl, do you know what time it is? It's almost time for the plane to leave.

Where is Sam? He was supposed to be here an hour ago. See, now he is really tripping."

"You know Sam, he probably got tied up with some Christmas shopping," I said, hoping that thoughts of a present would make her calm down. "He's probably buying gifts for us."

"The only thing Sam can give me is some space." My plan seemed to have backfired, making her mood even worse. "We all could be doing Christmas shopping. I'm not getting paid to do his job, and neither are you. That's it, Montana. I said it before, but I mean it this time. I'm writing his ass up. Where's the employee conduct forms?" Immediately Gail began searching her folders for the form.

"Gail, come on now. Don't write him up. It's the holidays. He's going to be here any minute. He's always a little late. Give him a minute."

"I'm not giving him nothing, I'm writing his ass up!" She ignored me and still searched through her files, finally finding the form she wanted and shaking it in the air, triumphant. "Ha! Found it! Employee name, Sam Benson. Reason for complaint: Rude, late, pink—"

With pen in hand, just as she was about to begin, Sam came skipping through the door full of life, laughter, and cheer. He was dressed in red velvet pants and a white ruffled tuxedo top with the sleeves covered with custom-made bells in all shapes, sizes, and colors. On his head he wore a lighted candy cane–striped Santa hat. Sam was the living, breathing personification of the holiday spirit.

"*Feliz Navidad! Feliz Navidad! Feliz Navidad! Prospero año y felicidad!*"

"Well, look who finally showed up almost an hour late. It's one of Santa's little elves. All ready to help Santa squeeze his fat ass down a bunch of tight chimneys."

"Somebody's not spreading any holiday cheer. I wonder whom? It must be the holiday horse. Gail, what's wrong? Did Santa not hire you to pull the sleigh this year?"

"Ha Ha. You're late and I'm writing your jolly little jingle ass up!"

"That's not very nice. I'm going to have to tell Santa you're being naughty, and you know what that means . . . no holiday hay under your tree this year."

"You know what, Sam?"

"What, Prancer?"

"Sam, I swear, I'm sick of you calling me out of my name."

"Oh, I'm sorry, Blitzen. Or is Comet or Cupid? Or Donner or Vixen?"

"I am not a horse."

"Gail, I didn't call you a horse, I called you a reindeer."

"What's the difference?"

"Oh, well let's see. There's antlers, pine needles, blinking red noses, candy canes, bells, peppermints . . . but you know, now that I think of it, you're right. There is no difference." Feeling Gail's anger nearing the boiling point, he offered, "Oh, lighten up, Gail. Let's sing a song. Your holiday theme song." Immediately Sam started singing and dancing, taunting Gail. "Dashing through the snow, in a one-horse open sleigh . . ."

"Sam, I swear . . ."

"O'er the fields we go—come on Gail—laughing all the way, ha ha ha!"

"Sam . . ."

"Bells on bobtail ring, making spirits bright, what fun it is to laugh and sing Gail's sleighing song tonight. Come on Gail—jingle bells, jingle bells . . ."

"I swear I hate you, Sam. I'm going back in coach, where I was supposed to be in the first place." Rolling her eyes, Gail left for the back while both Sam and I laughed out loud, nearly hurting our sides. I was laughing with Gail, Sam unfortunately was laughing at her. Any way it came, it was laughter that I needed. Laughter that felt good.

"Sam, I missed you so much. I haven't laughed like that in such a long time."

"I missed you too, girl. So how's it going? The engagement party is in a week, right? Have you made a decision yet? *Feliz Navidad!* Welcome aboard!"

"No, not yet. Happy holidays. Welcome aboard. I've got one more finalist. And the rules were that I wasn't supposed to make a choice until I've seen everyone, right?"

"Right, but you can at least have a favorite." Noticing the blank expression on my face, Sam's cheer faded. "Not even a favorite?"

"Nope. But I've got one more to see. That is, if he's flying on a commercial flight in the next few days."

"Montana. Always remember, the glass is half full. No matter how many times it's tipped over and spilled. No matter how many people have drunk from it, it's always always always half full. You remember that. You are a diva. Diva for life, diva for love. Never forget it."

Sam always knew what to say to make me feel better. At times he made me feel like he felt worse about my unmarried state than I did. Whether he did or not didn't really matter, because he was always uplifting and inspiring.

"You know what, Montana, it just hit me. You're not just a diva, you're more than a diva, you're a . . . a . . ."

"A what?"

"You're a Sadie." Suddenly his eyes lit up. I felt like I was looking through a telescope aimed at a night of shooting stars. He was alive, sincere, and impassioned. I could almost feel the inspiration that he was trying to share. It was the makings for a very warm, very tender moment. The only thing missing was that I didn't know what the hell he was talking about. Breaking him out of his glee, I asked.

"Sam."

"Yes?"

"Who is Sadie?"

"You don't know who Sadie is?"

"No, I'm sorry. I don't. Is that someone in your family?"

"No. Sadie is from the movie."

"What movie?"

"The *only* movie. *Funny Girl*!! Sadie was the only married lady in the neighborhood. That's who Fanny Brice grew up wanting to be like. And that's you. Sadie. Sadie, Sadie, married lady."

I sort of liked the sound of that. Saying it to myself over and over, I decided it had a ring to it. Sadie, Sadie, married lady. "Did she end up getting married? Fanny, I mean."

"Oh, yeah. She got married to Mr. Arnstein. They moved into a big house, bought big cars, and made lots of money." I had hope, even if it was vicarious. "But it didn't last."

"It didn't? They lost the house?"

"The house, the money, the cars, and eventually each other. Everything."

"That's not good."

"But in losing it all, she found what was most important."

"What?"

"What, what?"

"What was most important?"

"Oh! She found out that the most important love was the love she found for herself. Remember, Montana, the glass is always half full."

"Well, half full may be good enough for Fanny but I still want to believe that love's going to pour me a glass that's full."

"And it will, Montana, because you are a winner and winning means freeing yourself from negative thoughts and negative people. You are Sadie. You're Sadie, Sadie, married lady. And never ever ever let anyone rain on your parade! And if they try, you look them straight in the eyes and you know what you tell them?"

"What?"

Sam snapped his fingers twice, and on cue the big band Broadway score of *Funny Girl* came pouring through the plane's intercom as Sam began lip-syncing the theme from the film.

"Don't tell me not to live, just sit and putter. Life's candy and the sun's a ball of butter. Don't bring around a cloud to rain on my parade!"

Quickly, I grabbed a pen, trying to write down the words of the song as he continued.

Now in full voice, Sam began working his way through first class, dancing with passengers in business class, switching past Gail in coach, and working his way back up. The whole plane began cheering and yelling as their energy fueled Sam to even greater and more outrageous lengths of his performance. He was standing on seats, dancing and prancing up and down the aisle. The plane had been transformed into a Broadway stage, and Sam was the star. Finally, after he came to the big finale, the whole plane broke out in a standing ovation, everyone cheering, some throwing flowers, some throwing coins and dollars, some men even slipping Sam their numbers. Sam was the holiday belle of the ball.

Sam and I were still hugging, the passengers where still cheering, and Gail was in coach, still mad, when almost in slow motion an arm came rounding the corner. Then a leg, then a waist, chest, neck, and . . . no, it couldn't be. It wouldn't be. It was. Standing almost twenty feet away was Graham Jackson, boarding the plane and taking his seat in first class. I quickly grabbed a pillow from the overhead bin, covered my face, and headed toward the back of the plane.

"Flight attendants, prepare your cabin for takeoff."

First class was my scheduled post but there was no way I could confront Graham. I wasn't ready. What would I say? How would I act? How would I react to him still being married and me still being single? So, I did the only mature thing to do. I hid in the coach lavatory.

"Flight attendants, prepare your cabin for takeoff." Again the voice came through the loudspeaker.

"Montana, what are you doing in there?" It was Gail banging on the door. "The captain is ready to take off!"

"Do you mind if we switch posts?"

"Yes, I mind! It's a fine brother in 26B. What are you doing in there?!"

"Thinking."

"Thinking?"

"Yes, thinking."

"About what?"

"Life."

"Hello, flight attendants?" the captain's now annoyed voice shot through the plane's loudspeaker. "Cabin doors? Takeoff? Do either of these words make you want to do anything in particular?" By now, Gail's banging had increased and I could hear the passengers on the plane laughing at the captain.

"Montana, I swear if you don't open up this door . . ."

"Heifer, move out the way." It was Sam. "Montana, honey, it's me, Sam. Are you all right? What's wrong?"

"Who you calling heifer, stinkerbell? You move out the way! I was here first." Opening the lavatory door, I peeked out, making sure the coast was clear.

"Girl, what's wrong?"

"It's Graham."

"What's Graham?"

"Graham's in first class."

"Graham who?"

"Chicago Graham."

Again, only more frustrated, the captain came over the loud-speaker, "If anyone on board would like to begin a rewarding career as a flight attendant, I'll be passing out applications momentarily."

"Chicago Graham with the two kids Graham?"

"Yes."

"Chicago Graham that had you jumping in trash cans like a fool on Thanksgiving Eve, Graham?"

"Yes."

"Graham that ripped your heart into little ittly bitty—"

"Yes, that Graham!" I said, now irritated myself.

"You don't have to get an attitude with me. I'm not the one that had you fly to Chicago like a fool only to find out I was married."

"Thanks, Gail."

"Don't mention it."

"I can't let him see me like this."

"I tell you what, girl, I'll cover you in first class. Sam, you take my position in business class. As soon as we're up in the air, we'll figure it out." Gail quickly headed for first class, and closed the cabin doors to a round of thunderous cheers. Sam headed for business class, where he signed a few more autographs from his earlier performance.

Shortly after takeoff, Gail rushed to the back. "Girl, you were right. He does look like Billy Dee. And he smells good, too! You think I can get him to say, 'Do you want my arm to fall off?'"

"No."

"Okay, well, how about 'Success is nothing without someone to share it with.'"

"No Gail, this is serious. What am I going to do? I'm not ready for him to see me."

"The way you described your trip to Chicago, he's already seen you. Seen you, felt you up, filled you up, had you over for dinner, then took you below deck and had you as dessert. So what do you care? It's over. He knows what he did, and he knows you know what he did. What's the problem?"

"That's the problem. I know what he did. I mean lying to me about being married and all. And he knows what he did—because he was the one that was lying. But he doesn't know that I know, because we haven't spoken since he did what it was that I know he did that he doesn't know that I know. You know?"

"Montana, pull yourself together girl, you're blabbering. Has he at least tried calling you?"

"He's tried. But I haven't returned any of his calls."

"Why not?"

"After everything that happened, I was too embarrassed. I didn't want him to think I was that stupid."

"Girl, please, he doesn't *think* you're that stupid. He *knows* you were that stupid."

"Thanks."

"I'm just keeping it real."

Clanging his way to the back of the plane was Sam, looking like Igor after cleverly crafting a wicked creation. "Ooh, Montana, he's cute. It's a shame he flies to the right. You think he ever straightens out and flies down the middle or maybe even curiously drifts off to the left?" Sam said, batting his press-on lashes.

"Unfortunately no, Sam."

"Dare to dream, honey. Dare to dream. He is a dog. A cute dog. But a dog nonetheless. Punishing him is going to be so much fun."

"Sam, what the hell are you talking about?" Gail asked.

"I'm talking about karma. The universal law of reciprocity. The divine rule of retribution. Or in the words of the Godfather of Soul, the big payback!! Do you think it's a coincidence that he's on the plane, captive for two hours with nothing to do? Calm. Relaxed. Not a care in the world, thinking that he's gotten away with a crime of passion? Sitting there plotting on his next prey. I think it's time Graham learned a lesson on how it feels to be tampered with."

Gail's eyes lit up. For once, she and Sam were on the same accord. I was scared to ask what they were planning. But whatever it was, I wasn't going to miss one moment. First up to bat was Sam, grabbing the microphone, preparing to make the announcements.

"Ladies and gentlemen, we'd like to welcome you aboard Transcontinental Flight 587 with non-stop service to Chicago's O'Hare International Airport. Our travel time is two hours and ten minutes. In dog years that's fifteen hours and ten minutes. Today, in honor of one of our very distinguished first class passengers, we will be offering a choice of the following blockbuster films: *The Truth about Cats and Dogs, Dog Day Afternoon, Reservoir Dogs, Lassie,* and the Disney classics *Old Yeller* and *The Fox and the Hound.* And for all you intergalactic canine lovers, sit back and enjoy our in-flight song of the day: George Clinton's 'Atomic Dog.'"

Grabbing several bags of peanuts, Gail was next. Adjusting her breasts, raising her skirt, licking her lips, she sashayed down the aisle, stopping at Graham, wasting no time before beginning her patented peanut in the pelvic area move. Not wanting to miss a beat, I moved closer.

"Hello." She looked down her first class seating chart. "You must be Graham. Graham Jackson."

"Yes."

"Can I start you off with something to snack on? Maybe something hot. Something toasted. Something to sit on the tip of your tongue like the nipple of a bottle. Warm, wet, rubbery smooth, dangling from your mouth. Might I suggest a bag of mouth-watering nuts?"

As Graham nodded his head slowly, I could tell he was hooked. Pulling the bag from between her breasts where they had obviously been warmed, Gail opened them slowly and on cue, there they went—two bags of nuts fell into his lap. At first Graham tried to clean up the mess himself, but his hands were quickly replaced by Gail, who slowly began grazing her way along his thighs. Moving and shifting, tossing and turning, bumping and grinding. I could see Graham squirm and worm in his seat, at first fighting it off, but he was no match for Gail. Gail was a pro and the bastard was enjoying it. I could see his seat slowly recline. Slowly it reclined. Lower and lower it reclined. Until Graham, now hot and bothered, was lying in a nearly horizontal position, where I could see the steam racing from his head.

Instantly, Gail stood up, adjusted her breasts one more time, lowered her skirt, and leaned down, kissing Graham on the forehead. She then walked by Sam, handing him the baton like Marion Jones. Grabbing a pot of coffee, clinging and clanging, he weaved his way through the aisle, finally reaching Graham.

"Hello. Can I offer you something to drink? You look awfully parched. Would you like some coffee, juice, or an ice-cold can of Colt .45? I hear Colt .45 goes excellent with warm nuts."

"Coffee, please."

"Would you like one lump or two?"

"One."

"Coming right up." Sam poured the coffee and dropped in the sugar, all with a devilish grin on his face. I was afraid for Graham, and of what was to follow.

"All done." I saw it happen almost in slow motion. Graham's cup of coffee went flying through the air, landing straight in his lap.

"Aaiyeeeeeeeeeee!" He was scorched.

"Oh my God, what have I done?" Sam asked apologetically. "Are you all right?"

"No! You burned my leg, you idiot!"

"I did? Well, how does that feel, I mean, being burned and all? I wouldn't know, I've never been burned. Although, my girlfriend was burned once by a man who she thought loved her and wanted to be with her, only to find out he couldn't 'cause he was a lying, two-timing, reservoir dog. Let me get you another cup, since I spilled that one on your pair of thousand-dollar slacks."

"No! You've done enough, thank you."

"It's really no problem at all. Let's try some tea this time." Again in slow motion, the tea went flying into his lap.

"Aayeeeeee! What the hell is your problem?"

"Oh my God! I don't know what's wrong with me today! It's like things are just slipping through my fingers like love slipped through that same girlfriend's fingers when she found out that the man she loved was actually not a man at all, but the one hundred and first dalmatian."

"Get me something cold! Now!!"

"Yes, sir, coming right up! I'm going to get you something cold to cool you down." Grabbing an ice-cold pitcher of water, Sam commenced to pouring it straight in his lap.

"Aaiiyeeeeeee!!!" Graham shot up out of his seat, wet and enraged. "Are you on drugs? What is with you, pouring freezing cold water in my lap?"

"Oh, I'm sorry, is it cold? Cold like flying all the way to visit somebody thinking that you could possibly have a future together, only to find out that he has a past, present, and future planned with somebody else. That kind of cold?"

There was dead silence as Graham stood glaring. Seething with rage, he was slowly beginning to put two and two together.

"Well, I'm sorry, I'm just doing what you asked me to do. First you were hot and complaining about that. Now, you're cold, and now you're complaining about that. Which one do you want to be? Do you want to be hot or do you want to be cold? Do you want to be married or do you want to be single, 'cause now, I'm confused. I'll tell you what; hit the bell when you've made up your mind. Thank you."

Turning, switching, and smiling, Sam raced to the back where we laughed, high fived, and took guilty pleasure in watching the universal law of karma lodge its cosmic foot square in Graham's ass.

2:47 P.M. PST
LATER THAT SAME DAY

**7 DAYS, 2 HOURS, AND 13 MINUTES TO "E-DAY"**

From Chicago to Denver we howled. From Denver to Salt Lake City we hollered. From Salt Lake City to San Francisco laughter's tears came streaming down our faces. In San Francisco we had a three-hour layover. It was Sam's idea to catch a cab downtown. On our way from the airport to the city, as the sun set into the picturesque Bay Area skyline, my laughter came to a sudden end. It had just occurred to me that though I had laughed loud, Graham had laughed last and laughed best.

By now he had dried off, calmed down, and was sitting in front of his fireplace playing with his kids, petting his dog, and lying to his babies' momma about what had happened to his clothes. And I was still alone, still single, and still acting as though what had just happened hadn't affected me as much as it did. For whatever reason, probably an incredibly stupid reason, I still had feelings for him.

"Montana, are you all right?" Sam asked, being the first to notice my mood had changed.

"Yeah, sure. I'm just thinking."

"You're thinking about Graham, aren't you?" Gail asked.

"No . . . yeah."

"Girl, let it go. He isn't worth the space in your brain."

"Yeah, Montana, Prancer is right, let it go," Sam offered.

"Sam, I swear."

"Gail, this is not about you. This is about Montana. Can you for once think about someone other than yourself? My God!"

"Guys, it's okay. I've still got one more to go, right? All's not lost. Look on the bright side, right, Gail?"

"Yeah, I guess," she mumbled.

"The glass is half full. That's what you told me to remind myself of, right, Sam?"

"Right. And speaking of glasses and bottles, Gail, what's taking your brown paper bag hook up so long to come up with contestant number five? This is all your fault. If I had chosen who I wanted her to be with, she would have not only been married by now, but honeymooning on some exotic beach sipping on a piña colada while two bronzed and buttery servants in loincloths named Carlos and Miguel feed her freshly picked pomegranates."

"The ones you wanted her to choose were all gay, Sam."

"And? What's wrong with that?"

"Nothing if you're trapped in an episode of *Queer as Folk* but she ain't. Montana is strictly dickly, okay, gay cupid?"

"Gail, I swear I will scratch that one long painted-on eyebrow clean off your face if you open your mouth one more time."

"And I'll snatch that rat-infested ponytail clip-on from the back of your neck."

"Who's ponytail you calling rat-infested?"

"Yours, Ben!" She immediately started singing "Ben . . . the two of us need look no more—"

"Guys. Guys. Guys! It's nobody's fault," I interrupted. "It's the holiday season and Gail's hook up probably just got real busy, especially since these days people are flying more and planning less. No one's to blame. You guys didn't get me into this, and it's not your responsibility to get me out. I'm a big girl."

"Wait, Montana, I have an idea. Why don't you stay here in San Francisco for a couple days?" Gail said.

"San Francisco?"

"Yeah. That way, when my hook up calls me with the flight infor-mation, since number five lives in L.A., you'll save yourself the time it would take to fly all the way from Baltimore back out here to the west coast."

"That's *if* your hook up calls," Sam said, rolling his eyes.

"No, that's *when* my hook up calls."

"I can't stay here in San Francisco. I'm supposed to be working the flight back east."

"Girl, please, all the flying you do, you've got more than enough miles logged to take a whole month off, let alone a week."

"Yeah, Montana, Comet has a point."

"Call me Comet again, Sam—"

"Gail, this is bigger than you. Let it go!" Sam said, cutting Gail off mid-sentence then turning back to me. "Montana, we will totally cover for you. I wish they would try to say something about you missing a couple days. You know, I got Al Sharpton's pager number."

"And what am I supposed to do in San Francisco for one, or two, or however many days this might take?"

"You can hang out with some of my friends," Sam offered with a mischievous smile.

"It ain't Halloween, she don't want to hang out with none of your friends. Montana, I have a friend from my Raiderette days that works at one of the hotels downtown. She'll give you the hook up. You can hang with her and stay at the hotel. Not in some haunted house with Sam's freaky friends."

Once in the city, fancy cable cars we hopped while city fashion windows we shopped, until finally back in the hotel lobby on an old leather sofa we flopped. We were exhausted from the long day.

"Oh, girl, we got to get back to the airport. We're about to miss our plane," Gail shouted, realizing the three hours had almost com-pletely passed. "Get off me!" she yelled at Sam, who was almost dead asleep in her lap.

"Is Montana staying?" Sam asked in half yawn.

"Yes. I'm going to stay. Because nothing beats a failure but a try, right?" I said, finding new fervor.

"And the darkest hour comes just before the break of dawn," Gail gleefully added.

"And only seekers of love . . ." Sam announced, standing on the edge of the couch with arms open wide, warming the lobby with the fire from his eyes, ". . . ever become finders of love!"

"Must you always be so damned dramatic?" Gail shot while rolling her eyes.

They had to rush to make their connection. We hugged, Sam flagged a cab, and I watched from the lobby as they fussed and fought, nearly knocking each other down as they climbed into the cab.

Once again I found myself in yet another hotel room, my fate in the hands of chance. I fell into the bed exhausted and the night came and went with no call from Gail. The next day, more cable cars, and I even spotted a few Forty-Niner football stars, but no call from Gail. The third day there were even more cable cars and this time it was Oakland Raider stars, who just at the mention of Gail's name grew weak in the knees. But the night came and nothing from Gail. I was bored. So bored that I decided to call the only one on the east coast willing to talk at this hour. My eternal standby passenger: good ole William.

Dialing. Dialing. Dialing. No answer. No answer? Why wouldn't he pick up the phone? He's home. He's always home. Maybe he's in the bathroom or something. So again, I tried.

Dialing. Dialing. Dialing. No answer. What is going on? I hope there's nothing wrong . . . wait. If something had happened to William, his mother would've called my mother and my mother would've sent out an emergency satellite alert, which would have surely reached me by now. So why wasn't he answering the phone? Okay, but this time is the last time.

Dialing. Dialing. Dialing. "Hello?"

"William. Hey!"

"Hey."

"What took you so long to answer the phone? I thought something was wrong. You always answer the phone. Didn't you see my number on the caller ID?"

"Yeah."

"So why didn't you pick up the phone? Were you online?"

"No."

"Were you outside chopping wood?"

"No."

"Then why didn't you pick up the phone?"

"Montana, do you know what time it is?"

"Yeah, it's nine o'clock."

"Where? In Japan?"

"No, in San Francisco, silly. I'm in San Francisco."

"Well, I'm in Baltimore, and in Baltimore it's midnight."

"Okay, so it's midnight, I just, you know, figured that you weren't busy so I thought I'd, you know, call to say hi. You weren't busy, were you?" I asked, sensing his shortness.

"Yeah, actually I was busy."

"Doing what?" I asked, laughing, "taking the plastic off the couches?"

"No."

"Scraping the Spider-Man wallpaper off the walls in your old bedroom?" I said, laughing even louder.

"No."

"Then what could you possibly be doing at midnight alone without me?" Still laughing.

"William, where did you say the towels were?" My laughter came to an abrupt halt. Now I know I did not just hear what I think I heard. That woman's voice had better be coming from the television, a neighbor, something.

"William!" Nope, that wasn't the T.V., and didn't sound like the neighbor either.

"They're in the cabinet, third drawer from the bottom," he answered her.

"Uh, William. Who was that?" I asked, bewildered.

"Who was what?"

"That voice."

"A friend."

"A friend? At midnight?"

"Oh, so now you know how to tell time."

"Ha ha. William, what kind of *friend* comes over at midnight?"

"I have a lot of friends who come over at midnight."

"Like who?" I said, drilling him.

"Like you."

"Yeah, but we don't do what you're obviously about to do or just finished doing."

"Whose fault is that?"

"It's nobody's fault . . . and that's not what I'm trying to say anyway . . ."

"Then what are you trying to say? Would you rather it be *you* over here with me doing what I'm about to do or just got finished doing?"

"William! I can't find them. It's cold and I'm dripping wet!"

"Well . . ." I said, frustrated and admittedly flustered, "I guess I should probably let you go so you can help your *friend* who's obviously having difficulty navigating her way through the only cabinet in the entire room."

"Okay," he said nonchalantly.

"Okay?"

"Yeah, okay."

"Oh, so it's like that? Just okay, huh."

"Montana, did you or did you not just say you were letting me go?"

"Yeah but—"

"But what, then?"

"But, but . . . good-bye! That's but!" I said, pushing the end button on my cell phone over and over as hard as I could, wishing that it was actually the handpiece of a house phone so I could slam it down over and over.

No he didn't have some wet *skank* up in his house asking for some towels at midnight! Oh okay, so it's like that. Well, you're fired! How 'bout that? FYE—URRED! It's time to find a new standby!

I was incensed, irate, mad, molded. Suddenly I could relate to torching cars and burning clothes. To hell with Meg Ryan movies. Bring it on, Angela Bassett, bring it on! Just when you think you know somebody, what do they do? They go and stab you in the back. Okay, William, let's see how it feels next week.

I t was three days and counting and still no call from Gail. I awakened with the remote control surgically attached to my hand, content to spend yet another day watching movies that didn't matter. Then suddenly, out of nowhere, "RRRrrring!!!"

It was my cell phone. Quickly I answered.

"Hello?"

"Girl, wash your face, brush your teeth, scrub your booty, and put on the best outfit you got. Your latest, greatest, and last hope of ever getting married is making a connection in San Francisco in forty-nine minutes."

"I can't make it to the airport in forty-nine minutes."

"You're right, because now it's forty-eight minutes. Do you want to keep telling me what you can't do, or do you want to get off the phone, wash your face, brush your teeth, scrub your ass, and put on the best outfit you can find? Now it's forty-seven." Click! She hung up. I glanced at the clock. If I had any hopes of making my flight, I had to be dressed and ready in less than ten minutes.

Toothbrush in hand, brushing, brushing, brushing, done! Water turned on, scrubbing, scrubbing, scrubbing, done. Makeup in hand, painting, brushing, lip lining, done! Pulled out my fitted blues, slid into my designer shoes, squirted my favorite perfume, and I jetted out of the room with thirty seconds to spare. Come on, elevator. Come on! I can't wait. I'll take the stairs.

From the eleventh floor, I ran and I ran, bag hopping, sweat popping, floor after floor. Now at seven, then five, then finally, I was on the curb, flagging, waving, pleading, and needing just one cab with just one driver to bring me just one step closer to my goal, which was 33 minutes away.

*Sccrreeeeechh!*

The cab driver had slammed on the brakes looking as if he had seen a ghost. Well actually it wasn't a ghost, but rather me accentuating the positives while bending as if I had dropped my keys or my purse. There was no way I was missing that flight.

"Need a ride?" he yelled.

"Yeah! Can you get me to the airport in twenty minutes?"

"Not alive."

I leaned into the window, giving him a bird's-eye view of my breasts, now propped up like freshly picked peaches. His eyes bugged and his mouth flung open wide enough to fit his entire cab inside.

"Mr. Cab Driver," I said in my best Marilyn Monroe voice, "I really really need to be there in twenty minutes."

"Jump in, lady. I can't promise you twenty minutes, but twenty-one I can do!"

We sped off, dodging cars like Emmitt Smith dodging tacklers.

*Sccrreeeeeeeech!*

Handing him a twenty, and a tip of the same that made forty, I smiled and blew him a kiss. As an added bonus, I walked away switching, turning once to see his eyes enjoying a man's favorite pastime. He had gotten me to the airport in seventeen and a half minutes, so I was more than willing to oblige.

I raced through the airport security, waving my I.D. like Colombo at a crime scene, and made my way to the front of the line. Evil stares melted my neck like hot butter on a grill, but I didn't care. Lucky contestant number five was calling my name and I was all too eager to answer. Finally at the gate, flashed my I.D. again, boarded the plane, and headed quickly for the rear while managing to catch my breath.

"Hello, welcome aboard. Happy holidays, welcome aboard." I reached my post. Standing next to the rear lavatory was the perfect place to wait undetected. The perfect spot for my bird's-eye view of boarding passengers.

One by one they entered. One by one they boarded. And like clockwork, there he was, looking *foine,* leaping right off the pages of *GQ* magazine. It was my future husband to be, Quinton Jamison. Sporting an always fresh, closely cut, peppered gray haircut, Quinton was a product of the good old days when men were men. When they looked like men, smelled like men, and acted like men. Quinton was a trunk kind of man. A first class man. Actually, make that an *upper* first class man.

Aged like a fine wine, vintage like a well-kept coat, seasoned like a steak from Ruth's Chris, eyes still sparkling like newly polished china, face smooth like melted butter, skin tough as leather yet supple as lambskin. Go on, Quinton, you multi-millionaire textile guru, CEO of Jamison Enterprises. Looking like you just finished a choco-late-flavored viagra shake. I ain't mad at'cha, Quinton! Looking like the black bionic man. Better, stronger, faster. If the six-million-dollar man got a six-million-dollar raise, he'd still be six million dollars short. Short of your style, your flair, short of the essence that emanates from every pore of your body. Go on, Quinton.

"Flight attendants, prepare the cabin for take off."

Quinton was about twenty years my senior. A self-made man. Like a Ford truck, he was built to last, unmovable like a mountain, powerful like a locomotive, yet at the same time, gentle like a dove. Like your grandfather's clock, he always had time. Time to do whatever he pleased. Time to do for her whatever would appease. It was less than an hour's flight from San Francisco to Los Angeles, so whatever I had to do, I had to do it quickly.

Like a cheetah stalking my prey, I lay in wait for my perfect chance to get his attention. First, I would have to wait for the other ghetto Cinderellas to get out of his face. Look at them, giggling and staring, wiggling and baring all of their soul, or at least whatever was left of it. But Quinton wasn't the kind of man who was easily impressed, you silly rabbits. Tricks are for kids.

I met Quinton nearly a year ago. It was the perfect chance encounter. I was hurrying to make my flight and he noticed my scarf slipping from my neck. Stepping from his black stretch limousine, he yelled, "Excuse me, Miss."

Turning, I was frozen like Lot's wife, but not by Gomorrah's fire. I was frozen by my longing desire for a black knight on his white horse, or in this case, his black limousine, which was more than an acceptable substitute. For months after, frequent muses turned frequent excuses turned nothing. It was over. Not because of drama, or tension, or anything negative. It just ended like it never was. Like it was a dream. Clearing my throat, waiting for the coast to clear, I made my way forward. Wetting my lips, switching my hips, I was seconds away when I suddenly heard a voice barreling through the loudspeaker.

"We are experiencing severe turbulence. Passengers, please return to your seats with seatbelts fastened."

Passengers? Thank God he was only talking to passengers.

"Oh, and flight attendants too."

Imagine hips switching in reverse as I stumbled, barely reaching my seat, fastening my belt, and holding on for dear life during what turned out to be one of the most violent bouts of turbulence I had ever experienced.

There I sat, waiting for the captain to turn off the "fasten your seatbelt" signs and signal it was clear to move about the cabin. Minutes passed. Nothing. More minutes. Nothing. More than the fear for my life was the fear that my chance encounter would be bungled by nature, which for some reason obviously had it in for me. By now, a half hour had passed, my mouth parched from licking my lips, my back sore from shifting my hips in the ultra-hard plastic seats we were forced to sit in.

"Flight attendants, prepare your cabin for our final decent."

Noooooooooooo!!! The plane, like my hopes, was headed for the ground. Seconds turned into hours and minutes, years, as I slowly counted down, watching the plane grow closer and closer to the ground and my hopes for a chance encounter fade faster than April for taxes or black noses on Jacksons. We landed.

"Welcome to Los Angeles. Our local time is 11:14 a.m. Thank you for flying Transcontinental Airlines, where we promise to get you there on time and in one piece."

My goal was to get to the front of the plane in a matter of seconds, but my obstacles were at least 200 passengers of all shapes, sizes, and ages who themselves were eager to deplane. Grabbing my rolling bag like a football, lowering my head like a helmet, I was like Walter Payton weaving my way through the aisle. Passing parents, high stepping over children, and yes, sadly enough, even knocking down a few elderly along the way. It was a low moment. But they had insurance and over time their broken bones would heal.

Finally, I reached the front, but no Quinton. Reaching the gate, still no Quinton. Now standing on chairs, I hovered over the heads of passengers hurrying and scurrying, but no Quinton. He was fast. Obviously headed toward the baggage claim area where he would be greeted by assistants, drivers, and the demands of a hectic schedule that for sure wouldn't have room for me. If he reached the baggage claim area, my trip would be in vain. My mission was clear: reach Quinton before he reached the baggage claim. I had only one hope—the motorized passenger cart, normally reserved for the elderly or the handicapped, was calling my name.

Sneaking past passengers, throwing my bag in the back, hopping in the front seat, and turning the key, *vrrrrrooooooooooom!* I had lift-off. With my lead-lined foot, I pressed pedal to metal, hair flying in the wind, barreling down the concourse like Speed Racer.

Down the walkway past gate 25 I sped, knocking over gifts. Past gate 24 and the perfume counter I sped, inhaling whiffs. Gate 23, 22, and 21, passengers flagging and waving, wanting a lift.

"Sorry!"

Like Mario Andretti passing Al Unser, I passed gate numbers 20 and 19 and still no Quinton. Then finally, in the distance I saw him.

He was in full stride, walking at a brisk pace. My only hope was to race past him, pop in the restroom, and almost immediately walk back out like I was headed back to the gate.

*Vrrroooooooommmm!* The rpm's were tipping in the red as I covered my face, passing him. About one hundred feet ahead, I dismounted the cart like a jockey from a horse, hoisted my overstuffed rolling bag from the rear, snuck inside the restroom, and exhaled.

Quickly, having only seconds to spare, I adjusted the do, which had actually taken the shape of a helmet from the wind, lined up the lips, freshened the face, and walked out of the restroom, and in seconds I was standing right smack almost two feet from Quinton.

"Montana?" he spoke, looking rather shocked. But to my relief, pleasingly shocked. "Montana! What are you doing in Los Angeles?"

Grabbing me close, hugging me tight, I was holding my breath, hoping he wouldn't notice the rapidly pumping, violently raging, out-of-breath beating of my heart. He smelled good. Just like I remembered. He released me.

"You look amazing. What did you do to your hair? And you look like you've lost weight. Either that or gained it in all the right places. Either way, I'm not complaining." His eyes were sparkling as he glanced at my whole body from head to toe, never once blinking an eye. He was hooked.

"You don't look so bad yourself."

"Not bad for an old man, huh?" He laughed ever so smoothly. Quinton can downplay it as much as he wants, but the truth is he not only looked better, but was stronger, both mentally and physically, than most men barely half of his age. At any rate, I was more than willing to play along.

"I would've thought by now somebody would be wheeling you around," I said, shooting a smile.

"For a moment they were. After we lost touch, I lost the strength to walk. But sensing a chance reunion, I rehabilitated myself."

"Are you saying that losing touch with me made you weak?"

"Not at all. I'm saying that hoping I would one day see you again made me strong." His words were like silk, dressing my soul, gliding gently across my heart. Quinton obviously hadn't lost his way with words.

"What are you doing today?" he said. "If you're not busy, maybe we could spend it together." Just as I was about to answer with a resounding yes, his name came booming over the airport's loud-speaker.

"Quinton Jamison, you have an emergency phone call. Please pick up the nearest white courtesy telephone. Quinton Jamison, please pick up the nearest white courtesy telephone."

Selfishly, I hoped that whatever the emergency was it wouldn't interfere with our plans for the day.

"Just one moment, Montana. Don't move. I lost you ten months ago; I don't intend to let that happen again."

He walked over to the white telephone, and I could see his lips moving in obvious conversation with an assistant, or an executive in his company, or even worse, another woman. It had been almost ten months, and if I could find a husband in thirty days, he could have found ten wives in three hundred days. After only a couple of min-utes, he walked over. I was scared of the next words that would come from his mouth.

"Is everything okay?" I asked, really only wanting to know if everything was okay with *our* day.

"That was my driver. He gets a little worried when there's any delay in my arrival at passenger pickup, especially since airport secu-rity has become so stringent. Then he connected me to my assistant, who when I told her of my plans to interrupt my day's schedule, connected me to the vice-president of my company, who ran down an entire day of back-to-back-to-back meetings."

He paused, and I felt like the count was full, the ball was slowly passing the plate, I had my bat held high, and the umpire was preparing to yell "Sttttttttt-rrrrrrr-iiiiiike!"

Taking the high road, hoping to gain a shred of dignity, I offered an out, making it easier for him to reverse our potential plans.

"Quinton, I completely understand."

"You completely understand what?"

"That your schedule is full. I mean you were just on the phone with the vice-president of your company and she said—"

"Montana, she can say all she wants to say. She's the *vice*-president of my company, not the president. And being the president affords you certain conveniences, one of which is the privilege and power to not only change your mind, but your schedule as well."

"So, what did you say to her?"

"I asked her to connect me back to my assistant. And she did."

"What did you say to your assistant?"

"I asked my assistant to connect me back to my driver. And she did."

"And what did you say to your driver?"

"I said Richard, uncork my finest bottle of wine because I have been blessed with a divine alternative to an otherwise dull and monotonous day. So again, I ask, Montana Moore, are you busy?"

Almost shaking my head from my neck, I responded emphatically, "No, of course not."

My one hand in his, my other hand pulling my bag, we continued down the concourse, through the baggage claim, and out to curbside passenger pickup.

"Good afternoon, Mr. Jamison," came the voice of an older, fully grayed, black Mr. Belvedere–looking man. Professional yet warm. He grabbed Quinton's bags, and then my own.

"Richard, you remember Montana? From Baltimore?"

"But of course. How could one ever forget such a face, such a smile?" Smiling, he extended his hand and bent to gently kiss the back of mine. Richard was a pro. It didn't matter to me that with all the women that Quinton obviously meets, he was patronizing me with what I'm sure was his standard response. "Will you be joining us for the afternoon?"

Looking at Quinton, not knowing his plans, I was at a loss for the answer. Sensing my uncertainty, Quinton held my hand, taking it from Richard's, and answered.

"The afternoon, yes. But hopefully the afternoon won't be the only thing she'll be joining us for." Ahhh . . . music to my ears.

Richard opened the door of the asphalt-black stretch and we climbed aboard.

Inside, I could tell this wasn't the same limousine as before. Not that the last limousine wasn't above and beyond anything I had ever ridden in, but this limousine was obviously custom. Walnut-grained interior, a mini wet bar, and steel-colored carpeting that beautifully accented the charcoal-colored leather seats, each of which were embroidered with the letter Q. There was a flat-screen monitor built into the partition that separated us from Richard. We pulled away from the curb and into traffic, down Century Boulevard, and onto the 405.

"We'll make a quick pit stop past my home, and from there we'll just let it flow as we go. How 'bout that?"

"Sounds like a plan to me."

We entered the 405 and then exited onto the 10 freeway headed toward Santa Monica. We made it to the Pacific Coast Highway and drove along the coast. The views of the ocean were breathtaking. Bikers, skateboarders, mothers with children walking the boardwalk, lovers hand-in-hand running along the beaches. It was a Hallmark card.

"We should be there in just a few minutes. I live in an area called Pacific Palisades."

Not being overly familiar with Los Angeles, I had never heard of the Pacific Palisades, but I'm sure if Quinton lived there, it had to be something special.

Rounding a corner, we started to drive up a hill. Higher and higher we climbed, and then even higher. I reached in my purse for a tissue to catch the blood that would in any minute race from my nose. The limo reached the end of a magnificent driveway and my first instinct was to reach for the door. Quickly catching myself, I pulled back my arm. Remembering where I was, and trying to not be ghetto, I mustered up enough class to wait for Richard.

Richard opened the door and offered his hand, helping me out of the limo. Walking up Quinton's driveway, climbing his steps, I was expecting to see Robin Leach any minute welcoming me to another exciting episode of *Lifestyles of the Rich and Famous*.

Entering Quinton's foyer, my jaw dropped low enough to fit a thousand flies and their thousand friends inside. All I could say was "Wow!" And I thought Graham's house was big. Quinton's house could chew Graham's house up and shit it out. You could fit three of Graham's houses on Quinton's front lawn alone.

His foyer was bigger than my whole apartment. Greeting all guests was a knight's suit of armor holding a big knife, or a spear, or a gauntlet, I wasn't sure. Whatever he had in his hand, it was tall and heavy, and would hurt if it hit you. On the walls hung all kinds of art and antique clocks, from contemporary to classic, from urban to international. Antique furniture lined the halls, sculptures filled the corners, and indoor trees seemed to reach the sky, cut off only by the vaulted ceilings, lending shade and texture to the landscape above and accenting the light cast from its beautiful chandeliers. The floors were marble, probably imported from Italy. Or maybe it was from Spain. One thing's for sure, it certainly didn't come from Home Depot.

Next to Quinton, Graham was his Mini Me, a much smaller baller. Like a fake Gucci bag missing a C, Graham was the knockoff. I didn't dare pinch myself. If this was a dream, I had no intention of waking up until I had at least finished the day and ventured into the night.

Noticing my eyes had almost rolled out of my skull, Quinton offered to show me the rest of the house, or should I say, compound. We came to what looked like a wall, but with Quinton pushing it slightly, it opened to reveal a bathroom. You had to catch a bus from the sink to the toilet. The mural on the wall looked as though da Vinci himself had been the painter. The handles and faucets of the sink were all gold. Room after room, hall after hall, it was one breathtaking moment after another.

After touring the first floor, I needed a nap. But we weren't done. We moved to the backyard. Rather, *back forest*. Any moment I was expecting to see lions or tigers or bears come racing toward us. It was enchanting, the way I had always envisioned paradise: waterfalls, colored flowers, birds feeding, the fragrance of freshly cut grass and pine needles. Over to the right was a putting green with a flag embroidered with the letter Q.

We returned to the house and he led me up the winding staircase to the final room, the master bedroom. Two fifteen-foot doors swung open to the sounds of violins or cellos or something. The bed, made from hand-carved mahogany wood, was softened by a colorful tapestry made of textured silk from a thousand worms from a thousand cocoons over a thousand years. A sitting area with mahogany stained chairs guarded a table, set with what appeared to be pre-slavery china. Plush couches and lounge chairs lined the walls leading to the spacious bathroom. A detached five-headed shower-slash-steam-room-slash-sauna sat across from the tub that was fit for a king but designed for his queen, lined with candles, flowers, plants, and columns. Quinton flicked a switch and the ceiling began to open up, letting in the brilliant sunshine and cool crisp ocean air.

"You know, you can pick out constellations at night," he said, while looking up at the clear blue sky.

There were closets for days. Closets with room enough to fit the entire second-floor women's department at Nordstrom. Suddenly I had grown weak in the knees. My brain had gone into shock. This was too much.

"So, do you like it?"

"Do I like it? What's there *not* to like? Your bathroom is bigger than my bedroom. You know what that means, don't you?"

"Yeah. You need a bigger bedroom."

"No, that you need to convert your bathroom into a rental property and let me move in!"

"Why would you just move into the bathroom when there's an entire house?"

"How could I move into the entire house when I'd probably have to take out a loan just to rent the bathroom?" I responded laughing.

Not laughing, he replied, "Who said anything about renting?"

"Kaplump! Kaplump!" In stereo that was the sound of both my heart and jaw dropping. Wow. Again, Quinton was hitting hard—not throwing any jabs, only overhead rights and knockout punches. It wasn't fair, him having me against the ropes this early in round one. Not wanting to linger too long in the moment caused by his words, I shook them off and responded, "You shouldn't let your mouth write a check that your heart is going to have to cash."

While I was thinking I had said something clever, he responded, stepping closer and closer with each word that he spoke, "Then why don't I let my heart write a check that my mouth is more than willing to cash?" Holding my face in his hands, he leaned in close and we kissed. And we kissed. Down the hall, out the front door, we kissed. Into the limo, all the way from Pacific Palisades on down the coast we kissed, until finally we pulled up to a pier.

"We're here!"

"Here where?" By now my equilibrium had been altered by the constant pounding of my heart against my chest.

"We're at the pier. I hope you're adventurous." Little did he know that after the events of the last twenty days, adventure was my first, middle, and last name.

As I gazed out into the Pacific Ocean, the warmth of the west coast winter breeze blew briskly against my face. The view was amazing. Almost as far as you could see, birds were flying, waves were rippling, and boats were sailing.

"Beautiful, isn't it?"

"*Is* it? With a view like this, I can see why birds fly. If my view is this amazing, I can only imagine what theirs must look like."

"Well today you won't have to imagine. You'll know first-hand."

"Ma'am, the dressing room is around the corner." It was a teenage boy handing me a life vest and helmet. To my right, I noticed what looked to be several hang glides, jet skis, water skis, parachute packs, and harnesses hanging on a rack.

"You said you were adventurous."

"Adventurous, not suicidal."

"Don't worry; we're taking the hang glides made for two. I'll be right next to you."

"Good, even better, two suicides for the price of one."

He was laughing, "Montana, you are amazing. I had Richard purchase you something."

"What, life insurance?"

"No," he said continuing to laugh. "A brand-new set of hang-gliding gear. It's all waiting for you around the corner in the rest-room." Still noticing my hesitation, he added, "Come on. You only live once."

" 'Live' is the operative word."

Looking at him grinning like a six-year-old boy, I figured, what did I have to lose? The worst thing that could happen is I would be met with some fatal accident and die having never been married. With that thought I started toward the restroom, pulling the teenage attendant to the side.

"Cabin boy . . ."

"Yes, ma'am?"

"If something happens to me, for the record, Mr. Jamison and I had every intention of one day getting married. Got it?"

"Yeah, but—"

Cutting him off, slipping a twenty into the palm of his hand, again I asked, "Got it?"

Glancing quickly at the crisp bill, he nodded. "Got it."

Quickly dressing, I reached the deck where Quinton was already dressed and ready.

"You look incredible."

"Thanks," I said sheepishly, not exactly feeling too glamorous in a harness and helmet.

"We've got great winds. Let's go."

Mounting the artificial bird, we were seconds away from lift-off and I could barely hear anything over the rushing wind. Raising my voice for what might be my last time on earth, I shouted, "How do I know something's not going to go god-awful wrong?"

"You don't. That's what it's all about," he returned shouting.

"That's what *what's* all about?" I shouted above his shout.

"Life. Life is about having faith. Learning to trust someone other than yourself to get you where it is you've always wanted to go."

If these were to be my last moments alive, I needed more than the Zen philosophy on the real meaning of life to charter my journey to the hereafter. So, being a girl from Baltimore raised in the Pentecostal church, I closed my eyes and quickly began praying. In mid-prayer I felt myself being pulled ahead.

"Can you trust me?"

Looking into his eyes, helmet on, harness strapped, standing on a cliff a million miles from the ground, I realized I really didn't have a choice.

"Yes!" I replied.

Faster the rope pulled and faster we ran as slowly I felt myself running on air, my feet lifting from the ground. I closed my eyes, asking God to forgive all my moments of sinful indiscretion, vowing to never again sin, or lie, or cheat, or over-eat, or over-love, or—

"Montana! Open your eyes!"

"I can't!"

"You're missing the view. Open your eyes. It's okay!" Quinton said to me, squeezing my hand for reassurance.

Slowly opening my eyes, I saw he was right. We were okay. The air was crisp and fresh, the sun warmed our faces, and the view was unbelievable. Even the view from the cockpit or cabin couldn't compare. This time, there were no windows or windshields between the sky and me. This time we were one, and in spite of my fear and hesitation, I was actually having fun.

"What do you think?" he yelled. The wind had created an even stronger sound barrier.

"I think I like it!"

"You think or you know?"

"I know. I love it!"

"I thought you would."

"Did you think or did you know?"

Smiling, he responded, "I knew you would. So, are you still feeling adventurous?"

"You mean there's more?"

"There's always more if you're open to it. You have to be willing to explore."

"Well then, what the hell! Give me more!!!" Maybe the thin air was affecting my brain.

Finally reaching the ground, with only seconds to catch my breath, it was only a few minutes before we were once again in flight. The pier's attendants took us out on a boat and strapped parachute packs to our backs. Once on the water, we positioned ourselves in the back of the boat, pulled the cord on our parachute packs, and floated into the air, parasailing high above the waters.

After returning to the shore, I mounted the back of his jet ski and we went splashing and splishing over the waters, laughing and playing. I was wishing the day would never come to an end, but sadly, all good things do. We returned to the pier, dismounted our jet ski, dried off, changed, and hopped back inside the limousine on our way back to his home.

Relaxing and sinking into the plush leather seats, it occurred to me that maybe just surviving a day of hang gliding, parasailing, and jet skiing was probably Quinton's way of weeding out potential brides. And since I was still alive, I was probably still in the running. Either way I had fun. This was a different side to Quinton that I had never seen. The times we spent together before were usually pauses in business that evolved into causes for pleasure that usually ended in statements like "You know, we have to do this more often" or "It's a shame we don't have more time, more often" or "Wouldn't it be great if we could spend time, more often." But *this* time, I was being treated as if I was more than just a penciled-in diversion. This time he had used a Sharpie. I closed my eyes for a much-needed power nap to refuel for our evening ahead.

"Montana, wake up. We're here. After today's activities, I'm sure you've worked up an appetite. Let's go inside. If you'd like, you can freshen up before dinner in the guest room. I'll be down in just a few minutes. Make yourself at home." We entered his home as he kissed me on the forehead, walked down the hall, and raced up the stairs.

Freshening up sounded like a great idea, the only problem was finding the guest bedroom. He had shown me so many, I had forgotten which one was for guests. Okay, Montana, where is the guest room? Is it down the hall to the left, to the right, up the stairs, around the corner . . . hmmm. Suddenly feeling like a mouse in a maze, I decided to call for assistance. Surely there must be a butler, or someone around that could help me.

"Hello? Hello?" My words echoed through the house. "Hello? Hello?" No response. Then, just as I was about to venture off on my own, I heard a voice.

"Hello?" It was a woman's voice. I saw that it was a beautiful young woman, standing three feet away, and she was looking at me like I was a Jehovah's Witness. "Can I help you?"

"Yes, maybe you can. I was looking for the guest room. I kind of got lost, which isn't too hard considering the size of this house," I said, laughing lightly, trying to be friendly.

"Sure, it's down the hall, third door to your right."

"Thanks." Since she didn't ask who I was, I didn't ask who she was. As I turned and started heading for the third door on the right, her voice rang out again.

"Are you the new housekeeper?"

I stopped, turned, and kindly responded. "No," I said, giving her the benefit of the doubt.

"A new assistant? New cook, new driver, new valet? What?" Obviously she was someone important enough to ask me the questions, but not important enough to already know the answers. Either way, I wasn't going to let it spoil my already incredibly wonderful day or the potential for an equally wonderful evening. I smiled, gave the phoniest grin I could find, and responded.

"I'm not the assistant, the cook, the driver, or the valet. I'm Quinton's *guest,*" I said, adding a smidgen of stank to the word "guest." "That's why I'm looking for the *guest* room," I continued, serving sarcasm like I was Serena Williams and she was Jennifer Capriati.

"Well," she said, ball in air, racket in hand. "If you were his *guest,* then you should know where the *guest* room is." She slid her hand onto her hip, her neck straightened, and her eyebrows arched higher than they were already arched. It was 15-love. "And since you're on a first-name basis, then that would make you his . . ." Oh this was good. She was reaching, squirming, unsure of my response. 15–All.

By now, I myself was wondering what response would be fitting. So, deciding to err on the side of caution, I replied, "I'm his *friend*."

"Friend?"

"Yes, friend. I'm Montana Moore," I said, extending my hand.

"That's an odd name. Valencia. Valencia Jamison," she said, not extending hers.

Ooh. 30–15. Now I was fishing. "Jamison? So that would make you his . . . ?" God, please, don't let this woman be his wife, or an ex, or his next. Not now. The day is going too well.

"I'm his daughter." Whew! 30–All. Daughter. Thank God. That, I could handle. "So, you and my father must have obviously just met."

"No," I said, switching to my sistah girl mode. "We didn't just meet. I've known your father forever."

"Forever?"

"Yeah, forever!"

"And your name again is?"

Now, this little brat knows she remembered my name. But to play along with her childish games I answered anyway, "Montana. Montana Moore."

"Funny, he's never mentioned your name to me before." Once again she scored. It was now 40–30. Break point, Valencia.

"Let me see, there was Sheila Morgan, Lisa Morris, Melissa Morales, but no Montana Moore."

First game, Valencia.

"But then again, he only talks about the women that made an impression." Make that first set, Valencia. Count to ten, Montana, count to ten.

"If you don't mind me asking," she said, realizing she was now serving aces, "how *old* are you?"

"Thirty-five," I said proudly, knowing I looked twenty-five.

"Hmm. You're thirty-five and my father is almost fifty-five? Hmmm. Is the dating pool that shallow that you have to chase after older men? Or even worse, is the problem that you couldn't find anyone your *own* age, or that you couldn't find anyone your own age with as much money as my father?"

Suddenly I felt like Keanu Reeves in *The Matrix*. But instead of dodging bullets, I was dodging 115-mph tennis balls shooting from her lips. Just then, Quinton appeared.

"Valencia, so nice of you to drop by . . . again . . . without calling. By now I'm sure you've had the pleasure of meeting Montana," he said, rubbing my arm. "An incredible woman who afforded me the pleasure of sharing what turned out to be an unforgettable day. And Montana, by now I'm sure you've had the"—pausing to carefully select his words—"*displeasure* of meeting my spoiled daughter, who was born with a silver foot in her mouth."

Shocked but gratified, I took great pleasure in seeing her face crack like a crash test dummy flying headfirst through the windshield. She had won the battle but *I* had won the war. Match goes to Montana Moore.

"Now, Valencia, if you will excuse us."

Turning and rolling her eyes, she walked away huffing and puffing like someone had just taken her Barbie. C-Ya!

"Whatever she said, which I'm sure was inappropriate, please accept my apology."

"Apology accepted." I sighed. A man that knew how to gracefully put an opposing woman in check was refreshing, even if it was his own daughter. "So, did you get a chance to freshen up?"

"No, I was looking for the guest bedroom and got lost."

"It won't take long before you learn your way."

It won't take long for me to learn the way? He's doing it again, dropping hints.

"I'll wait for you in the den, which is down the hall this way, just left of the staircase. And the guest room is down the hall that way—"

"I know, third door to the right. Thanks."

"But before you freshen up, I like to give you something." He handed me a long, black, velvet-covered jewelry box. My heart stopped.

"What is it?"

"It's something for you to wear after you freshen up."

"What is it?"

"Open it up and see for yourself."

"Right now?"

"Yes, Montana."

"Okay," I said, like a contestant on *Let's Make a Deal*, thinking that behind door number one could be a . . . diamond tennis bracelet? It was a diamond-studded tennis bracelet. And not just any tennis bracelet, but one that looked like it had been hijacked from Elizabeth Taylor's personal collection.

"Quinton! Oh my God!"

"You like it?"

Do I like it? Thinking to myself, there's not a woman on earth that would not only *love it,* but chop off her good arm to *have it* just so she could wear it on the one remaining luckiest one arm in the world.

"Yes. I like it! Whose is it?" I answered, knowing it couldn't be mine.

"It's yours." Imagine my head making yet another 360-degree turn.

"Mine?"

"Yours."

"But, why?"

"Why not?"

"I'm sorry," I said, still not believing my ears and wanting to hear him say it one more time. "Whose did you say it was?"

"It's yours, Montana."

"Quinton, this is lovely, but I can't take this."

"You're not taking anything. I'm giving. There's a very distinct difference."

"It's beautiful."

"It's ten carats. I bought it the last time we were together. It started off as a necklace that only had a few diamonds totaling one carat. Then each month we remained apart, I added more diamonds until finally it became a tennis bracelet, though I wouldn't recommend that you play tennis in it."

"So, if I had waited ten more months . . . ?"

"If you had waited ten more months, I would have been bankrupt."

He took the bracelet out of the box, wrapped it around my wrist, and then snapped it closed. "Take your time. I'll be waiting in the den."

Now I was really afraid to pinch myself. What I had once feared to be a dream had now turned into a full-blown fairy tale, complete with knights and princes riding in black limos. I was Cinderella, the belle of the ball, a princess adorned in priceless jewels.

I walked inside the guest room and fell against the inside of the door, sinking to the floor in disbelief. Okay, Montana, now, take it easy. Relax. Breathe. Relax. This is real. Quinton is real. And the diamonds on your wrist are . . . *"Diamonds!!!"* Quickly I stuffed my fist in my mouth to muffle the sound. Okay, Montana, relax. Breathe. Relax. I remembered Sam's words when he cautioned me about filling myself with helium. Same actions, same outcome. Different actions, different outcome. Okay, I'm all right. *Diamonds!!!*

Finding the strength to stand, then willing myself to the bathroom, I turned on the water, showered, and began washing away what seemed to be layers and layers of years after years of getting closer and closer to finding my one.

After my shower, I searched my bag, looking for an outfit to complement the occasion. I pulled out a classic black dress with thin straps. Simple, yet regal. The perfect dress for my ensuing proposal. Fixing my hair, lining my lips, spraying once, twice, perfume on, I was ready.

I reached the den and there he was, sipping on wine, looking as eager to see me as I was to be seen. Taking my hand, he led me onto his terrace, where under a night full of stars we dined on Chilean sea bass in a teriyaki ginger glaze, with wasabi mashed potatoes served over a bed of green beans. I was so hungry, I finished my meal and wanted to finish his, but I decided to chill instead. Too close to the finish line to commit an unnecessary foul. For dessert we had a banana soufflé covered with vanilla bean sauce. The plate was yelling, "Lick me, lick me," but again, I mustered restraint and like a lady I left just enough on the plate to appear grateful, but not greedy.

"All done?" he asked, wiping his mouth like a monarch.

"Yep. All done."

He rose from his seat, walked behind mine, and reached for my chair, pulling it from under me. We held hands as we walked from the patio into the yard.

"Have you ever imagined what it would feel like taking a year off to travel the world? Anywhere, anytime, anyplace?"

"Yeah, sure, I've thought about it. Every woman's thought about it. I guess I've just never had the time or the means."

"If you were given the means, would you then find the time?"

"Quinton, what are you saying?"

"What I'm saying, Montana, is come travel with me. Around the world. See places you've only read about in *National Geographic* magazines or seen pictures of on the Discovery Channel. Let's visit the pyramids in Egypt, the Coliseum in Rome. Let's do something silly like box with a kangaroo in Australia, or something dangerous like join a safari in Tanzania. Montana, what I'm saying is, if you'll give me the time then I'll give you the means."

In a *George of the Jungle* kind of way, was this a proposal? I mean, why else would he ask me to travel for a year? I mean, didn't he not-so-subtly ask me to move in earlier today? And when we were at the airport, didn't he tell Richard that I was staying for the afternoon and "Hopefully the afternoon won't be the only thing she'll be joining us for . . ." Oh yeah. It was a proposal. It was definitely a proposal.

"So what are you *really* saying, Quinton? Are you asking me to leave my job, give up my apartment, detach myself from my friends, family, the twenty-four-hour video store?"

"Yes. Do you want me to hire a plane and have him skywrite it in the air? Yes, Montana, yes."

"Oh my God, Quinton. Oh my God."

Hugging him tight, feeling him lift me off my feet, I was on a magical merry-go-round, body spinning, face grinning. Finally I was winning with love, with fate, and with chance. It was a *Pretty Woman* moment and Quinton was the black Richard Gere. There was only one minor detail missing. I still wanted him to ask me the question in a more traditional way. Not that I had a problem with his more roundabout approach, but after thirty-five years of waiting, a girl wants to hear those four magical words. The four words that would remove the shackles and free me from the vise grip of the dreaded Moore family curse. Yes, I wanted to hear those four words: Will-you-marry-me?

"So, does your smile mean you accept my invitation?" he said, for the first time looking unsure himself.

Invitation? That's an odd way of describing what was obviously a proposal. I figured maybe I should guide him to the obvious with a subliminal hint.

"Are you asking do I accept your proposal?" Okay, so I didn't have time for subtleties, especially with Sheree's party only four days, five hours, and fifty-seven minutes away.

"If that's what you want to call it, then yes, do you?"

Wait a second, if that's what I want to call it? I was confused. "Well, what do you want to call it, Quinton?"

"I called it what it was, an invitation. An invitation to live life the way it was meant to be lived. Montana, this isn't that deep, I'm asking you to come travel with me for a year."

"And then what happens after the year is up?"

"I don't know."

"Quinton, I need to know. A woman needs to know."

"Needs to know what?"

"What's going to happen next! You want me to just say okay and just set aside a year and go travel with you? I wouldn't even know what to pack because I wouldn't even know where I was going or when I was coming back or how long I was going for or if we ever made it to where we were supposed to be going because I didn't know where we were going in the first place."

"What's wrong with that?"

"Everything. Quinton, I just can't live my life like a participle and dangle."

"But that's what you do for a living, Montana. You dangle. And you make thousands of people a day feel safe and secure with the thought of dangling. So now all of a sudden, why would you be afraid to dangle?"

"What about marriage?"

"I've tried it, Montana. Twice. It doesn't work. All it did for me was ruin two very good friendships."

"And kids? What about raising a family?"

"Sometimes they don't work either. You love them, care for them, but they just don't work. After meeting my daughter, I'm sure you would agree. Listen, Montana, if marriage and a family are what you really believe that you need, then you should find someone who will give them to you. But if you can handle a life filled with romance, adventure, and the courage to dangle, then you're staring at a man who's more than willing and able to give you just that."

"What if that's not enough?"

"And what if it is? Either way, it's a choice you'll have to make."

Echoing through my mind were the words "a bird in the hand" and standing less than a foot away from me was a prehistoric-sized pterodactyl. Yet and still, my hand was closed, and my heart unsure.

"I tell you what, Montana. We've waited ten months already. What's a few more days? Think about it. I'm passing through New York next week on my way to London, then to Rome, and then to Greece. I'll have my travel agent book you a ticket just in case. Now, for the rest of the evening, let's laugh, dance, dangle, and pretend that this night never has to end."

As we danced under the moonlight I wondered if my road to pretend would ever end.

N ow I've heard it called a lot of things before, but an "invitation" had to be the classiest way I've ever heard of being asked to be international travel booty. But I guess I can't be too mad at Quinton or his "invitation," especially since I've never been invited anywhere close to Rome, Greece, or London. I was once invited to Paris. Well, Paris, Texas, by my aunt. I was invited to Detroit a couple times. Even Chicago. Though I'm really trying to forget about Chicago. But Rome? Greece? London? Quinton's game was seamless and his gifts were priceless. But for all the bling bling that would linger, there was still no ring ring on my finger.

I was still undecided. Not about the bracelet—'cause I kept the bracelet—but about Quinton's "invitation."

"Happy holidays and welcome aboard Transcontinental Flight 581 with non-stop service to Baltimore's BWI Airport."

Nestled tightly in a coach window seat in the rear of the plane, I decided this time to simply be a passenger. I had a lot on my mind and not very much time to sort through the haze.

On one hand, Quinton was offering everything a woman could ever ask for. On the other, he was denying the very thing that a woman spends most of her life waiting to have.

My life was an oxymoron, a series of contradictions, misnomers, and inconsistencies. My road to happiness was once again covered with potholes, speed bumps, and flashing yellow caution lights. I was a contestant on *Who Wants to be a Millionaire?* having made it to the final question but having used all of my lifelines. It was just Regis and me. Regis, me, and that one question with four possible answers, none of which seemed like the right one to pick. Would it be A or C, B or D? Would I choose Damon's drama, Langston's Juicy, Curtis's Mahalia, or Quinton and his never-ending episode of Lifestyles of the Rich and Jaded?

Whatever my decision, it was now three days before the event that my family had now branded "The Late Great Announcement." The unveiling of my husband-to-be had, like a Tyson fight, turned into a media circus. By now I'm sure my mother had made a six-figure deal with pay-per-view or scheduled a prime-time interview with Barbara Walters, or optioned my rights to the Lifetime Channel for a made for T.V. docudrama. There were at least a hundred messages on my answering machine. Messages from relatives I had never seen or ever heard of up until now. Like second cousin Mertile from Macon, or Great Uncle Clarence from Cleveland, Aunt Daisy from Dallas. All with well wishes, all promises of kisses, all waiting for "The Late Great, Oh God we can't wait" announcement.

I was scattered and my brain was in emotional overload. I needed some rest. I needed to relax and let go. Let go and let God. I was due a God moment. Especially since nothing else up until now had proven to work. So again I prayed, asking God to get me out of what I hadn't had the courtesy of asking Him to get me into. Closing my eyes, quickly saying my prayers, I drifted off into a blissful rest. Nothing would wake me up. Not turbulence, not annoying announcements, not crying children, or a restless three-hundred-pound man whose body and booty had oozed from his seat into mine. Nothing. I managed to stay asleep, not waking until we had arrived at BWI Airport.

"Welcome to BWI Airport, where the local time is 6:35 p.m. We know you have several choices for air travel and since none of them were available, we thank you for choosing Transcontinental Airlines."

The passengers gathered their bags, standing in the aisle for what seemed to be hours as they slowly exited the plane. I pulled my over-stuffed rolling bag from the overhead bin and casually made my way down the aisle. I was happy that this was the last time I would see the inside of an airplane prior to making my announcement at the party.

In a way, the moment was bittersweet. The inside of the airplane was where I first entered the world, an unexpecting, unsuspecting, unpretentious baby girl. The plane was in many ways like a parent. Nurturing, comforting, a protective shield providing a layer of secu-rity between me and the rest of the world. Okay, I'm sure that sounds a little silly, but I guess you'd have to have been born on a plane to really understand. So indulge me for a minute while I take a moment to pause and reflect. Pausing. Reflecting. Still pausing. Still reflect-ing. Done.

"Montana?" asked the captain, who was killing some time as he relaxed between flights, "expecting anything special from Santa this year?"

"As a matter of fact I am," I said, smiling to myself. "Have a good holiday!"

"You too."

Once out of his sight, I could relax and let my hair down. Tonight was going to be a candle lightin', warm bubble bath takin', classic soul music listenin' evening to unwind. Thank God I didn't have to run into anybody tonight, because they might be introduced to a Mon-tana they had yet to meet.

Walking up the stairs headed for the airport exit, with my rolling bag in hand, I was making a beeline to the airport shuttle past gate 25, then to 24, down to 17 when I noticed a familiar hat and match-ing cobalt blue suit from behind, staring out into the distance, hold-ing a dozen red roses.

It was Curtis. Curtis? What is he doing here? Oh my God, I for-got. I told him about Sheree's engagement party. He must've gotten the dates confused and come here to surprise me. Oh, no, Curtis, why did you do that? Bless his heart. He has no idea that he's been cut from the team. And look at him. Aw, I feel so bad. I liked Curtis, just not enough to deal with him or his missionaries and their impossible standards. Still, he was a decent man and I owed him the respect of at least acknowledging his effort and thanking him for at least trying.

"Curtis?" I called, walking up on him from behind.

"Montana?" I could tell from the look on his face that he was shocked and disappointed that I spotted him before he could spot me. With him standing there speechless, frozen in the moment, I took the dozen roses from his hand and began the task of delicately letting him down, but before I could, he started stuttering while pulling out a powder blue hanky to wipe the sweat from his brow.

" 'Be ye also ready, for the Lord cometh like a thief in the night.' That's in Ephesians. Had you been the Lord, I would've been burglarized. Montana, I wasn't expecting to see you. How did you know it was me?"

"How could I not know it was you?" Noticing his eyebrows raising, I cleared my throat, trying to cover up what I had just blurted out. "I mean, you have a unique sense of . . . style." He looked down at his suit.

"Oh. You mean the suit?"

"The suit, the matching crocodile shoes, coordinating coat, hat, belt, and tie."

"You like it?"

"Yeah! It's umm . . . It's you! It's . . . blue!" I said, for lack of a better word.

He was still looking nervous and I started feeling bad. It must have taken a lot of courage to fly to Baltimore unannounced, putting his feelings out on the line. Letting him down wasn't going to be easy. Easy Montana, think easy, think delicate, think how you would want to be handled if this were you.

"So, Montana, it's so good to see you. And you're looking lovely as ever. I guess I owe you an explanation for being here at the airport all dressed up carrying flowers and everything."

"Curtis, no. It's okay, you don't have to explain."

"No, but I should, really."

"No, really you don't. I know all about it."

"You do?"

"It's pretty obvious, don't you think? I mean, look at you. You're so nervous, you're sweating. Curtis, you're here because you wanted to surprise me. And you did. I'm surprised. You were the last person I expected to see in Baltimore when I got off the plane. Curtis, what you did is very sweet, and very thoughtful."

"It is?"

"It is. Curtis, what you did speaks volumes."

"Yeah, but Montana—"

"No buts, Curtis, you have nothing to be ashamed of. You are a man of character, integrity, and more important, courage. Some day some woman is going to be very lucky to have you as her husband. But Curtis, today is not that day, and unfortunately, I'm not that woman."

"Montana, I already know that."

"You already know what?"

"I know that I'm not the man for you."

"If you already knew that then why did you fly all the way to Baltimore to see me? And bring flowers?"

"Montana, I didn't come to Baltimore to see you."

"You didn't?"

"No."

"Curtis, come on now. We're two adults. It's okay. I know being let down isn't easy, but you don't have to create some fantasy scenario for why you're here. It's okay. God knows I've gone through enough letdowns in my life to know how it feels a thousand times over."

"Montana, I need you to really hear me. I didn't come to Baltimore to see you. Really, I didn't."

Okay, now I was getting a little irritated with Curtis. Not to mention I was losing respect for him not only as a man, but also as a man of God. He was playing games. Games that I was no longer interested in playing. I was tired, worn out, and my feet were hurting and this fool was standing here looking like Bluey Vuitton wanting to play some kinda high school "who quit who first" games. Okay, Bluey, you asked for it. Gaining attitude by the second, I let it rip.

"Okay, Curtis, if you weren't coming to Baltimore to see me, then why don't you tell me, who were you coming here to see?"

"Montana, I was coming here to see—"

"Curtis!! Oh my God, Curtis!!" Imagine my head doing multiple 360-degree turns as the voice of Gail rang through the air. She ran quickly toward Curtis, coming to an abrupt halt when she spotted me.

*Screeeeeeetch!* Her heels, like the wheels on a Formula 500 racing car, began smoking. Her eyes nearly popped out of her head.

"Montana?"

"Gail."

"Hey, girl. Hey Curtis."

"Praise the Lord!"

"Well . . . now that everybody knows everybody, would somebody like to tell me what's going on?"

"Girl . . ."

"Damn it, Gail, don't 'girl' me right now, I'm not in the mood."

"You know the Bible says in Corinthians that a swearing tongue—"

"Can it, Curtis!"

"I guess you don't care too much for Corinthians, amen."

"Gail, what the hell is going on?" I glimpsed Curtis out of the corner of my eye squirming and making the sign of the crucifix.

"Well . . ."

"Well what?!"

"Well . . ." She stood there squirming, at a loss for words, finally blurting out a response, "You didn't want him. So . . ."

"So since I didn't want him, you went behind my back and got to know him for yourself."

"You know, Adam *knew* Eve. And Eve bore Abel. That's what they used to call it back then. But Gail don't *know* me like Adam knew Eve. Praise the Lord, amen! That was in Genesis." Both Gail and I shot Curtis an evil stare. Clearing his throat, he said, "Maybe you didn't get to that part in the Bible yet."

"Montana, you said he was a free agent, so I drafted him."

"Yeah, but I thought we were on the same team. I didn't know I was talking to somebody from the enemy's camp."

"You know God will send angels to encamp all around you. That's in Ephesians."

Together we yelled, "Can it, Curtis!"

"Amen," he mumbled.

"Curtis, would you excuse us for a second?" I said, desperately needing some real girl-to-girl talk with my best friend, who was quickly becoming my less friend.

"Of course. Maybe we should pray first. Men ought to always pray and not faint." Again he felt our stare. "Or not, amen. That's in Galatians." He cleared his throat again. "I'll just be over there. Let the Lord use you."

"Gail, how could you do this? I thought you were my friend?" I hissed, fuming with anger, trying to keep my twitching fist from punching her dead in her face.

"I am your friend."

"Friends don't do this to friends."

"Do what? Try to be happy? 'Cause that's the only thing I see that I did."

"Try to be happy? With Curtis? Gail, please, give me a break."

"Oh, what, I can't be happy with Curtis? 'Cause he's a minister?"

"Uh . . . yeah. Curtis is looking for the first lady of his church, Gail."

"And?"

"And? First, you would have to *go* to church; and second you would have to *be* a lady. Neither of which you have ever done or ever been."

"So what exactly are you saying, Montana? You calling me a ho?"

"No, Gail. I'm calling you a whore. It's in Ephesians, right, Curtis?"

Pausing, Gail took a moment to digest my words. "You know what, Montana, I'm really sorry you feel that way. And I'm sorry for going after somebody that *you* said *you* didn't want. But Montana, you ain't the only woman in this got-damn world that wants to be happy, okay? Did you ever think that maybe listening to you talk about getting married every freaking day for the past ten years may have made me want the same thing? I know I joke and play a lot and I may say some things that make you think I don't care about love, but I do. I'm just like you, Montana. I'm looking for the same things you're looking for. Somebody that I can love and somebody that will love me back. And I'm sorry if I hurt you, and I'm sorry you had to find out about it this way. I was going to tell you, I just didn't know how. I am still your friend. And I hope you feel the same way about me." She turned away from me and signaled to Curtis. "Come on, Curtis. It's time to go. My *friend* and I are finished."

"You know in Ephesians it says, 'There is a friend that sticketh closer than a brother.'"

"Shut up, Curtis!" I said, this time wanting him to sticketh his Bible where the sun don't shine.

Clearing his throat for the umpteenth time, Curtis offered, "Montana, I'm real sorry about all of this. It just kinda sorta happened out of nowhere. I hope you'll forgive me. Just like Paul in Ephesians talked about Jesus forgiving us our trespasses. Oh, and one more thing."

"What, Curtis?"

"The roses."

"What about them?"

"They're for Gail. Do you mind?"

I couldn't believe he asked me for the roses. I thought about breaking them over his head, but then I paused, deciding to be civil.

"I mean, if you want to keep them you can, but—"

"Here!" I handed the roses to Curtis. He then turned to Gail and handed them to her. They both turned and began walking away.

"Happy holidays, Montana," he said.

"Eat shit and die, Curtis."

"I believe I'll pass on that one, amen."

Watching them both walk off into the distance, I must have stood in the same spot for at least an hour. I couldn't believe that Gail had actually moved in on my man. So this is what it's all about? Everybody's in it to win it for themselves. Cool. I get it now. I really get it now. Every woman for herself.

With cell phone in hand, dialing, dialing, dialing. Ringing, ringing, ringing. Finally, a voice picked up on the other end.

"Hello?"

"Hey, it's Montana."

"Montana, I was just thinking about you."

"I was thinking about you too. Which is actually why I called. I've got some good news. At least it's good news to me. Hopefully it'll be good to you too. I've had time to think about your offer and . . ."

"And what?"

"And I accept. We'll make it official Christmas Eve at my sister's engagement party here in Baltimore. Plus, that'll give you an opportunity to meet my family. I can't wait to see you again either. Bye-bye."

Cell phone off and with a sinister grin, I started walking down the corridor, thinking to myself that if revenge was sweet, I was sure to have a mouth full of cavities by Christmas morning.

## Chapter 16

**10:30 A.M. EST
TUESDAY, DECEMBER 24TH "E-DAY"**

**9 HOURS AND 30 MINUTES UNTIL
THE MOMENT OF TRUTH**

The alarm clock buzzed. Rolling over, I squinted while my eyes focused on Muggly, who was staring at the flashing red numbers on the clock.

"Meoowww."

"Yep, Muggly, it sure is. Today is the day."

It was December 24. Finally it was here. After nearly thirty days and thirty-five years, Christmas Eve was finally here.

Running just enough water over my face, brushing just enough strokes across my teeth, quickly throwing on some kick-around clothes and grabbing my coat, I ran out of my apartment headed for my manicure, pedicure appointment. Manicure and pedicure done. Now on to my hair stylist. A few snips. A few flips. Done. Then headed back home, where it was now a couple hours and counting until the event.

There was a knock at the door. Judging by Muggly's barrage of uncontrollable purrs and yelps, it had to be . . . looking through the peephole, I saw that it was. It was William. Muggly always knew when it was William. Not that he's over here all that much, but I guess since he found her first, they have a special bond.

"Meoooow! Meooooooow!"

219

"Okay, Muggly, okay."

Sliding the latch, turning the bolt, I opened the door.

William was standing with a gift in hand. We had a tradition of exchanging gifts and opening them before Christmas Day. Remembering our last conversation and how it ended, I manufactured an attitude, not wanting to let him off the hook too easily.

"Can I help you?" I asked.

"Merry Christmas!" he exclaimed, ignoring my funk.

"Can I help you?" I repeated with an even more wrinkled frown.

"Come on now, Montana. Are you still trippin' over the other night?"

"Trippin'? Over what?"

"You know what."

"Oh, Dirt Devil? Dustbuster? No William, I think that was honorable of you. She was obviously soiled, homeless, and musty, you were just giving her shelter, water, soap, and towels. You're like the YMCA. You're a rest haven!" I said, grinning.

He handed me his gift, smiling, I'm sure expecting to receive one in return. "Merry Christmas, Montana."

"Thank you, William. You know, I've been so busy, I haven't had a chance to go shopping for you yet."

"I know. I know. That's cool. I'm not tripping. I just wanted to keep our tradition. And in keeping our tradition, you have to open it today. And I wouldn't wait too long, it's got an expiration date." I held the box to my ear, shaking it.

"Just open the box, silly."

"I will. Not now though, but come on in. I'm kind of rushing to get ready for tonight, but I have a couple of minutes."

"Oh, so you *are* going?"

"Why wouldn't I be going?"

"I don't know, it's just that no one's been able to reach you for the past couple days. Your mom called my mom. My mom called me, and—"

"And then you came over here to spy on me and make sure I wasn't drowning in my own pool of self-pity."

"Yeah, pretty much. And, of course, to give you my gift."

"Well, as you can see, I'm fine. No pool. No pity. I'm perfectly okay. And I wouldn't miss it for the world."

"Good. I'm glad." He paused with his hands in his pockets, fidgeting, looking like he obviously had something else to say. "Hey, Montana, look, I know it's a little difficult for you, you know, with your little sister getting engaged and with all the attention your family puts on marriage. So, as your oldest and dearest friend, I came up with a solution."

"A solution for me?"

"Yep."

"So what is it?"

"That we get married."

"We who?" I asked, looking at him as if he had lost his mind.

"We, us," he answered. I began laughing. "What's so funny? I'm serious. So what do you say? Tonight at the party, we can make the engagement announcement, and since your sister Sarah's husband is a minister, he can marry us right there at the party. Then we can whisk away to a romantic honeymoon in Italy. That's where you always wanted to go, right? Tour the island of Capri or Venice and take a romantic ride on a gondola while a man named Gianni pours us vino under the moonlight."

"Okay, sounds like somebody's been watching the Travel Channel. And what about Dirty Girl? Where's she gonna be while we're whisking away on a romantic honeymoon?"

"Montana, I'm serious."

"You're serious?"

"Yes!"

"William, you've never been gone for two days, let alone two weeks. Who's going to run the family business?"

"I don't know. Maybe I'll get my mother to come out of retirement."

"Your seventy-year-old mother?"

"Yeah. We can hook up her pacemaker to my power drill battery, I don't know. So, what do you say? You, me, Venice, tonight. Is it a date?"

Staring at him standing there looking more charming than ever, if I thought for a moment he was serious, I would have taken him up on his offer in a heartbeat.

"William, though your proposal is very sweet and quite flattering, and though the bubble gum from your ring would go quite well with the ice cream and cake, you'll be relieved to know that someone has once again beaten you to the punch, and this time once and for all, releasing you from your thirty-year obligation of playing ghetto Prince Charming, saving me from the big bad wolves of the world."

"Montana, what are you talking about?"

"I'm talking about tonight."

"What about tonight?"

"Tonight I will introduce my man to the entire Moore family clan."

William stood expressionless, almost looking like he was affected by my news. "You're kidding, right?"

"Nope. I'm not."

"So, the talk about you making some kind of announcement tonight wasn't just a rumor?"

"Nope. By nine o'clock tonight I will be transformed into the new and improved Montana Moore." Out of nowhere William laughed, looking at a loss for words.

"What? What's so funny?"

"Nothing."

"Then why are you laughing? You think I'm crazy, right?"

"No, I think that . . . I think that . . ."

"You think what?"

"I think . . . that I owe you a congratulations. Congratulations."

"You're coming tonight, right? You have to meet him!"

"I'll be there. For a minute or two at least."

"Well, just don't leave before nine o'clock. Because that's when he gets there."

"I'll do my best," he said, heading for the door.

"So, wait, don't you want me to open your gift?"

"It's no rush. Besides, your audience awaits you."

"But I thought you said it had an expiration date."

"It did, but I think we may have just missed it."

"Okay silly, suit yourself. I'll open it later."

William kissed me on the cheek, turned, and walked out of the apartment. Something was obviously on his mind, but now was not the time to focus on William. It was time to focus on me. My alarm clock sounded again as I closed the door. It was 7:00 and the engagement party started in one hour.

I reached in my closet, pulling out the red Valentino dress Sam had picked out in New York for this very occasion. Slipping into the dress, for the first time I felt like a woman. As silly as that may sound, it was true. Today I was a woman and after tonight, with the whole Moore clan of looky-loos, whisperers, and naysayers, I would finally become a lady. Vindicated. Emancipated. Finally free from the dreaded Moore family curse.

Taking a last-minute check for quality control, I turned off the lights, grabbed my coat and purse, and headed out the door and down the stairs. Perfect, a cab was waiting right on the corner.

"Where to?" the driver asked.

"Sheraton Inner Harbor, please."

"Right away."

After a few minutes we had arrived. I paid the cab driver, popped open the door, and stepped onto the curb. I stood staring at the top of the Sheraton while bright lights glistened from the Inner Harbor waters. I entered the hotel, hopped in the elevator, and headed for the Crystal Ballroom.

After climbing what seemed to be a million floors, the elevator finally stopped. The doors slowly opened to reveal a beautifully adorned room full of family, friends, and a festive jazz band playing all the favorite holiday tunes.

I waltzed into the room like I was the queen of England, waving my right hand ever so slightly. The right hand with, of course, my ten-carat diamond tennis bracelet sparkling in the air. Flashing the diamonds, blinding anyone who would dare to stare. Yes, I had diamonds. Look at all my diamonds, you bunch of nosy, jealous heifers. Past Aunt Daisy I flashed my diamonds.

"Hey, Aunt Daisy."

"Montana, baby I was trying to—Good Jesus, look at your wrist!" I ran them past her eyes, giving her just enough time to catch a real good stare. "Is them real?"

"They sure is!" More real than that crooked synthetic wig you've been wearing for the past thirty years, I thought to myself. Smiling, "All right Aunt Daisy, you be good now!"

I was working the room. Sticking and moving. There was Uncle Clarence from Cleveland. "Hey, Uncle Clarence!"

"Hey, baby girl . . . now, how come you didn't—My God, girl, I need a pair of shades to look at all that! That man must be some kinda sweet on you!" he said smiling, with every other tooth in his mouth missing, looking like he had been chewing on a bag of rocks.

"Like candy, Uncle Clarence!"

And then passing Cousin Mertile from Memphis who stutters.

"M-M-M-Montana, you-you-look—" I'm sure she had another compliment but I didn't have time to wait for her to finish her sentence.

I continued working the room, one by one, table by table, flashing, and grinning, finally I was winning. Every mouth from every table was open. All eyes were on me. I was in a state of blissful joy. Unspeakable joy. The kind that nothing or no one could quench. No one except—

"Montana, what the hell are you doing?"

No one except my mother. Grabbing my arm, pulling me to the side, she was, as usual, overdressed for the occasion. Hair over-done, makeup too made up, and full of drama. I was tempted to make a citizen's fashion arrest, but why ruin my chance of grabbing even more laughs throughout the evening at her expense?

"Happy holidays to you too, Momma."

"Save it, Montana. This is still your little sister's engagement party. And you're prancing around the room like it's yours when I have yet to be introduced to this man that you claim to have."

"First of all, mother, I'm not prancing. I'm sashaying. And second of all, the man that I 'claim' to have will be here at nine o'clock. And then I will not only introduce him to you, but to the entire family as well."

"Nine o'clock?"

"Nine o'clock."

"Um hmh." Both of us looking at the large clock on the wall that by now read 8:12.

"Nine o'clock?"

"Nine o'clock."

"Well, in the meantime, try to act like you've got some sense, please. The entire family is here and I don't want you embarrassing me any more than you already have. Now, come say hello to Mitchell. He's lonely because he doesn't know anybody yet."

Not wanting to argue, I did as she asked. Luckily for me, Sheree was there with her fiancé. Unluckily for me, she and her fiancé quickly moved on as they continued to work the room. I spent the next five minutes with Mitchell talking about nothing, then five more with my sisters Sarah and Sharon and their husbands talking about nothing.

"Nine o'clock," I said to all who inquired as to the whereabouts of my date. "You'll meet him at nine o'clock." Smiling to the next table. "Peanuts! Popcorn! Nine o'clock! He'll be here at nine o'clock!" In retrospect, it probably would have been easier for me if I had gotten a neon sign that read "nine o'clock" and attached it to my forehead.

The clock on the wall was now reading 8:45. Any minute I was expecting him to walk through the doors, when suddenly from behind I heard the voice of—

"Sadie, Sadie, married lady!"

"Sam?! Oh my God, what are you doing here?"

"Girl, I wouldn't miss this for the world. And look at you! You look fabulous! That dress is working, girl. I told you it would!"

"Thank you! And look at you! All dressed up in a suit and tie!"

"Am I working it, girl?"

"You are *working* it!" I said, laughing, glad that my friend had showed up to support me.

"So, spit it out. Who is it?"

"Who is what?"

"Montana, don't play with me. I just passed up the Barbra Streisand Holiday Look-alike contest to be with you, okay? Who did you choose?"

"I want it to be a surprise."

"A surprise?! To who? Me or you?"

"To you and everybody else. I'm expecting him here any moment. He doesn't live in town and the earliest he could make it here was nine o'clock. But he promised me he'd be here." Both of us looking at the clock on the wall that now read 8:51.

"Nine o'clock?"

"Nine o'clock."

"It's almost nine o'clock now. Don't you think you're cutting it close?"

"He'll be here. Wild horses couldn't keep him away."

"For your sake, I hope you're right. And speaking of wild horses, where is Gail? I thought she would be here too."

"She's probably somewhere getting engaged herself."

"Oh, that's why the horse-drawn carriage was missing a Clydesdale . . . Gail's getting engaged? To who?"

"Curtis."

"Curtis who?"

"Curtis."

"The Lord is my Shepherd I shall not want, Curtis?"

"Yes."

"Seek ye first the Kingdom of God, Curtis?" I nodded my head yes.

"In the beginning God created—"

"Yes, yes, yes! That Curtis."

"Hmmph, straight folks."

Just as I was about to spill the whole Gail thing, we were interrupted by the sounds of tapping on a microphone. "Testing testing, one, two." It was my mother settling in at the podium.

"Everyone, may I have your attention, please?" The band stopped playing their Christmas medley, and everyone in the room grabbed their drinks, their mates, and quickly made their way to their seats.

"I'm so happy you all could make it to Baltimore this year to join me on one of the happiest days of my life. As you all know, my youngest daughter Sheree announced almost a month ago that she is getting engaged to a very fine young man from Philadelphia. And in keeping with our family tradition, we wanted to welcome him into our family in advance, giving him a chance to meet everybody, and one final chance to back out before we all started spending our money on gifts." The whole room erupted in laughter. My mother was a ham and loved being the center of attention.

"And my oldest daughter, who is also Sheree's maid of honor, has an announcement to make of her own. So, without any further ado, I present to you Montana."

Almost instantly the whole room broke out in cheers and a standing ovation as I reached the podium and approached my mother, who leaned over and whispered into my ear while still faking a smile.

"Don't make an ass out of yourself. And don't look at me that way. Ass is in the Bible." Smiling and waving, she stepped down from the podium, leaving me alone.

As I approached the microphone, you could hear the sound of a pin drop as everyone in the room sat with anticipation, eager to hear my announcement. As I grabbed the microphone, the bracelet swung around my wrist, causing the entire room to gasp. Noticing William walking into the back of the room, I began talking, trying to buy myself a few minutes before my date arrived. Looking at the clock on the wall, it was 9:06.

"So, everybody's here and safe and sound and in one piece. That's good. It's always important to be in one piece. Because if you're not in one piece, then you're in many pieces and that is definitely not good. Unless of course, you're a slice of pizza." Laughing to myself. "Get it? Slice of pizza . . ." The room was dead silent, and the faces of my family were expressionless. My first joke had bombed. "So, I probably should first tell you a little bit about Sheree and why she picked me as her maid of honor. Okay. My relationship with Sheree started even before she was born when I used to talk to her through my mother's stomach." That went on for the next ten minutes and still my date hadn't arrived. It was now 9:16. I continued babbling. "Then, finally, she learned how to talk, and believe you me she hasn't stopped talking since." Again, another bombed joke. My family was beginning to grow restless, as my stage performance was dying a slow and painful death.

For the next ten minutes, I moved on to Sheree's years at elementary school as the sweat beads started to form on my forehead. Then ten more minutes through middle school as my heart began pounding out of my chest. Ten more through high school, the prom, the graduation, college selection, freshman, sophomore, junior, and senior year.

Suddenly, in what seemed like slow motion, the doors to the back room flung wide open.

"Montana!" shouted a voice that sounded familiar. No. No. It couldn't be.

My eyes nearly shot out of my head as walking through the doors looking as pompous as ever was . . . Langston. Langston? What the hell is he doing here?

"Langston, what the hell are you doing here?"

"Hell is in the Bible!" shouted my mother from her seat as the entire room looked on in confusion.

"I was flipping through the Calendar section of the newspaper and saw an advertisement for your sister's engagement party. I figured I'd find you here. Montana, I was just thinking about us and we're a great team, you know. And, well, I have another donation dinner. And the last one, that you attended, we all know what happened there . . . Mr. Donaldson donated twice as much money as he was going to in the first place. Montana, there are a lot of opportunities for a congressman's wife. I mean, look at Hillary. Big things happen when you stand by your man. So, anyway, I've concluded that my life would benefit most with you in it. So, what the hell, let's get married! I have a date set, a dress picked out, and all I need for you to do is show up and say 'I do.'"

Instantly the whole room began cheering.

"Stop cheering!" I yelled. "Langston, what kind of proposal is that?"

"Obviously better than what you've received thus far," he responded.

"He do got a point," Aunt Daisy added. "Do that mean we can start cheering again?"

"Yes, you can," Langston answered.

"No, Aunt Daisy, you can't," I countered. "Where's the romance? Where's the fairy tale?"

"Look Montana, I'm past childish fantasies and you should be too. You want romance? You want fairy tale? Okay. On the way here, I stopped at Tiffany's and picked this up."

Slowly he opened the ring box as the entire room gasped and started to cheer. He then began making his way toward me as the radiance from the ring filled the room.

"Mother Mary, full of Amazing Grace!" screeched Aunt Daisy as she stood up and began doing the holy dance.

"Mmm—mmm—my—gooood—goodness!" stuttered Aunt Mertile. The room erupted in cheers.

"Stop cheering!" I shouted.

"Montana, be rational. All I need to hear you say is 'yes, I will.'"

"Yes! She will," my mother belted.

"No, I won't, Momma!" I belted even louder.

"Yes, you will!"

"No, I wont!"

"You will!"

"I won't!"

"I'll marry you!" yelled Aunt Daisy.

"You're already married, Daisy, to some old man who's barely alive. Langston, I'm not going to marry you, okay?"

"Okay, I get it. Well, at least, are you available the week after next? I've scheduled another donation dinner. I'll pay you. I'll pay you ten percent on what you bring in. No. Fifteen percent. No. Twenty-five percent, and that's my final offer."

"No, Langston! No!"

"Why?"

"Because I don't love you."

"What's love got to do with it?" My mother stood up and blurted out.

"Everything, that's what, Momma," I said as the whole room grew still. "Here I am, I've got one man I wanted to marry who's already married. Another man wanting to marry me that I don't want to marry. Then, there's another man who's divorced and doesn't want to get re-married. And I'm doing all this for what, love? Love? No. This has nothing to do with love. Marriage in this family never has anything to do with love. Momma, you're always telling me that love is overrated, right?"

"It is," she said stubbornly.

"No, Momma, it's not. Love is *underrated* in this family."

"Listen here, young lady—"

"No, Momma, don't you think it's time you listened for once? Now, sit down."

To my amazement, after a few moments, she slowly rested in her seat. The whole room again broke out in cheers.

"Stop cheering! We've all been brainwashed by some stupid rule to think that love doesn't matter, that only marriage does. And that it's a woman's sole duty in life to rush to the altar and find somebody. Just to be married. Just to be accepted. Just to be admitted into some social club full of a bunch of women who don't want to be married to the men they're married to."

"Amen!" screamed Aunt Daisy.

"Amen," I softly replied. "I spent the last three weeks running all around the country so I could show off something so that you all would think I'd won. But the truth is, no matter who or what would have walked through that door at nine o' clock, I would have lost. Because that person wouldn't have been able to give me the most important thing. And that thing is love."

Again, the whole room erupted in cheers.

"Stop cheering," I said calmly.

I turned to Sheree, who was seated at her table with eyes full of tears, and tenderly offered, "Sheree, if you really love whatever his name is, then you should marry him. But if you're doing it to avoid some mythological make-believe Moore family curse, then you're making the biggest mistake of your life."

Feeling the weight of the entire family on my shoulders, I held my breath, waiting for a response. After a few moments Sheree mouthed the words, "Thank you." The look on her face was all I needed to see to know that whether she got married or not, the curse had been broken.

And then, that very moment, I saw the truth. The real truth. I did have love. I've had it for almost my entire life. I've had it in the kindest, most sincere, most honorable man in the world. A man who has loved me since I was six years old.

"William!" I said aloud. "William! I've been blind. I've been stupid. If your offer still stands, and you still want me, I'm here! I'm right here," I said, willing to put it all on the line for one shining moment. "William!" I shouted, scanning the room from the podium. By now everyone in the room was calling his name, searching, hoping that he would respond. I could feel my moment swiftly starting to dim when I felt a hand on my shoulder.

"Montana, William's not here. He left fifteen minutes ago," my mother whispered into my ear.

"He did?"

"He did. So now that you've made a complete ass out of yourself, and this time I don't mean the one that's in the Bible, and you've alienated every woman in this entire family, are you happy?" she said, staring in my face, seeing in my eyes that my whole world had just crumbled.

Dropping the microphone on the podium, as the feedback rang through the room, I ran down off the stand, past Sheree and her fiancé, past Sam, past Aunt Daisy from Dallas—"Baby?"—past Uncle Clarence from Cleveland—"Good Lord!"—and past second cousin Mertile from Memphis—"M—M—Mon—" I ran through the room and out into the hallway where I burst into tears, hearing my mother's voice through the door.

"Okay everybody, wasn't that nice? Now, it's time for more music and merriment as we celebrate the happiest day of a young girl's life.

My youngest daughter Sheree is headed down the road to becoming a woman. Clarence, wake up! Daisy! Mertile! Let's hear it for Sheree and her new fiancé! Her new fiancé—whatever his name is!"

Sam burst through the door, himself almost in tears. Seeing me as distraught as I was, he came and hugged me.

"Oh Montana, this isn't how the story was supposed to end!"

"Well, how did *Funny Girl* end?"

"Like this. But I thought things were at least going to work out better for you. If you don't stop crying you're gonna make me start crying, and I don't want to start crying 'cause once I get started, I can't stop."

"I'm sorry, Sam, but I can't stop crying. I can't help it."

After a moment Sam burst out into tears. "I was supposed to be at the Barbra Streisand look-alike contest being fabulous and you got me here with you, crying! Aaaaaah! Jesus!!!! Why?!!! Why, Jesus, why?!!!"

## Chapter 17

It was like a scene from a Black funeral. Sam was weeping, wailing, and rolling on the ground bemoaning, "Take me, Lord!!! Take me!!!" Even in his despair he was dramatic.

After a few minutes of fanning himself with both hands, Sam pulled himself together and suggested that we head back to my apartment. I agreed. We made our way downstairs, headed out of the hotel lobby, and hailed a cab. Reaching my apartment building, we made our way up the stairs and inside, where we flopped on the couch, exhausted from the evening's emotions.

"Well, girl, you sure know how to throw a Christmas Eve party, that's all I got to say."

"I'm sorry I ruined your chance to win the Barbra Streisand contest."

"Oh please, girl, I win it every year. I barely have room in my apartment for all the trophies. So, don't worry about me."

"I made a pretty big fool out of myself."

"Why? For daring to find love? Montana, no, you did the right thing. Remember, only seekers of love are finders of love. You remember I told you that, don't you?"

"I remember. But is that really the case? I've been a seeker all of my life, and I have yet to be a finder."

"'Yet' is the operative word."

"Christmas Eve has always been such a magical time of year. I guess this year, I ran out of magic."

"Christmas Eve isn't over yet. It's only ten-thirty. There's still an hour and a half left. That's more than enough time for magic to happen. Remember, the glass is half full. Who knows, any second magic could come knocking on your front door."

Almost immediately there was a knock on the door. Sam and I looked at each other.

"Are you expecting company?"

"Not that I know of." Walking to the door, Sam looked through the peephole.

"Is it magic?" I playfully asked.

"Yeah, Black magic," Sam said as he begrudgingly opened the door. "Well, look what the wind blew in. It's the boyfriend burglar, Man Thief!" Gail stood in the doorway with her hand on her hip.

"Hey, Sam. Is Montana here?"

"Yes, but I've been instructed to tell you that she's not talking to you."

"Sam, please, okay? I really need to talk to her."

"Shouldn't you be in Atlanta tarrying for the Holy Ghost or something?"

"Sam, please. Can I talk to her?"

"Okay, but make it quick." He backed out of the way, allowing her to come inside.

"Montana?"

I remained with my back to her, not acknowledging her presence.

"Montana, you have every right in the world to never talk to me again. But I wanted to at least try to explain."

"Get on with it, Gail, you're wasting precious time," Sam said, annoyed.

"Anyway, Curtis met me in Baltimore on his way from New York to Atlanta and we flew in together. We prayed before we took off. Then we prayed after we touched ground. We got to his house and prayed when we walked in the door, and again before we left out. We prayed before service, in the middle of praise service, before the offering, after the offering, before the sermon, and after the sermon. After the service ended, the missionaries took me to a back room, closed the door, and we prayed some more. Now, you know me, I'm used to spending a lot of time on my knees, but they took being on your knees to a whole 'nother level. Anyway, while I was on my knees praying I realized how wrong I had been for going after Curtis. If he was off-limits to you, then he should have been off-limits to me too. No man in the world, I don't care how perfect he may be, is worth losing my best friend over. 'Cause girl, well . . . hell, you're all I got, really. So, after we prayed at least three more times, I lotioned my knees and said good-bye. I hopped a plane to Baltimore, rushed straight to the engagement party, and they told me what happened. Then I came straight over here. Girl, I'm sorry, and I know I may not have much tact, or sense, or—"

"Class!" Sam added.

"I may not have any class either, but I got love. I got love for you, even if me wanting to have somebody so bad temporarily clouded my judgment. I love you, girl. And I'm your friend. And I'm sorry." Gail broke down with emotion. "Montana, girl, please don't make me stand here like this. I can't take it anymore. Can I have a hug?" Feeling her sincerity, I got up, walked over to her, and we hugged. "I love you, girl."

"I love you too, Gail."

Watching us, Sam started swelling with emotion himself, until he could no longer take it. "Awwwwww, don't y'all start crying! You're gonna get me started again and I already cried once. Aww, see that? Now I'm crying again. Group cry! Group cry!" Together we embraced as our crying quickly turned to laughing.

"Look at us. Back together again. Just like we started."

"I know. I guess misery really does love company," Gail offered.

"Honey, speak for yourself, I am not miserable," Sam proclaimed.

"Of course you're miserable, Sam! You're a black man who dresses up pretending to be a white woman."

"At least I don't go stealing someone else's man, like somebody we know. You, Gail, are like a Ziploc bag: a rest haven for leftovers!"

"Who you calling a rest haven?"

"Hmmm, let me see . . ." He looked around, rolled his eyes, tapped his chin, and finally said, "You!"

"Take it back, Sam!"

"I ain't taking nothing back, Gail. Ye shall know the truth and the truth shall set you free. Now, you're free! Freee! Frrrrreeeeeeeee!"

"Damn it, Sam, that's it!!!" Grabbing each other, tugging at each other's clothes and hair, they both wrestled down to the floor. Oh yeah, we were definitely back where we had started. As usual, it was me, the very one who needed consoling, who would be responsible for stopping them from killing each other. As I began pulling them apart, there was a honking sound outside of my apartment building.

"You better be glad she pulled me off you, Gail."

"You're the one that should be glad, Sam."

The honking continued.

Sam wiped the dust from his suit and crossed to the window. "Somebody is honking awful loudly outside of your window."

"Who is it?" Gail asked.

"I don't know. But whoever it is is in a long black stretch limousine."

"Limousine?!" Rushing to the window, looking below, I couldn't believe my eyes.

"Are you all right, Montana?" Gail asked.

"Girl, is this limo for you?" Sam asked.

I nodded my head quickly as Richard jumped out from the car, ran and opened the side door. Stepping out in a long black wool trench was Quinton.

"Ooooh, girl. Somebody hand me a halo 'cause I have just been touched by an angel!" Sam exclaimed.

"Girl, who is that?" Gail asked as her eyes nearly popped out of her head.

"That's Quinton."

"*That's* Quinton?!"

"That's Quinton?! Ooh, and in a long black limousine. Girl, now I know what Grace Jones was talking about. He could pull up to my bumper anytime!" Sam instantly began singing. "Pull up to my bumper, Quinton . . . in your big black limousine!!!"

"Sam, stop it, okay?"

"I'm sorry, girl," he said, but started right back up. "And drive it in between!!!!"

"Sam!"

"Girl, I'm sorry! Is that who was supposed to be at the engagement party at nine?"

"Yes."

"Well, girl, you better say something. 'Cause in a minute, you about to come up short."

"I know that's right," Gail added.

"You know *what's* right, Gail? You've already exceeded your stolen boyfriend quota for the year, so back up, you hoochie!"

Richard continued to lightly tap the horn.

"Girl, you better answer that man."

"Why should I answer him? He was late."

"Better late than never."

"Girl, that man flew in all the way from California for you. I thought that's what you wanted."

"He was what I wanted. But that was an hour ago."

"Well, what changed, Montana?"

"I don't know. I guess I did."

"You did?"

"Yeah. I was going to settle for something less than what I wanted just to have somebody to show up at the engagement party. But now, since it's over, I figure what's the use?"

"Well, girl, you better say something."

"Yeah, Montana, or he's gonna wake up all the neighbors."

Slowly I walked over to the window, and stuck my head out.

"Montana, thank God you're home!" Quinton said. "I'm sorry, but I had some last-minute business meetings and had to catch a later flight. I hope I didn't ruin anything. Are you all packed and ready to go?"

"Quinton, I changed my mind."

"What?"

"I'm not going, Quinton. What you said in California made a lot of sense."

"Which part? I said a lot."

"The part about if what I needed was more than what you were offering I should find somebody that is willing to give that to me. I'm not ready to give up on having it all."

"And that's your final answer?"

"That's my final answer." Staring down at my wrist and the diamond sparkling tennis bracelet, I began undoing the clasp. "Girl, where did you get that from?" Gail said, noticing my bracelet for the first time.

"Quinton gave this to me in California, and I'm giving it back."

"You're what?"

"I'm giving it back."

"Why?"

"Because it doesn't belong to me."

"Well then, let it belong to me. But don't give it back."

"I'm giving it back."

"Montana, you're obviously under emotional distress right now. You're not thinking clearly." Grabbing my arm, Gail snatched the bracelet in an attempt to stop me from throwing it to Quinton.

"Gail, let her hand go!"

"Sam, get off me, I'm trying to stop her from doing something she'll regret in the morning!"

"Gail, let go of her hand, you gold-digging heifer!"

"No!"

Shoving, pulling, tugging, the bracelet flew out of my hands and into the air while we three watched it travel in slow motion out of the window and into Quinton's outstretched hands. Holding it in his hand, Quinton smiled.

"I'll hold this for you, just in case you change your mind."

"Thanks, but I won't." Hopping in his limo, Quinton drove away into the distance as we watched and marveled.

"Girl, I can't believe you did that."

"I can. Montana, you have honor. You have courage."

"And she has a case of mental retardation. We all could have retired off of that bracelet. I can't believe you let him walk out of your life like that."

"I wanted a commitment. He wanted travel booty."

"And what's wrong with that?"

"Nothing, if you're a ho ho ho," Sam said, staring at Gail.

"Montana, where are you ever going to find another man that's willing to take you around the world, buy you diamonds, and make a commitment?"

I walked over to the window and stared into the night.

"I'm trying to think of somebody and I can't think of nobody," Gail said, thinking out loud. "How 'bout you Sam? Can you think of anybody?"

Shaking his head, "Nope."

"William!"

"William what?" Gail asked.

"William asked me to marry him and travel with him tonight to Venice."

"William? When it's Wright, it's right, William?"

"Yep."

"And what did you say?" Sam asked.

"I laughed. I thought he was joking."

"You thought he was joking? Did he have a 'Def Comedy Jam' T-shirt on? Why would you think he was joking?"

"Because we always joke like that."

"Well where is he now?" Gail asked.

"I don't know. He walked out while I was waiting for Quinton to show up at the engagement party."

"Do you know where he went?"

"Nope. He came by earlier and dropped off a gift and that was it. Then I saw him tonight at the engagement party but we didn't speak. I was at the podium pouring my heart out to him, but he had already left."

"Well, where is the gift?"

"It's over there."

"What was it?"

"I didn't open it up. I was going to open it earlier, but after I told him about my plans, he made another joke and said that whatever was in the box had already expired."

"After you told him about your plans?"

"Yeah, I told him after he asked me to marry him and travel to—"

We all looked at each other with our mouths hanging wide open. We rushed to the box, yanked it open, and shredded the wrapping paper. Inside the oversized box was an envelope with a red bow on top. I opened it slowly, pulling out something that seemed to be shaped like a card or a ticket or a—oh my God!!! It's a ticket.

"It's a ticket."

"Girl, it's a ticket to Italy!" Sam yelped.

"He was serious."

"Girl, what time does the ticket say the flight is scheduled to leave?"

"Eleven forty-five."

"Eleven forty-five?"

"Eleven forty-five?!" All three of us looked at the clock on the wall that read 11:15.

"That's in thirty minutes."

"We can't get to the airport in thirty minutes."

"Sure we can, if we leave right now. Come on, Montana, we have thirty minutes of magic left!"

We ran around the apartment nearly in circles trying to digest all that was happening. "Okay, but I have to pack." I rushed to my bedroom but almost immediately Sam grabbed my arm, stopping me.

"Montana, forget about packing. Girl, for once, it's time you left your baggage behind and claimed your future!!!"

Staring at Sam's face, I thought that was the most profound thing I had ever heard in my life. It reminded me of what William had told me that late night in the car when he talked about how ironic it was me being a flight attendant with so much baggage. And he was right. It was like an "Ah ha" moment, a light bulb moment, a moment of clarity. And for the first time, I reached for my coat and left without my overstuffed rolling bag, feeling lighter than I had felt in my entire life.

With thirty minutes and counting our mad dash began. Racing down the stairs and out of the building, we all three ran into the street each desperately trying to hail down a cab. Yelling, screaming, whistling. Finding no luck, Sam ran over to Gail, stood behind her, and pulled up the back of her coat and skirt, flashing Gail's hot red holiday panties. Almost every cab in Baltimore came screeching to a halt as we all jumped in the first one and raced down the road.

"To BWI. Get us there in fifteen minutes and there's a hundred-dollar tip."

"Hold on!"

The driver slammed his foot on the gas sending us almost flying through the back of the cab as he broke almost every law from speeding to running red lights to driving on the opposite side of the yellow lines. Obviously short on holiday cash, he was pulling out all the stops. We swayed and swerved like a pinball machine as the cab changed lanes, zooming through the highways, finally making his way through to Trans-Europe airlines. Hopping out of the car, throwing him all the crinkled up bills we could find, we were cutting it close, as it was now 11:35. We had no clout to get us through the international travel line that seemed to wrap around the entire airport.

"This is going to take us forever. It's a million people in this line. No way can we make it in time."

"Where there's a Gail, there's always a way."

Handing Sam her coat, adjusting her breasts, and raising her skirt, Gail made her way to the front of the line and up to the male gate agent. As she whispered in his ear, he began to smile. Then she slid her hand between his inner thighs, and his smile grew wider and wider until we saw his hand waving us to the front of the line. Sam grabbed my arm and we ran past angry passengers cussing and fussing in foreign languages, but since we couldn't understand what they were saying, it had no effect. Once to the front of the line, waving my ticket, I passed through. Sam and Gail followed behind.

"Sorry, only passengers with tickets past this point."

"But they're with me."

"I'm sorry, it's airport policy."

"Forget about us, Montana, go!"

"Go get your man, Girl!"

Hugging them both quickly, I was off, hearing Sam yelling, "Remember, only seekers of love are finders of love!"

"Sam, do you have to be so dramatic *all* the damn time?"

"Yes, I'm gay!"

Racing past gate 1 headed to gate 12. Past gate 2 I sprinted, throwing off my jacket, hoping to gain more speed, past gate 3 I threw off my shoes, running in stockings, past gate 4 and then 5 and then 6, past a policeman taking a break.

"Hey! Slow down!" The policeman yelled.

Still I ran. At gate 8, glancing over my shoulder, I noticed that by now there were at least half a dozen policemen behind me shouting, three concession workers yelling, and one police dog barking, all chasing me. But like the fugitive, I ran.

Still I ran, past gate 9 all the way to gate 10, and finally up to gate 12, lunging for the door as several policemen caught up to me, guns waving, night sticks poking, workers yelling, and dog growling. As they held me from behind, I was waving my tickets, yelling and screaming like a mad woman while I watched the gate doors slowly close.

"Noooooooooooooo!"

They grabbed my arms while I yelled and they yelled back. I could see the plane slowly pull off from the gate when they finally released me.

"I'm sorry, Ma'am, but you were running, and with airport security as it is . . ."

"I know. I know. It doesn't matter now. It's too late."

"Well, uh, Merry Christmas," they said, walking away, seemingly compassionate and apologetic, but having no idea of the impact they had just had on my life.

Sighing, I sat on the floor, watching the airplane head for the run-

way and then take flight into the air, fading into the distance. Looking at the clock, I saw it was eleven fifty-five and I had just about run
out of holiday magic.

I stayed on the ground, almost paralyzed with pain. Thinking to
myself that I had just let the only man who had ever proposed to me
slip through my fingers twice. Thirty years ago and then again today,
thirty years later. Another almost fairy tale gone bad.

I headed toward the airport exit while every possible scenario
went through my mind about what William was probably thinking
about me, and what he would probably be doing in Venice alone
without me, and how by now he probably didn't want to have anything else to do with me. Finally I reached the airport exit and stood
on the curb, attempting to hail a cab.

"Can I help you with your bags?"

"No, thank—" Turning my head, I noticed a man standing in a
skycap uniform with his head lowered. He slowly raised it, and I saw
it was . . . William?

"I think you should really let me help you with your bags."

"Oh my God, William, what are you doing?!"

Not believing my eyes, I leapt into his arms. We embraced. Spinning, crying, hugging, and squeezing until finally, he managed to
pull himself away while wiping the tears from my face with his hand.

"William, what are you still doing here? I thought you were supposed to be on the plane! We almost got hit by a truck and died, then
I almost got shot, and then the dog, the dog almost—"

"Montana, Montana! It's all right, I'm here, and I'm not going
anywhere."

"What about your flight to Venice?"

"I got to the airport and waited, hoping you would show up. But
when I saw that you weren't going to make the flight, I got off the
plane. Going to Venice was about being with you. If I couldn't go
with you, I wasn't going without you."

"So why are you dressed like a skycap?"

"I got off the plane, and figured I'd give it one more try. I borrowed the uniform and was on my way to your apartment. I always

heard you say that with all the baggage you had in your life, maybe it wasn't a man that you needed but a skycap. So, I figured, I'd show you that I was both. Montana, I don't just want to be the man in your life that helps you carry your baggage. I want to be the one to help you check it, and then walk away from it.

"Montana," he said as he pulled out a ring box and handed it to me, "this is for you." I opened it slowly and it was the most beautiful ring in the world. The exact same ring William had offered me almost thirty years ago from inside the Cracker Jack box. My eyes swelled once again with tears. Then removing it from the small box, and kneeling down on one knee, he held my hand and asked.

"Montana Christina Moore, for the third and final time, will you marry me?"

Hardly able to breathe, barely able to utter the words, catching my breath, grabbing my heart, I answered, "Yes, William, yes. I'll marry you!"

Grabbing me, lifting me, spinning me round . . . I felt lighter and lighter, pinching myself, hoping that this wasn't a dream. This time I wanted it to be real. And it was. I was not only claiming my future, I was kissing it too.

*H*aving grown up in a Pentecostal church, and being raised by three generations of women (one being the Pastor), it's no wonder I write the things I write. Really, I just love the Lord. And the way I praise Him is through sharing my gifts with you. I'd like to thank God for the gift of words—and more importantly—the gift of love. Who knew that a broken heart, a scratched Al Green record, and comp tickets to see a stage play would have turned into all of this. I've finally decided to stop trying to figure it out and let God keep working it out! (See, I told you I was raised Pentecostal.)

Next, I'd like to thank and acknowledge the four remarkable women who taught me the love of God, the love for myself, and the love for humanity. Those women are my great-grandmother and the best friend ever, Pastor Annie M. Woods (boy oh boy do I miss you, Ma!). My mother, my first love, and the baddest woman I know, Diane Harris. And lastly my two Grandmothers, Alice McPherson and Evangelist Catherine Kilgore.

To the men in my life who helped bring me into manhood: my late uncle, Elder Ronald H. Woods, who I know is grinning from ear to ear at how his two nephews turned out; my big brother and original soul superhero, James T. Talbert, Sr.; my dad, Lenwood Harris; and my father, Reverend Jim Talbert.

To the millions of playgoers, to the pastors, bishops, church folk, and everyday folk that have supported me over the past twelve years: You mean more to me than words could ever express. Sincerely, I say thank you!

To all my friends at radio, television, newspapers, and magazines, their owners, their program directors, promotion directors, and jocks: Thank you for letting me year after year promote play after play. With your help I'll be promoting novels and pretty soon films and television shows. Consider yourself forewarned.

To all the authors, booksellers, and publications in the literary world: I'm truly in awe of the industry you've nurtured and grown over the years. I'm honored to be a part of your community.

Thanks to Sha, Enoch, Andre, and the entire Ecclectic Salon family for listening to me as I rambled about my novel every week. To Kelcey Newman for making regular late-night trips to the house, then to Coffee Bean to work on yet another version of the cover art. You're the best! To Haminot, Laura, Bridgett (a.k.a. sexy toes), and the ladies at Gordon and Associates for your love and support. To my lawyer, Darryl Miller, for making me laugh and keeping me out of trouble.

To Cindy Stox—my prototypical Montana. And her friends Dan Graham and Donna Oglesby: Thanks for taking time to give me insight into the world of flight attendants.

To all of my close and personal friends and the national chapter leaders of the David E. Talbert Book Club (which you know by now isn't really a book club, but rather a collection of my close and personal friends across the country who wouldn't charge me for help). For real, I thank you all.

To my circle of dear friends, family, and fabulous ladies—Chelia Saddler, Diane Houslin, Sandra Azor, Sandy Sisson (momma-in-law), Lisa Deveaux, Patrice Wilson, and Leneé Harris (Lil' Sis): Thank you all for your insight, encouragement, and enthusiasm. God knows I needed it.

To Ms. Cathy Hughes, and the support of the entire Radio One family: I don't take it lightly that while being one of the busiest and most enterprising women in the world, you find my work important enough to invest your time, insight, and creativity. Thank God for you!

To the entire D.C. Metropolitan Area, the Oakland/San Francisco Bay Area, the city of Baltimore, my folks at Morgan State University, and WEAA: Thank you for embracing me, educating me, and giving me a platform to discover and develop my gifts.

To my extended family members who have opened their homes, their hearts, and some even their churches: Bishop Noel Jones, Bernard and Shirley Kinsey, Reuben and Linda Cannon, Dr. Frank and Marla Reid, Tim and Pam Watts, and Scott Julion.

To Holly Davis Carter, a.k.a. "Flouie Vuitton"—one of the most aggressive and hardest working sistahs in the industry. Thank you for believing in my work enough to invest your time, energy, and connections. To the super-assistants and some ex-super-assistants—Karima, Maria, Ina, Mindy, and Amy—one, thanks for keeping me on point, and two, thanks for giving me greater insight into the mind of a woman.

To my literary agent, Alan Nevins—who after seeing my play *Love Makes Things Happen*, cornered me in his office and demanded that I write novels: And you didn't even know I could write! In a town built on the fake, phony, and pretentious, you are one of the most genuine people I know.

To my manager Mike Prevett, who always jumps off calls, and hops on phones to brainstorm with me: Mike, you are truly one of a kind! Thanks for always being on point and giving the best story notes ever. Your office with a view is right around the corner.

To my editor, Cherise Grant—okay, so now I know why editors get such huge shoutouts!: Thanks for taking the time to give such wonderful notes. Handwritten notes. Email-able notes. Hundreds and hundreds of notes. From you I've learned that it truly does take a village to raise a novel. Big thanks to you, David Rosenthal, and the amazing publishing house for breaking convention, embracing my world, and cultivating my career in literature.

Lastly, but certainly not leastly, to my wife, my buddy, and my in-house editor, Lyn: If it wasn't for you reading every page, catching every line, one can only imagine how this novel would have turned out. Thank you for fighting *for* me and sometimes even fighting *with* me. When folks see my name, what they really see is a result of the countless hours you invest in securing your husband's legacy. For all you do . . . Baby, this one's for you.

—*David*